Hanna—
Can't chain
someone onc[e]
they've been set

free souls

Susan Kaye Quinn

Love Quinn

Free Souls is the final novel in the Mindjack Trilogy.

Summary: Kira Moore has joined the Jacker Freedom Alliance
and lives for the day she can destroy jacker-hating FBI Agent
Kestrel, but when the National Guard surrounds Jackertown, she's
forced to take on a mission that may be her last: assassinating
the world's leading anti-jacker politician, Senator Vellus.

December, 2012 Edition

Cover and Interior Design by D. Robert Pease
www.WalkingStickBooks.com

Edited by Anne Victory

ISBN-10: 1481177060
ISBN-13: 9781481177061

"You don't have a soul. You are a Soul. You have a body."
— C.S. Lewis

For my mom,
a free soul if I've ever met one.

praise for FREE SOULS

"Quinn paints a picture of a not-too-distant America where politicians inflame the hatred of one section of the populace for another—all for their own gain—and you worry that her world is not so far off from our own."

—**Dianne Salerni**, author of *We Hear the Dead, The Caged Graves*, and the forthcoming *The Eighth Day*

"Free Souls starts with a bang and doesn't let up. Like a mash-up of all your favorite science-fiction adventures from Star Wars to The Legend of Korra, it blends nonstop action, nail-biting escapes, and great romance. I absolutely loved it! A great series conclusion—a must-read."

—**Leigh Talbert Moore**, author of *Rouge and The Truth About Faking*

"Susan did it again. Free Souls was WOW! I expected Kira to step up to her role as heroine but not like this. Surprises kept coming until the very end which tied up more loose ends than I knew existed. Warning: Don't start reading until you have time to finish. I didn't want to put Free Souls down for a second. It's that kind of book."

—**Sher A. Hart**, Goodreads Review

chapter ONE

*J*ulian's whispered words drifted past my ears and disturbed the dead quiet of the street, still hushed by the early morning hour.

"You don't have to do this, Kira."

I didn't respond, just leaned into the concrete wall next to him and watched the thin trails of smoke lace the frosty November air. A slow-burn acid was eating through the metal door hinges of the Crawford power plant, and we were close enough that the acrid smell singed my nose.

Julian's second-in-command, Hinckley, pressed flat against the wall opposite us, huddled tight with his squad of mindjackers in an attack formation. Hinckley's extreme talent was his ability to manipulate many jackers at once, but it was his military background that made him so valuable to Julian. Some of Hinckley's men were ex-military as well, bringing their urban-combat training along when they joined Julian's revolution, but today they were armed with dart guns in accordance

1

with Julian's no-kill policy for the mission. I reached my mind out to Hinckley, pushing through his tough mindbarrier to link a thought. His mindscent was crisp, like rubbing alcohol, and stung almost as much as the acid.

You ready to do this?

He flicked a look to his men, probably doing a wordless check. *Yes, ma'am,* came his reply. *As soon as the acid is through, Jameson will take the door and toss the smoke bomb. Then we'll be right behind you, laying down suppression. Just like we trained.* His fingers drummed the barrel of his dart gun but still kept discipline, his trigger finger staying clear until ready to shoot.

My own dart gun was safely tucked in the back of my pants.

"Kira," Julian said quietly. "I mean it. It's not too late to do this differently." I turned to face him in our tight spot against the wall, and his words floated on a ghost of breath that caressed the air between us. A familiar tug inside wanted me to breathe in his soft words and drink in the concerned look in his glacier-blue eyes. I almost leaned closer to him, but it wouldn't be mesh to hug Julian right before an op. Or any time, really. I blinked and focused on the flak jacket snugged tight over his ultralite winter coat. It wasn't mesh to whisper in front of a door we were about to break down, either, but Julian's extreme jacking ability included mental defenses that scared up my worst nightmares, so linking in to his mind wasn't an option.

I kept my voice low. "You want this to be a covert operation, right?" If the Feds knew we had taken the plant, they would send

2

a battalion of jack police to take it back. "Someone needs to stop the staff from calling for help. Last I checked, you don't have any other jackers who can run up two floors to the control room in under three seconds."

The Crawford plant was three stories of crumbling red brick on the outside, but inside, a state-of-the art hydrogenerator pumped life-giving power to Jackertown. Unfortunately, the mindreaders held the plant, and with winter creeping up on us, they could shut down Julian's revolution simply by turning off the power and freezing us out. We needed to get in, scribe the twenty workers into being jacker-friendly subversives, and get out before anyone suspected a thing. But a mindwave disruptor shield encased the building, which meant they expected an attack, or at least were prepared for one. Inside, they would have anti-jacker helmets, conventional weapons, and whatever jacker-tuned technology the government had cooked up in the last three months.

"Once we take out the door," Julian said, "we'll be past the shield and able to jack anyone on the first floor. You can hold back, wait for us to clear the room. Then, with your extended reach, you can stop anyone inside the plant."

"Unless they've got helmets," I said. "Then it'll take time to fight our way in, time we don't have. They'll be shooting bullets at us, Julian, not tranq darts."

"Which is precisely why I don't want you charging in first."

"And precisely why you need me to get to the control room fast. If they've got helmets, the only way to stop them from alerting the Feds is to go up and knock on their door."

It was the same argument we had back at the headquarters of Julian's Jacker Freedom Alliance while planning the operation. An argument Julian had lost when I convinced his twin sister, Anna—who was in charge of all JFA operations and more Attila the Hun than Julian would ever be—that my nascent ability to hyper-control my own mind meant we could take the plant with a low profile and minimum casualties the way Julian wanted.

"What if you're not fast enough?" Julian asked.

I couldn't exactly outrun a bullet in my hyped-up state, but it would be difficult to track me with a gun, especially if Hinckley and his men did their part and gave me some cover.

"You worry about your part of the op," I said. "I'll worry about mine." I was part of the assault force, with Sasha and Julian bringing up the rear as the support team. As much as Julian seemed to worry about me, Sasha was more important to the operation. He was the only one who could scribe the workers, permanently rewriting their minds so they would be jacker sympathizers. But he needed to touch them to do it. "Just get Sasha up to the control room as fast as you can. I don't want to go through all this for nothing."

"What if your blowback hits before you've disabled the crew?"

He simply wasn't giving up.

"Then make sure you're not late."

Julian sighed and looked like he was holding himself back. From a hug? More likely, he wanted to shake some sense into me. I closed my eyes and pretended to start the meditation routine that helped me enter my hyped-up state. I used to think that thoughts of inappropriate hugs were just a leftover from when Julian used his ability to "handle" my instincts—my mating instinct, to be precise—to make me fall in love with him for about ten seconds. That feeling kept surging back, days and weeks after we escaped from Agent Kestrel's cells.

I thought maybe Julian had done something permanent to my brain.

Then I realized nearly everyone in the JFA had intense feelings when it came to Julian, and it wasn't due to his handler abilities. He drew them in with the words he used, the things he did. He was setting up schools for the changelings we rescued, bringing the mindjacker clans together, creating a future for jackers seemingly out of thin air. Members of the JFA were fiercely loyal, every last one of us willing to die for him and the cause. I first noticed it in my fellow long-distance jacker and best friend, Ava—the shine in her eyes, the way her face turned radiant when she spoke about Julian. It looked a lot like love. My eyes probably shone when I looked at Julian too.

That didn't mean we were *in love* with him.

Real love wasn't just instinctual attraction or passionate loyalty to a charismatic leader. Real love was the way Ava gazed at her boyfriend Sasha, like she lived on the air he breathed. And Sasha looked at her like she was his reason to keep breathing. Being in love was something I used to have until a jacker named Molloy shredded the memories of my boyfriend Raf, leaving a hole in my heart that still whistled, cold and empty. Only a few things quieted the ache. Focusing on a mission. Shooting a target into oblivion at the practice range. Meditating myself into that hyper state where I could do impossible things.

I was jerked out of my ruminations by Julian tugging on my flak jacket. I pushed my combat helmet back off my forehead. My hair was getting long again, making it slide way too much. Julian avoided my stare as he tightened the straps of my jacket.

Any tighter and I wouldn't be able to breathe. "Easy, boss. I'm pretty sure the bullets can't sneak in the side."

He pulled the strap one more time. "Be careful, keeper," he said softly, then fixed his gaze on the door over my shoulder. Julian hadn't called me keeper in a long time, not since I showed up on his doorstep, ready to join his revolution. Maybe he really was worried. The tug inside demanded my attention again, and I almost reached out to reassure him, but Hinckley's hand signal saved me from it.

Hinckley pointed to Jameson, who had shifted in front of the door. The wisps of smoke from the acid had trailed to nothing, and the dawning sun glinted off the barrel of the battering ram as Jameson held it at the ready. Sasha stood slightly back from Julian, and in spite of the stone-cold look on Sasha's face, his normally dark skin had paled to almost gray. Scribing twenty people was no small feat. His deep brown eyes used to seem empty to me, soulless, but now I knew they held more souls than he could count.

I brushed against his mindbarrier, and he let me in. *Are you all right?* His normal potpourri mindscent, a trace reminder from every soul he had ever scribed, was laced with a sour tinge of anxiety.

I will be. He gently nudged me out of his mind. I didn't press back. He didn't need me in his head, distracting him from the task ahead.

I closed my eyes again, needing to clear my mental decks for real this time. Julian's sister, Anna, had helped train me in relaxation and meditation techniques, in between pushups and hand-to-hand close-combat drills. I imagined going down a mental elevator, floor by floor, slowly breathing in on the count and out on the pause. I quickly passed the thinking centers of my mind, sinking deeper to the parts that controlled heart rate and breathing. Below them were vast networks, like a mass of spaghetti, that orchestrated every function in my body. I was convinced that Sasha worked on this level most of the time, but I hadn't figured out how he did his scribing thing. Yet.

Focus. Breathe in. Breathe out.

I searched for the thread I needed, the one that would change every muscle strand in my body from slow-twitch to fast. The ratio of fast- and slow-twitch muscles was set at birth, although athletes (illegally) used gene therapies to enhance it. What they took serums for, I could trigger with a simple thought. Which meant I could move, well, fast. Faster than should be humanly possible, even with gene therapy and a ton of training.

I would pay the price for it later.

I plucked the neural string that sent the signal. It zinged through my body, racing chemicals and rapid-fire electrical impulses to every muscle. They quivered with the sudden conversion to fast-twitch. I catapulted out of the depths of my brain, pumping up my adrenaline on the way. The conversion would last until I triggered a reversal, but the adrenaline boost would help my muscles handle the speed for longer.

I opened my eyes. Hinckley was waiting for my signal. I gave a shaky, jerking nod, clenching my jaw shut so my teeth wouldn't rattle. My fingertips gripped the rough concrete wall, anchoring me until it was time. My entire body vibrated with the need to run, to purge this speed that was coiled in my muscles like electricity in a bottle.

Jameson slammed the door open with one loud bang of the battering ram, and it acted like a starter gun going off. My body broke loose and shot through the doorway like a bullet screaming from a sniper rifle. The adrenaline keyed up some senses— my peripheral vision and balance—and dimmed others, notably my hearing. I heard the smoke grenade chitter behind me and detonate, but then I moved into a cone of silence. The smoke was too slow to obscure my passage as I raced past two helmeted guards toward the stairwell on the far side of the room. Human reaction time was about two-tenths of a second—by the time they could move, I had already blurred across the floor.

I tore through the doorway and leaped up the metal-grated stairs, taking several steps with each bound. My senses slowed further, and I saw where each foot would fall right before it hit. Something shoved me in the back, making me over rotate and slam into the wall at the top of the stairs. I was going so fast, I

8

literally bounced off. The recoil carried me to the next flight. I pivoted, my toes barely kissing the ground before I flew up the next set of stairs, no time to think about what had just happened.

Beats counted in my head. My heart was a slow drum roll tolling through my body and pounding out the seconds. *One*: in the building and up the first flight. *Two*: for the next three flights. *Three*: and I was at the top of the stairwell, on the third floor, hurtling through the door of the control room. Half a dozen middle-aged men in stiff-collared shirts stood by their screens, manipulating the mindware interfaces. One had a phone to his ear and a wild-eyed look. I ran straight into him, not slowing in the slightest.

He never saw me coming.

We fell together. His phone skittered across the floor and cracked against the wall. My momentum carried me over his head, and I flipped and landed on my back on the concrete floor. I bounced a couple of times before the energy of my body was spent, and I lay sprawled, face up on the floor. My muscles still full of fast-twitch action, I flipped over onto my hands and feet. The toes of my running shoes gained traction on the smooth floor, and I was ready to charge again, like a wild bull hyped on frothy anger. Which probably wasn't far from the truth.

The downed power-plant worker lay motionless and the others gaped at us, stunned. They all had anti-jacker helmets. Six against one. Even a raging bull was going to have problems with that. I jerked up from the floor, pulled out my dart gun, and started shooting. I got four, but the last two came behind me and grabbed my shoulder and gun hand. My shot clattered against the screens. Anna's close-combat training kicked in. I curled the gun in close to my chest, pulling the guy holding it forward, then drove my other elbow into the second guy's body. He huffed stale coffee breath over my shoulder. I whipped that same elbow over his bent head and around to catch the first guy across the chin. His head flung to the side. The momentum of the strike rotated me out of his hold, and he staggered under the blow.

I shot them both at close range and they dropped at my feet.

I slowly lowered my weapon, quivering from head to toe. If they hadn't been practically on top of me, I would have missed them. Footsteps clanged up the stairs, which my brain cycled through as strange. The steps didn't make noise before, which meant my hearing was coming back. I aimed my gun at the door. My hand shook so badly that I actually missed Julian as he came through. He ducked, far too late, screeched to a stop, and held up his hands.

He watched me lower the gun, took in the bodies around me, then hurried into the control room. "Did you tranq them all?" He eyed the bodies as if he expected them to pop up off the floor.

I nodded in a jerky motion I hoped he would see was a *yes*. My lungs gasped for the oxygen they had neglected to use in the mere seconds I had taken to fly in here and disable the command center. I shook too much to speak, so I turned and gestured to the plant workers at my feet.

"What the—" Julian cursed behind me. I tried to turn, but he held my shoulder and dug into the back of my flak jacket. A dull throb of pain raced between my shoulder blades, and I wanted to ask what he was doing, but my brain was starting to cloud. I felt it coming: the blowback. The moment when all my muscles would scream their fatigue at once and lose the cohesion that allowed me to stay upright.

Julian turned me around and held out a small and coppery lump. It looked like a smashed bullet. "They shot you."

His face turned darker than its normal creamy-brown color. I couldn't answer him and wondered if he was mad at me, like it was somehow my fault that I got shot. I tried to work up a suitably sarcastic response, but the blackness rushed my brain all at once. My vision went first, and gravity pulled me through a vacuum of the senses, devoid of light and sound and feeling.

I had just one thought: I hoped Julian would catch me before I cracked my head on the cement floor.

chapter TWO

Ava and I camped out on the roof, our yoga mats laid side by side. We faced each other, cross-legged, as though we were about to meditate. Which was partially true.

I slowly twisted myself into a lotus position, rotating my hips like Ava had taught me until I reached it. Every muscle in my body ached, even the ones behind my ears, between my toes, and tiny, screaming muscles in the crooks of my arms that I didn't know existed. I had tortured them into superhuman feats in the assault on the power station this morning, and now they were paying me back.

It was totally worth it.

The mission was a success. Sasha scribed all twenty-three employees of the Crawford power plant into being jacker sympathizers who would never turn the lights out on Jackertown, no matter who ordered it. We left a JFA member behind as an undercover staff member and even repaired the door on our way back out. Well, someone did, probably Sasha, given his handiness with a welder and distaste for broken things. I was passed out from the blowback and they had to carry me home. At least I had managed to keep the mission covert. Even Julian acknowledged as much. When I woke up a couple of hours later, sprawled on my bunk in the converted door factory that still served as the JFA headquarters, he was by my side. He had resumed the normal calm and attentive demeanor that made everyone love him, leaving me no chance to formulate a witty jab about him being mad at me for getting shot.

I relaxed into the lotus pose, stretching the muscle strain out of my body, but I couldn't help wincing as the bruise from the bullet moaned its complaint. Julian's worries weren't entirely unfounded. It was a good thing I had been wearing a flak jacket.

"How are you feeling?" Ava asked. Her rail-thin body seemed to be holding her lotus position effortlessly.

"Like I've been run over by a tank," I said. "With a couple kidney punches for good measure."

She nodded. A tuft of her long, blond hair lifted with the breeze and she tucked it back. My ultralite coat warded off the cold wind that gusted up from the streets of Jackertown below and brought the tempting smell of bacon from someone's late-morning breakfast. My stomach grumbled, even though I had already fed it a huge post-blowback meal.

Ava's gaze drifted to my upper left arm where my jacket covered a giant purplish bruise, another souvenir from the mission. The momentum of the bullet had shoved me into the wall, giving me two bruises for the price of one.

"We don't have to do this now, Kira," Ava said. "We can try again tomorrow."

"No, no, I was just whining. I'm fine."

She dipped her chin to peer at me. Her normally soft blue eyes were sharp with skepticism, and it clashed with the graceful lotus pose she held.

"Really," I said. I didn't want her to back out of our search today. We'd already had to skip a couple of days to prep for the mission and every day I wasn't looking for Kestrel was a day further away from killing him.

The war had begun in earnest four months ago, when Julian finally got his chance to blow up the gate to Agent Kestrel's secret facility and rescue the changelings Kestrel tormented there. Julian's Jacker Freedom Alliance had been born on that day—we liberated hundreds of jackers and swelled the ranks of the JFA overnight, bringing all the clans of Jackertown together—but Kestrel had slipped away again.

Ever since then, I had been honing my jacking skills and marksmanship, imagining a hundred different ways I could kill him. *Way #13:* a long mindjacked walk off Navy Pier. *Way #65:* death by choking on his own spit from cyanide poisoning. *Way #52:* slow death by asphyxiation from a blow to the Adam's apple. It was probably wrong to have that one be my favorite, but I didn't care. One way or another, when the time came, I would be ready.

And Kestrel would finally be dead.

"We'll keep our search short today, okay?" I said, trying to smile away Ava's concern. "Only a few sweeps and then we'll try again tomorrow."

Ava nodded her acceptance of my compromise. We both closed our eyes. I had to dive into my mind to do my part, and she needed to calm hers to allow me in.

Early on, when I had managed to fight off Kestrel's tranquilizer by ramping up my heart rate, I discovered I could manipulate my own mind. But I really had no idea of the depth of that ability. Over the last four months, I had explored and strengthened it. I was still finding new skills, but the most useful discovery was one of the first. When Kestrel wanted jackers hyped up to the fullest expression of their abilities in his experiments, he used jacker-specific adrenaline to boost them. It was the same stuff Julian had in his med-patches. I could trigger its production in my own body by following a particular neural pathway, like a street map that pointed the way to the Shot of Adrenaline department in my mind. I had used it before to amp up my endurance when I was SuperFastGirl.

And I could do it for other jackers, too.

I slowly breathed in and out, concentrating as I hunted down the right neural spot and dosed myself with a little adrenaline to help with the search. The chemical coursed through my body and eased some of the achiness of this morning's mission, but I wouldn't push it too much—one blowback per twenty-four hours was plenty.

Ava couldn't jack into my head—no one could, at least no one so far had been successful—but I could reach into hers. Ava's mindbarrier was weak, easy to push through, but I took care to be gentle. Her strawberry mindscent lingered at the back of my throat as I repeated the steps, finding her adrenaline release center and dosing her, only stronger. Outwardly, the two of us were the picture of a couple of Buddhist monks, calmly holding the lotus position on our mats. Inwardly, the quiver of excess adrenaline shook my too-full stomach, and Ava had to be feeling it even more strongly. Soon we would look more like junkies hyped up on some kind of psychedelic drug.

A small price for the possibility of finding Kestrel.

My unenhanced reach was at most a few thousand feet, double that with an adrenaline dose, but even unenhanced, Ava could reach for tens of miles. Enhanced, she could touch Wisconsin, a hundred miles away. When I synced my abilities with hers, our reach was... well, we hadn't exactly tested the limits. We had tried to pay a visit to Senator Vellus—mindreading politician and the country's most avowed hater of jackers—in his office in Springfield, two hundred miles from Chicago. We hadn't made it past the mindwave disruptor shield surrounding the capitol building, but it had been fun to try.

Syncing my mindfield with Ava's was tricky. There was a natural resistance when one jacker mind encountered another: the strong could invade the weak, or two minds of equal strength might fight, like oil wrestling with vinegar. But merging was a foreign idea.

Are you ready? I asked Ava, wanting to be sure.

Don't tax yourself, Kira. But yes, I'm ready.

I was more worried about taxing her. Her jacking skills were almost nonexistent, but when we synced, my jacking ability carried over. It seemed to be rough on her, leaving her already too-thin body drained of its normal spark.

I slowly eased our minds outside the confines of Ava's head and toward the street. Everyday life rambled below us. Changelings played while on break from their lessons and training sessions. Contractors traded mindjack favors between the Clans, respecting Julian's ban on trafficking with mindreaders. JFA patrols neglected their duties at the perimeter of Jackertown, curling smoke from their cigarettes and chatting instead.

I pulled Ava's mindfield along, reaching for one of the minds below. We needed something to focus on to sync up our mindfields properly before casting out for the larger search. I heard Ava pull in a long breath and let it out slow. Her mind relaxed, and the moment we synced, a tremor rippled through my body.

Ready? Ready? Our thoughts vibrated together.

Let's go. Let's go.

We reached past the edge of Jackertown, skipping over the vast ring of abandoned brownstones and businesses that comprised a buffer zone of sorts between downtown, where mindreaders still commuted to work, and the suburbs where they lived. A hundred years ago, before the change, this part of the city was a vibrant mix of people living in stacked apartment complexes along bustling train lines. Then all our leftover medications, flushed into the water and forgotten, brewed into something new: a cocktail that triggered a change in our brains. The world quickly filled with mindreaders, and that was when the depopulation started. Mindreaders could tolerate the close quarters of skyscrapers for work and play, but no one wanted to hear their neighbor's thoughts in their sleep. People fled to the wide-open spaces of the suburbs, and much of the city was abandoned to the demens, people driven mad by the adolescent change into mindreaders.

Dipping into the minds of the demens was dizzying at best and gut-wrenching at worst, so we took care to avoid them. We normally started our spiraling search for shield-protected facilities in downtown Chicago. Some important government buildings had them, like the mayor's office, but we were looking for something out of place, like Kestrel's secret facility we had destroyed over the summer. Of course, we would love to find Kestrel himself, but our luck wasn't the kind that would drop him into our laps without a helmet. But finding a shield-protected facility where it didn't belong was a step in the right direction.

A cluster of helmeted minds on the move caught our notice. We scanned the un-helmeted minds nearby for information—the entourage was Senator Vellus's. What was the senator doing in Chicago? He spent most of his time in the capitol building in Springfield, when he wasn't working the Senate floor in Washington DC, promoting his anti-jacker agenda.

My eyes popped open to look at Ava. The surprise registered on her face as well, but her eyes remained closed, holding tight onto our mental merge. I closed my eyes again, careful not to break our link.

Can we take Vellus? Maybe jack a passerby to go after him? No, they're too well guarded, plus they're on the move. Our synced thoughts twined around each other, asking and answering our own questions. *Let's follow them for a while. See where he's going. Maybe he'll take off his helmet—*

"Meditation on the roof?" Anna's voice broke into our thoughts, snapping our mind sync apart. "Isn't it a little cold for that?" Breaking the connection meant we couldn't reach as far we could on our own, especially me. My mindfield whipped back to my head like an overstretched rubber band, adding mental soreness to the physical fatigue that still prodded my body with dull sticks of pain.

I cracked open my eyes to look up at Julian's sister, the glare of the morning sun making me squint. Anna towered over us with her fists on her hips. Her straight hair hung to her shoulders like a sheet of black rain. She had the same creamy-brown skin and intense blue eyes as her twin brother, Julian, but while Julian's face was usually warm and inviting (unless he was mad at me), Anna's was almost always drawn as sharp as the knives she liked to throw in our training area downstairs.

"There are usually less interruptions up here," I said, which was as much as I could complain about it. Anna didn't know that Ava and I were searching for Kestrel. No one did, not even Julian. It was my own private obsession. One that Ava indulged me in because she was mesh that way. She understood how

19

much it fed and quieted the aching hole left inside me from losing Raf. I knew she pitied me from the time I spent in her mind, but it was in a kindhearted way. I understood why Sasha loved her so deeply.

Ava did the searches not to find Kestrel, but to help me.

Anna wouldn't understand, and Julian... well, I didn't want him to think I had gone demens. He trusted me, confided in me. Hinckley was his second-in-command, but I was his friend-in-chief. If he knew I was obsessing over Kestrel, he would worry, and he already did too much of that.

"Sorry to interrupt." Anna glanced at Ava, then back to me. "Kira, can we talk?"

Anna and I both had impenetrable minds, which meant I couldn't just link in to her head to make this discussion private. And Anna wasn't much of a "talker," so this must be important. I frowned an apology to Ava, who smiled brightly and climbed off her mat. She rolled it up and tucked it under her arm, then glided in that light-stepped way of hers to the stairwell. I unfolded gingerly from my lotus pose, stood, and took my time rolling my mat, waiting until Ava was out of earshot.

The stairwell door slowly swung shut. "What's up?" I asked Anna, searching for something I had done to make her angry, but coming up empty. She had been in favor of my part in the mission, and it had gone well.

"Kira, I want to take you off mission duty." Anna's face was the picture of a commander in control, yet her tone had an unusual softness underneath.

"What?" Fear gripped my vocal chords and hiked up my voice. I needed to be in operations the way I needed to search for Kestrel. "Why? Because of the blowback? I'm fine, really. It's not that big of a deal, but if you want, next time I won't push so hard."

"It's not that." She shifted from foot to foot and studied the broken pebbles on the concrete rooftop as if the words she was searching for were hidden in the random pattern of stones. Which made no sense. No one made Anna uncomfortable, least of all me.

She finally looked back to me. "You would better serve the cause on the political side of things."

Suddenly it became clear. "Not you too!" From the moment I joined the JFA, Julian had wanted me on his weekly political talks, which sent waves of revolution rippling across the chat-casts. He urged jackers around the country to join us, successfully building the population of Jackertown to nearly three thousand. I was fully on board with Julian's revolution, but joining his PR campaign was the last thing I wanted to do.

Anna was a good three inches taller than me and could probably take me in a fight, even if I were hyped up on fast-twitch. But there was no way she was taking me off ops, least of all to do Julian's chat-casts.

I glared up at her. "I belong on ops, Anna. You know it. Remember last week? With the Fronters?" The Readers' First Front made more incursions all the time into Jackertown. Their propaganda accused us of everything from baby-stealing to animal worship, and they liked to haul off unsuspecting jackers for their vigilante justice. "If I hadn't been there, scouting beyond the perimeter, we would have lost someone. Probably several someones, just like last month, when they took an entire patrol near the perimeter." That one had hit everyone hard. I jabbed a finger at Anna's camouflage ultralite. "I've got skills the JFA needs right now. You know it's true. You need me on ops."

"I'm not saying your skills aren't... useful." Her face drew tight, like she was forcing the words out. Then her voice became even softer, so unlike her that it made my heart race. "I know you want to do ops, but we don't always get to do what we want, Kira. Sometimes we have to do what's needed of us. Although, for you..." She paused, like this part was especially difficult for her to say. "...it's a little more complicated."

"What are you talking about?" Now I was genuinely confused. "I would do anything for the JFA!"

"I know," she said. "I know you would. It's just that Julian thinks it's important that you shouldn't be on ops. And what he thinks matters." She paused as if this was a grand revelation and not something Julian and I had been quarreling over for months.

"I would do anything for Julian." I said it flatly, daring her to contradict me.

She didn't say anything, just shook her head, then ran both hands through her hair, leaving it mussed. Normally, Anna was about as subtle as a right hook. Reading her wasn't difficult, and she didn't try to make it so. But today she was a thousand crossed signals that made my head hurt. Or maybe I was still recovering from the blowback. That was possible.

"Julian is important, Kira," Anna said finally, her voice falling into her familiar command mode, as if Julian were an objective we were going to reach by deploying all our assets. "He's more important than any of us. Jackers will listen to me, they'll carry out my orders, but they *follow* Julian. Do you understand? He's the heart of the JFA, and we can't have anything messing that up. We can't have him distracted by things that aren't central to the cause. He needs to keep his focus."

"So what are you saying?" I said. "That I need to go on Julian's chat-casts because we can't have him worrying about me on ops?" My chest tightened and triggered a strange light-headed feeling. I couldn't help it if Julian worried about things he shouldn't. The op had gone fine, and I had been right after all—the plant worker would have called in the assault if I hadn't reached him in time. It was stupid for me not to be on ops, and it was dangerous to go on the chat-casts. Julian wanted me to be something that I couldn't. That I wouldn't, not if it endangered the people I loved.

Anna bit her lip and stared out over Jackertown, avoiding my question.

"Anna." I took a breath, trying to calm the panic-fueled storm brewing inside me. I had to appeal to her rational side—that was where Anna operated ninety percent of the time. I could reach her there. "I can't go public the way Julian wants me to. Vellus is just waiting for me to pop up on his radar screen again. The only thing keeping my family safe is that, as far as Vellus knows, I'm long gone."

"He has to know you're here, Kira."

"Maybe," I said. "He's probably watching my family to see if I go back home, but so far, he hasn't made a move against them. I want to keep it that way. If I'm splashed all over the casts, Vellus will use my family to flush me out. I would be forced to leave the JFA and go to ground for real. *Forced*. I won't put them in danger again." I hadn't spoken to my dad since I left—just scrit Xander every once in a while to check on them. I was afraid Vellus might go after Raf, too. Even though Raf hated me now, as far as Vellus knew, I still cared for him.

"We could send a few JFA members to protect them," she offered.

"A couple extra jackers?" I asked. "Against the entire federal government?" This was the same argument I'd had a million times with Julian.

"Or we could bring them here to keep them safe."

"Jackertown's getting better, but it's still no place for a reader like my mom." I ran my hand over my face, trying to rub the frustration from it. "It's not going to work, Anna."

I saw my argument take hold, trapping her in a box of logic. Backing Anna into a corner wasn't the safest thing to do, but I'd rather take my chances with her than risk the alternatives.

I leaned in close and dropped my voice to press my point home. "Julian doesn't need me to be a figurehead in the revolution. He really doesn't. People follow *him*. They love him. He *is* the revolution. He doesn't need me up there, appealing to jackers and the public. I can serve the cause better on ops, even if he can't see that."

"What can't I see?" Julian asked, his voice breaking in from the door of the rooftop stairwell. I jerked back from my close whispering with Anna, my face heating up. How much had Julian heard? He claimed that he never controlled Anna's instincts, but could he read her thoughts? Or was he locked out of her impenetrable mind, like he was with me? I spun back over my words. There wasn't anything I hadn't more or less said directly to him. Except maybe the part about leaving the JFA if I had to.

Anna and I stared at each other and flicked looks to Julian as he quickly strode over to us, neither one of us apparently knowing what to say.

Julian folded his arms. "If you're done conspiring against me," he said, seeming to include both of us in that statement, "I could use your help with something." Those words were for me, and relief flooded through me followed by an echo of concern. Was Anna an advanced scout, prepping me for Julian's latest bid to bring me into his jacker-recruiting program? My head hurt from all the jumping to conclusions. Better to simply take it at face value.

"Sure thing, boss." I eased the tension out of my voice. "Have some new recruits you want me to whip into shape? I'm ready to go. What do you do need?"

He grimaced. "No, I have something much more difficult for you. It might be at the limit of your capabilities, but I'd like you to at least give it a try."

He was completely baiting me, but I let him, just to show I could play along. "We'll see about that."

He turned toward the stairwell, but not before I saw a grin play across his face. I nodded to Anna as I left, but she didn't look reassured. In fact, the lines on her face were even sharper than when she had come up on the roof.

chapter THREE

I followed Julian down the stairwell, trying to guess his intentions from his cryptic smile when he stole looks at me and the way his long-fingered hand lightly skimmed the rail.

I had no clue.

At the base of the stairs, to my surprise, we didn't turn toward the central meeting area at the front of JFA headquarters or even the privacy rooms Sasha had built along the side, but instead strode past the training area, heading for the back door. When we reached it, Julian grabbed a white-hooded jacket off a rack and held it up for me to slip my arms into, even though I already had my ultralite. I tried not to grimace as all the obscure muscles in my body protested my every movement. Julian chose to ignore the signs that I was still recovering from the blowback, so maybe we wouldn't argue about ops after all. Which only made my curiosity spike to a new level.

Julian slipped on his jacket as we stepped outside into the blustery cold. "So, what were you and Anna talking about?"

"You," I said, casting a look from under my hood. "About how impossible you are to deal with. We're seriously contemplating a coup. We're going to put Hinckley in charge." Hinckley was born to be second-in-command; he would rather fall on his own jacker-tuned Taser than join a coup against Julian.

"At least put Ava in charge," he said with a grin. "Then I can be sure that the changelings will get taken care of."

"Ava was our second choice."

His light laugh was good to hear, like all his worried thoughts about bullets and ops had been scrubbed clean in the bright midmorning sun. We crossed the street, striding past half a dozen changelings playing kickball. They were underdressed for the late fall cold, their breath leaving puffs of steam in the wake of their frenzied chase after the ball. A dark-haired girl stopped to beam and wave at Julian, and he smiled in return. Down the street, a cluster of JFA sentries, black armbands over their ultralite jackets, saw Julian coming and scattered. Maybe they finally remembered where they were supposed to be.

As we neared a large furniture store, abandoned long ago when the city depopulated under the range ordinances, I finally realized where we were headed.

"The Mediation Center?" I asked as we slowed in front of the door. "Did I get a traffic ticket?"

Julian didn't smile, just pulled the door open for me. "I want your opinion on something."

"My opinion." That sounded like Julian wanted me involved in something that was decidedly not ops. The dimly lit interior of the Mediation Center waited past the open door, but I didn't step through.

"Mediation is important, Kira," he said patiently, his hand bracing the heavy wooden door open. "If we're going to have a civilized society of jackers, we need to have laws and people to enforce them."

Of course he was right, but I didn't want to encourage him. "I know. I'm not saying it's not important."

"I'm glad you think so." Julian handed me a small, tinfoil-covered pellet. It looked like a bullet, but I knew it was much more powerful than that.

"A thought grenade?" I asked, eyebrows arched.

"Just in case. I'm hoping you won't have an occasion to use it." He swept his hand through the open space. "They're waiting for us."

I gently closed my fist around the thought grenade, careful not to crush it. It was an anti-jacker weapon designed by the government, specially tuned to jacker mindwaves but completely harmless to mindreaders. Julian and I had used one to bust out of Kestrel's prison, which only worked because the thought grenade didn't electronically scramble my brain like it did most jackers. What possible use could there be for one here in Jackertown?

I stepped over the threshold of the Mediation Center, and a gust of wind rustled the photofilms that papered the windows inside. They were pictures of the jackers who had gone missing. The ones Julian and the mages had rescued and returned to Jackertown. It afforded privacy to the proceedings and a vivid reminder of life before Julian had arrived in Jackertown full of hope for the future and the conviction that we all deserved to be free.

We hung our jackets by the door. The room still hinted of furniture polish from the long-ago time when it was home to bedroom sets and armoires. Now it was empty except for a few people in rickety chairs. They faced an elevated stage and a single, battered table that served as the magistrate's bench. An older jacker, dressed in long black robes that pooled on the floor, sat on another spindly chair. Behind him stood one of Hinckley's men with a military buzz cut and the square jaw to match. I didn't recognize him, but Hinckley had acquired a whole new batch of recruits when Senator Vellus purged the government of suspected jackers last month.

As soon as the magistrate saw Julian, he hustled to his feet, his chair creaking behind him. The three people seated below took their cue from him and rose as well. One of them wore an anti-jacker helmet, with his hands bound in front, and my curiosity went into overdrive. No one in Jackertown wore helmets. It was like waving the enemy's flag in the face of an armed militia.

The cage fit snugly around his head, held in place by a chin strap. A quick mental brush verified the disruptor field was fully functioning. No one, not even Julian's strongest jacker, Myrtle, could breach the shield when it was active. The man was mid-twenties, thin, and had the crazed look of a demens on a very bad day. The two jackers on either side rested their hands on their holstered weapons, but they acted like the guy was radioactive, staying close enough to guard him but keeping their distance as much as possible. The helmet clearly wasn't to protect the person wearing it, but to keep others safe from the mindfield inside.

The thought grenade in my hand took on new weight—it would reach through the man's helmet to scramble his brain. *Just in case*, as Julian put it.

Julian motioned everyone to sit as we approached the stage, but they remained standing. Behind the magistrate's bench, a wall-mounted screen was split between a database of adjudicated cases and a listing of the Jackertown Code: no kill jacks, no stealing, no mental or physical assaults, no forced jackwork, no contracting to mindreaders, no unauthorized memory wipes, and no vigilante justice. The system was mostly held together by a universal respect for Julian's judgment and stiff penalties ranging from banishment to scribing. There were no jails in Jackertown and not much in the way of second chances. A lot of dangerous jackers passed through the Mediation Center, but I had never seen someone helmeted before.

As Julian led me up the three wooden steps of the stage, the Mediation room suddenly felt like a duty I had neglected while playing with guns and ops. Julian was building a new society for jackers; the least I could do was understand the mechanics of how it worked. Maybe that was why he had brought me here.

Or maybe he needed someone to wield the thought grenade if things got out of control.

When Julian took his place by the bench, the magistrate finally sat. The guards and their prisoner took their seats as well. I stepped back two paces and nodded to Hinckley's enforcer who had his rough, meaty hands clasped in front of him, having not moved through the entire display of courtesy and officiousness. Julian frowned at me and tilted his head, indicating I should step forward to stand next to him, which I dutifully did.

"Magistrate," Julian said in his official *I'm in charge* voice, "I understand that you've found this jacker guilty of murder, is that correct?"

"Yes, sir." The magistrate's wrinkled face barely moved with the words. It was strange to hear him call Julian *sir*.

The helmeted man leaped up, his chair clattering to the floor behind him. "I am *not* a jacker!" The man's mouth trembled like he had trouble forming the words. "I didn't kill nobody!" The two guards next to him were on their feet in an instant. Hinckley's man stepped forward, a dart gun in his hand. I searched for a hard surface to crush the thought grenade against. Without looking back, Julian flung an arm out to stop all of us.

"So you keep saying," Julian said to the prisoner, his face falling into the blank look he reserved for jackers he would soon be scribing or banishing. "We have several dead bodies that would seem to indicate otherwise."

"I didn't kill them!" The man's voice climbed an octave,

almost hysterical. "They attacked me! I... I didn't do anything. I *couldn't* do anything. I'm not one of you!"

The man's impassioned plea struck me as strange. Was he just crazy? A demens jacker? I'd seen a lot of things, but that would be a new one. Julian's face twitched. Normally, he could to dip into the man's mind and read his instincts, his intentions, his most basic desires. Julian could read any jacker or reader that way—the sole exception being me, with my impenetrable mind. He knew what was going on inside people's heads better than they knew themselves. But with the prisoner's helmet on, Julian's ability was useless.

Julian surprised me by turning around. "This person," he said, emphasizing the word, as if his jackerness was actually up for debate, "was found with a JFA patrol beyond the perimeter. He claims they attacked him."

I swallowed. Julian didn't say I would have to give my opinion in court, especially on a murder case I knew nothing about. "What does the patrol say?" I asked. Everyone was watching me, including the magistrate, who had twisted in his seat to stare.

"They aren't saying much," Julian said. "They're dead."

My stomach hollowed out. Six dead jackers. What kind of ability could wipe out an entire patrol? Once upon a time, I'd knocked out a warehouse full of jackers, but I had caught them by surprise. A JFA patrol would be very difficult to surprise, and it was practically impossible to get a kill jack on all six at once.

My fingers brushed the smooth metallic surface of the thought grenade. "Why does he say he's not a jacker?"

"That's the part we don't understand."

The prisoner's skin was pale and sweaty, as if he was living inside a nightmare and couldn't wake up. Definitely freaked out.

"Could he be a changeling?" I asked. "Maybe he just came into his power, so he's not sure what's going on?" It had been over a year since I had discovered my ability, but I still remembered the day it happened—and the terror that came with it—with crystal clarity.

"He's at least a decade older than any changeling I've ever seen," Julian said.

I nodded.

"I... I told the judge here," said the defendant, waving a shaky hand. "I can prove it." He pointed his bound hands to a spot near his shoulder. "You can check for yourself! They took my DNA. They tested me. I'm not no jacker."

He had been tested? I knew Vellus was herding people through testing stations to sift the readers from the jackers. Most jackers left with a J inked on their cheeks, while some never came back, detained indefinitely under Vellus's latest laws reducing jacker rights. No one knew why some jackers were set free while others were held—it seemed a cruel, random lottery—but mindreaders left the testing station with a Band-Aid of Honor from their DNA test and a special designation in Vellus's national registry as "normal."

"If I was one of you," the helmeted man said, "they would have tagged me. You... you gotta let me go! I didn't do nothin', and I don't belong in this freak town. You can't keep me here! I got rights!"

"Did he really just get released from a testing station?" I asked. "That's kind of a strange lie to make up."

"That's what he claims, and he has a bandage and recent puncture wound on his arm," Julian said, face grave. "However, I'm not inclined to take the chance of sending someone into his head to search his memories. A second patrol found him passed out next to the bodies of the first patrol. When they realized he was alive, they jacked him awake. He nearly killed the jacker waking him—permanently wiped half his mind—before they put him under again. We were lucky he was still half-tranqed when they figured out what he was."

"Which is?"

"I don't know, precisely," Julian said. "But Myrtle's got serious competition for the *Strongest Jacker I Know* award."

"Are you going to banish him?" I asked. "He doesn't want to stay, anyway."

"If he's as powerful as he appears, I'm not sure that's wise. He seems..." Julian glanced at the man, whose gaze was shifting between the magistrate, Julian, and me in a bouncy dance that made me dizzy to watch. "...unstable. But we can't take the chance of unhelmeting him for scribing or... any handling that I might be able to do."

That gave me pause—I only knew of one other time that Julian had permanently altered someone's instincts, and it still haunted him. It wasn't an option he would even consider unless there weren't any others. The rough justice of the Clan approach, where killing was as common as jacking, was slowly giving way to the rule of law, exactly as Julian wanted. I knew he didn't want to go backward, but the only place equipped to keep someone like this was Vellus's Detention Center. And I couldn't stand the thought of sending another jacker there, even one as dangerous as this guy.

"I know it doesn't seem likely, but maybe he really is a changeling." I had captured the attention of the man now, his flighty gaze landing on me and sticking. "How old are you?" I asked him.

He flicked a scattered look around the room, then came back to me. "Um. Twenty-seven."

"If I'd been a reader all that time and suddenly changed... well, I'd be a bit freaked out too." I was talking directly to him now. "There are a lot of jackers who, when they first come into their abilities, can't control them. Especially when it comes on quickly." That was painfully close to what had happened to me with Raf. "Jacker changelings need someone to guide them, to help them understand what's happening, so they can learn to control it. Your ability doesn't have to be a weapon that kills. It's like a gun—just because you have it doesn't mean you have to use it."

He blinked, his eyes bloodshot and rimmed in red. His chest heaved a little with his labored breathing, but his body seemed to calm along with the tension in the room.

"We haven't harmed you." I gestured to the guards hovering on either side of him, their hands still on their weapons. "Any one of them could have killed you at any point, but instead they brought you here for trial. An ability as powerful as yours is dangerous. Anywhere other than Jackertown, and you would likely be dead by now."

The man pursed his lips and slipped a glance at his guards.

"Out in the mindreading world," I continued, "you might be able to rook for a while, passing for a mindreader, but eventually you'll be caught. Especially if you can't control it. If you don't get yourself killed first, the readers will happily throw you into Vellus's Detention Center. Your brain will rot away under the gas until you not only can't jack, but you won't even know who you are."

I let my words tighten around him for a moment.

"It's not up to me," I said, "but in my opinion, you should be given a chance to learn to control this ability of yours. If you can, you could make a real difference in the fight to build a better life for jackers everywhere. Or you can take your chances with a world that thinks you don't deserve to share the same air now that you're one of us instead of one of them."

His face fell, but there seemed to be a new rationality dawning. Less panic. If he had somehow just changed, maybe the craziness was because he felt trapped in the middle of Jackertown with all the lies and rumors that mindreaders believed about us. I looked to Julian, but his eyes had a fire that made my face heat up, so I quickly looked away and stared at a rusted nail poking out of the raised platform, avoiding his gaze.

After a moment, Julian spoke and, thankfully, it wasn't to me. "The normal punishment for murder is scribing, a complete rewriting of your mind, something that's not possible in your case. Banishment isn't an option I'm ready to consider until I can be assured that you can control your ability enough to be released. You'll be incarcerated for the time being, but I'll appoint a jacker to work with you to develop your skills. Should anything happen to that jacker, we will have no choice but to remove the threat you pose. However, if you can learn to control it and prove you're no longer a danger to others, you will have the choice to stay here in Jackertown or leave."

The man blinked rapidly, his head swinging from Julian to me and back again.

"Do you understand the sentence?" the magistrate asked.

The man's gaze jumped to him, like he had forgotten the magistrate was there. "Um... you... you're not going to kill me, right?"

"That is correct," he said. "You are sentenced to one month of incarceration with release pending remediation." He banged a gavel that made us all jump.

The guards gingerly took hold of the man's arms and led him away. I had no idea where they were taking him. They'd probably have to build a cell just for him.

Julian turned from the others, his face still burning with the same intensity as before. He stepped close before I could dodge him.

"This is where I need you, Kira." His voice was a whisper full of meaning. "Not in ops."

I had already figured out that was where he was going with

this. "You want me to be a magistrate? Because I really don't look good in black robes."

He smiled wide. "I wouldn't mind seeing you in black robes. If I'd known you could talk down a crazed super-changeling, I would have put you in the judiciary rotation sooner." His smile mellowed. "Just think what you could do on the chat-casts."

The chat-casts again. He just wasn't going to give up on that. Why couldn't he understand that all I wanted was to serve the JFA, get revenge on Kestrel, and keep my family safe?

"The people want to hear from you on the chat-casts, not me," I said, my hands spread wide with exasperation. "You inspire them. Your words give them hope. I would only be repeating what you say, anyway. You don't need me."

"I do need you, Kira."

"No you don't." Somehow it seemed like we had veered off into talking about something else. Time to change the subject. "But if you want my opinion, I can think of a few things around here I'd like to have taken care of."

His voice dropped further. "Like what?"

"Like, what's the JFA's plan for dealing with the testing stations? We're losing jackers every day to Vellus's round-up efforts. When are we going to put a stop to that?"

He touched my shoulder, his hand warm even through the ultralite. "Soon, but not yet. An assault on the testing stations would bring Vellus's forces down hard on Jackertown. We've got the power plant secured, but we're not ready for the siege that would bring. We need to ensure our food and water supplies first. Patience, Kira. I promise we will shut down the testing stations eventually."

"A promise?" I smirked and shook my head in mock chastisement. "Anna wouldn't approve." His promise-making got under his sister's skin, but I thought it was part of what drew people to him.

His smile made me suddenly aware of how close we were, whispering on the stage together, his hand warming my shoulder. The idea of inappropriate hugs crossed my mind again. I should have pulled back, but I saw an opening in the way his eyes were lit with promises and possibilities.

"I know a certain female jacker with extraordinary abilities," I said, peering up at him. "Someone who's exceptional in operations and that just might be able to conduct a covert op for you. We could be in and out of a testing station, with no one the wiser, like the power plant today. All you have to do is say the word." I wished I could persuade him with just my smile, but instead his face drew into a scowl.

"The last place I want you is somewhere Vellus can—"

A banging sound from the back of the Mediation Center cut him off. The door had flung open and Hinckley rushed in, his boots screeching on the polished wooden floor of the Mediation Room and his jacket flapping at his sides like it wanted to take flight and carry him across the floor even faster than his long-legged strides. Julian and I quickly broke apart.

"Julian!" Hinckley called, not waiting until he crossed the room. "Vellus has called in the National Guard. Jackertown is surrounded."

Chapter FOUR

I'd never seen Julian so angry.

We had nearly sprinted back to the JFA headquarters, and now tension radiated from Julian's body like waves of heat. His shoulders were stiff as he stared at the angry red words of the breaking tru-cast scrolling across the screen. Jackers drifted into the kitchen from the racks in the back. They must have been drawn by the palpable unease up front, or perhaps they had just heard the news about Vellus and the National Guard.

Hinckley leaned against the weathered wooden table where the JFA shared meals, talking in hushed tones with a half dozen of his men, some with their jackets still on after being called back to headquarters. Hinckley broke from his men, nodded to the new arrivals, and stood next to Julian. He folded his arms, and his stringy fingers tapped a silent rhythm on his well-defined bicep. His early-morning training sessions with Anna seemed to be bulking him up, but he was probably used to it from his time working jacker Special Forces in the government.

I brushed Hinckley's mind. *What news do they have?* I asked when he let me in.

They don't know anything more than we do, Hinckley thought.

Did somebody discover we scribed everyone at the power plant?

That's what I'd like to know. Apparently no one near the perimeter has their short comm on. His mindscent was sharper than normal, and his jaw worked as if he wanted to chew on whoever at the perimtere had neglected their duty.

Where's Ava? I asked. Headquarters was dead center in Jackertown, which meant the perimeter was out of my reach, but Ava could easily find out what was happening there.

Hinckley nodded. *I've got someone looking for her.*

Julian didn't notice either Hinckley or me, his gaze still trained on the screen. It played an image of the National Guard troops at the edge of Jackertown, all sporting black automatic rifles and standing at attention in the middle of the intersection. Julian's knuckles turned white as he clenched the short comm radio in his hand, holding it close to his mouth.

"What do you mean, Yee's not checking in?" he shouted far louder than necessary. "Find him!" His face was three shades darker than normal and getting worse.

Yee was supposed to be on sentry duty at the perimeter. Had the National Guard troops already taken prisoners? The tru-cast kept cycling the same images, then an interview with Vellus from days ago looped in. He didn't say anything about the National Guard, just blathered on about his testing station program and how it was slowly solving the "jacker problem" as he now called us.

Julian had switched channels. "Mary!" he shouted into the short comm. Every face in the kitchen area turned to stare, and the only sound was a door creaking closed in the back. I stepped closer to Julian, then stopped. He finally looked away from the screen, to me, and the lost look in his eyes made my heart seize up. In that frozen beat of time, he searched my face. I couldn't tell what he found, but he frowned and turned back to the screen. When he spoke into the short comm, his voice was smooth and warm, the normal voice that held everything together, including my frayed nerves.

"Mary, how are things at the plant?" he asked. She must be the jacker we left at the power station this morning. "So everything's secure, then," he said, for the benefit of everyone listening in. Shoulders around the room relaxed, probably as much from his tone as anything else. His words washed relief through my body, too. I clenched and unclenched my hands, trying to shake the remaining tension away.

"Good," Julian said into the short comm. "You're sure there are no Guard troops waiting outside?" There was a pause. "No, stay there. Things here are more... complicated. Maintain your post and keep your short comm with you. I want you in constant contact. If we need to come get you, I want to know immediately."

If the power plant was secure, Vellus's sudden movement

against Jackertown didn't make sense. Finally, a live tru-caster broke in through the repetitive looping images with a pulsing blue news alert scrolling across the bottom of the screen. Vellus appeared, along with Illinois' Governor Rancin, another politician riding the anti-jacker sentiment of the state. The background was out of focus, so it was hard to see where they were, but it hadn't been that long since Ava and I sensed Vellus's entourage in downtown Chicago.

The boom mics picked up the thought waves from Vellus and the tru-caster who was interviewing him.

Governor Rancin has wisely decided to deploy the National Guard in this tense situation, Vellus thought. *I fully support him exercising his duty to keep the state's citizens safe from any domestic emergency that might threaten them.*

On screen, a tan camouflage troop carrier rolled to a stop and spilled out Guardsmen onto the sun-bleached street. Their pitch-black riot gear and anti-jacker helmets drew an invisible *do not cross* line between them as they took up positions facing Jackertown.

What domestic emergency prompted this action?

The tru-caster had directed her question to the Governor, but Vellus answered. *A small, armed group of jackers from the lawless area known as Jackertown attempted to take over a power generation station in Crawford. They were unsuccessful, I'm happy to say, and the power station is secure. It's only used for peak power usage for the suburbs, in addition to powering Jackertown. There were no service interruptions, but the*

Governor's timely deployment of the National Guard will keep jackers from making any more excursions out of Jackertown to threaten areas where normal mindreaders live and work.

"Vellus is right," Julian said. "The power station is secure—securely under our control." That knowledge seemed to help return Julian's face to its normal color.

"But if Vellus knows about the assault, he has to know we've jacked people there," I said. "Why is he leaving it in our control?"

Anna spoke up from behind us. "Vellus doesn't want to publicly acknowledge that the JFA has a win." Hinckley stepped aside to let her stand next to Julian. She eyed the screen, crossing her arms. "We left the station workers well-armed. Vellus would have to do a full assault on the power station to take it back. The media would be all over that, and the Guard might not win, not right away. Instead of taking back the power plant, Vellus is using it as a pretext to roll out his anti-jacker National Guard unit."

Julian templed his hands and touched them to his lips, the way he did when he was pondering something. That simple motion, that return to normalcy, eased the jitters working their way into my stomach.

"Vellus can claim victory without ever having fought the battle," Julian agreed. "He knows we can't dispute it without bringing an attack. And now he has a justification to set up security around Jackertown to keep track of our movements."

The screen switched to another shot of the troops. Most were busy forming a human barrier, but a few were unloading giant panels from a white convoy truck. They looked like plastifoam from the ease with which they were handling them, two Guards to a panel.

"Um, Julian?" I pointed to the screen. "That does not look good."

We watched as they placed one panel next to another and left them standing. A wall. Around Jackertown.

Julian's face darkened again. "They're fencing us in."

"That's not much of a fence," I offered.

"Those are mobile anti-jacker shields." His voice was dead calm, his gaze trained on the screen. "Probably electrified as well. With those in place, they can keep anyone from getting in or out. They can stop all trade, all flow of goods, food, medical supplies. They plan to keep us here a good long time with those."

This was the siege Julian had worried about. The one we weren't prepared for yet. Julian closed his eyes, ran a hand over his face, and I sensed a coiled anger underneath that small move. He was wiping the signs of it from his face so he could keep that calm expression for the rest of us. It sent a shiver of alarm shooting through my body.

"What are we going to do?" I asked.

"It's time, Julian," Anna said, facing him.

"No." Julian didn't look at her, still transfixed by the white panels that were undoing all his careful planning.

"Time for what?" I had no idea what they were talking about, which just bumped my alarm up another level.

Anna dropped her voice. "She has a way to stop him, Julian. Let her use it."

"I said no." He refused to look at her. Or me, for that matter.

"What are you talking about?" Maybe Anna had a mission that she hadn't shared, a secret plan in the event of a siege.

She looked past Julian to me. "Kira, your father still has access to Vellus." She stated this as a fact. At my dubious look, she explained, "He may not be mindguarding for Vellus anymore, but he knows how to contact him. He could arrange for you to meet with Vellus. Take Sasha along."

No, no, no. The idea of using my dad to go after Vellus made my head spin. It was flat dangerous. If we were caught... "I don't think—"

Julian turned his head to Anna and cut me off. "I'm not sending Kira anywhere near Vellus." His voice left no room for objection.

Anna objected anyway. "We need more time, Julian. We're not ready for a siege. Kira can buy us that time, a lot of it, if Sasha is successful in scribing Vellus. He has to be stopped before he becomes any more of a threat. It's worth the risk."

Julian stood straight, fists slowly clenching at his side. "No." They were nose to nose in a staring contest.

"There's another way," I said, desperate to avoid returning home as much as Julian didn't want to send me there. "Let me take Sasha and go after Vellus directly. Right now. He's here in Chicago New Metro."

That got their attention. Both Julian and Anna swung their heads to me.

Shock registered on Julian's face. "How do you know that?"

Oops. "Um, well." There was no time for hedging. "Ava and I have been doing long-distance surveillance, looking for Kestrel." Anna gave me a knowing look, like she had already guessed we were doing more than meditation on the rooftop. "Anyway, this morning we sensed an entourage coming out of the mayor's office. I'm sure he's still somewhere nearby. If we move quickly, we can catch him before he leaves Chicago. Let me and Ava search again, find him, take a strike force, and take him out."

Julian's face pulled into a frown as I talked, but he didn't question why I was looking for Kestrel. "I don't want you going anywhere near Vellus."

"She doesn't have to," Anna said. "She and Ava can pinpoint Vellus's location, and Sasha can lead the team against him."

Thank you, Anna. If this worked, it would not only remove Vellus as a threat, but I wouldn't have to endanger my family to do it.

"If we attack the senator in broad daylight," Julian said, "and he suddenly is turned into a friend of the JFA, everyone will know he's been jacked."

"Which is why Sasha will have to be subtle," Anna said. Sasha's ability was powerful—he could change the personality of a person down to their core. He could change Vellus into our best friend, but Anna was right. That would be too obvious.

"Most jacks are temporary," I added. "Even if they know he's been attacked, most people would expect him to return to normal afterward. Sasha doesn't have to make Vellus an instant revolutionary. He could scribe him into being a subversive, like the power-plant workers. Vellus could be our double agent on the inside of the anti-jacker movement, feeding us intel and working to sabotage his own plans."

I saw Julian struggling to find the flaw in the plan.

"We have to move fast." I gestured to the screen. "Before they get that fence up and turn all of Jackertown into a concentration camp. Plus, Ava and I won't be able to reach through the shield once they get it up. We should move closer to the edge of Jackertown now. From the rooftops at the perimeter, we should be able to reach over the shield if they activate it before we get there."

Julian ran his hand through his hair, then dropped it. "Okay, but you're doing surveillance, Kira, nothing else. Don't engage the Guard at the perimeter."

"Surveillance. Got it, boss."

"I mean it."

"I'm exceptionally talented at surveillance."

That drew a slight smile out of him. "Take Sasha with you for backup. He'll want to go if Ava's going, anyway. Short comm back as soon as you know Vellus's location. We'll organize the strike from here. Under no circumstances do you go after Vellus on your own."

"Aye, aye, Captain."

But I had no intention of following Julian's orders. If the opportunity presented itself, I would take out Vellus myself.

Chapter FIVE

S asha, Ava, and I threaded through the maze of Jackertown's alleyways, staying off the main arteries in case Vellus started rolling tanks into town. We dodged potholes and abandoned furniture left over from the days when the demens were the sparse and rambling inhabitants of this slice of Chicago New Metro. They had been driven out when the jackers moved in. Normally these streets would be bustling with the daily life of Jackertown, but today they were empty again. The sounds of changelings at play had been replaced by the silence of shuttered windows and the hushed whispers of JFA sentries. They were stationed on the street corners with black armbands and rifles while everyone else was inside, hovering over their short comms or watching the tru-casts.

Ava and I both reached a full 360-degree circle around us, scanning for Guardsmen who might be making incursions into Jackertown, although there had been no report of it on the short comm that Sasha carried. He followed behind us, his dart gun drawn. The three of us slowed our pace as we crept up on the perimeter at the eastern edge of town. We paused at a side alley that emptied onto a mid-sized street at the limits of jacker-occupied land.

The perimeter of Jackertown stretched for miles, but even this small strip had a half dozen Guards patrolling it, hanging out in pairs. Vellus must have hundreds of Guardsmen at his disposal. The rough sound of their voices, unused to talking out loud, drifted down the alley. Their helmets not only kept us from jacking in, they kept the readers' mindwaves from beaming out. The Guardsmen were all effectively zeros, an irony I didn't have time to dwell on.

I brushed the soft mindbarrier of Ava's mind, asking her to let me in. *Are you sure this is the least-protected strip of the perimeter?*

Yes, Ava thought, and I sensed Sasha's presence in her mind, joining us. *Since they haven't activated the shield here, we should have a straight shot to downtown. If Vellus is still there.*

Don't you need to get up higher? Sasha pointed to the fire-escape ladder of the three-story brownstone we were huddled against.

Ava's eyes unfocused for a moment, then she blinked. *They're assembling the shield along the southern edge, so we can't search in that direction. If we don't find Vellus in our first sweep, we may need to go up higher to reach over the shield.*

Then we better get started. I took Ava's hand and led her behind a dumpster that was bashed in and leaning perilously to one side, forming a small cove between the rusted metal and the crumbling cement of the brownstone. We needed a safe place to hide while we searched, in case the Guardsmen decided to take a stroll. Sasha followed, keeping his gun and his gaze trained on the opening at the far end of the alley. The dumpster reeked of yesterday's pizza and day-old salad—someday I hoped picking up the garbage on time would be Jackertown's biggest problem.

Are you ready? I asked Ava.

She nodded. Sasha pulled out of our minds, but watched us with high interest. We sat cross-legged on the rough pavement, hands resting on our upturned knees. I counted down from ten, trying to breathe through my mouth to avoid inhaling the nearby garbage stench, and dosed myself, then Ava, with adrenaline. We reached for Sasha's mind to get synced.

What the... His mind did a contorted dance, caught between reflexively shoving us out and holding onto Ava. We were synced and gone before he could decide.

Where do we start?

We knew the answer even as we asked it.

Tribune Tower.

The *Chicago Tribune* reporters were no doubt tru-casting the breaking news of the siege right now, and they might know Vellus's itinerary. We reached to downtown and found our favorite reporter, Maria Ramirez, working on a story about families torn apart when a member turned jacker, something that hit uncomfortably close to home for both of us. We brushed Maria's mind, lightly, not wanting to ransack her memories, but also concerned about alerting the other reporters to our presence.

Maria, we thought. Would she recognize our twinned thoughts or freak out? *We are Kira.* Well that didn't come out exactly right.

Maria bolted up from her desk and panic spun through her thoughts. We were tempted to jack her into calmness, but that wouldn't be mesh. We would have to talk her down.

We... I'm Kira, I thought with some effort, trying to project my thoughts with a little more authority, although Ava's were dominant at this distance. *Please be calm. We're not going to hurt you.* This was a lot trickier than it seemed, controlling our thoughts.

What do you want? Sour panic trickled through her normal apple-flavored mindscent.

We're trying to find Vellus, we thought, giving up on trying to separate our thoughts. *Do you know his itinerary?*

Kira, is that really you? Why are you so... different?

Don't worry. We tried to think reassuring thoughts, but the distance was hard to overcome. *We're just trying some new skills. Can you help us find Vellus?*

He was here a few minutes ago, she thought. *Doing an interview with another reporter. I was definitely not invited.* We had no doubt about that. Vellus would never take the chance of a one-on-one interview with Maria again, not when the last time Julian had been there and handled Vellus into releasing prisoners from his own Detention Center.

I think Vellus is headed for another interview on site at the perimeter of Jackertown.

What? Our thoughts rang strong in her head. *Thank you, Maria. That is very helpful.* We would call Maria later to explain. Or maybe not, because the less she knew about our operations, probably the better. We pulled back from Maria's mind and started sweeping the major streets of downtown Chicago near the Tribune Tower. There were thousands of mindreaders working in the skyscrapers, but relatively few in the streets. They bustled through the early-winter chill in search of lunch or their next appointments. We quickly found Vellus's entourage, a cluster of anti-jacker helmets heading south, toward Jackertown.

It's true. He's coming here.

I pulled our twinned mindfields all the way back to our heads, then disentangled my thoughts from Ava's. The rapid mental shift and the excitement surging through my body made the alley walls spin. I braced myself up from the grimy pavement and shook my head to clear it.

I met Sasha's expectant look and whispered, "Vellus is coming this way!" I pulled Ava up to standing, and she brushed muck from the seat of her pants. I motioned with my head for them both to follow me down the alley.

When we were out of earshot of the guards and around the corner, I whispered, "Vellus is doing an interview along the perimeter."

"Why would Vellus come here?" Sasha glanced at Ava who confirmed it with a nod.

"Maybe he's doing a photo op with the troops," I said. "Maybe he wants to inspect the troops personally. Who knows? I don't care, Sasha. He's coming here!"

Sasha pulled his short comm radio from his pocket to call Julian, but I stayed his hand.

"We don't need a strike team," I said softly. "You and me, Sasha. We can do this together."

"Julian won't like that," he said carefully. But he wasn't saying no.

"Look, this has a much better chance if we work together. If nothing else, I can boost your scribing power with adrenaline, so you can scribe Vellus without having to touch him. But I'm pretty sure I could sync with you too. I think I know what level you're working on."

"What level I'm what?" Sasha's face twisted up, as if I'd gone demens right in front of his eyes.

"Never mind that part," I said. "I think I can boost your range even farther by syncing with you the way I did just now with Ava. Our minds would work together. You could scribe Vellus from far away. We wouldn't have to get close, and Vellus would never know what hit him."

"If I can get in and out without having to do a physical assault..." He was thinking out loud now.

"No one would have to know he was attacked," I said. "Or that he was turned. Plus Vellus is coming straight to our doorstep. We won't get another chance like this." I wasn't absolutely sure it would work, but it was an opportunity we couldn't pass up.

"Vellus and his entire entourage are helmet-protected," Ava said. "How are you going to get past that?" She was asking questions, but she wasn't saying no either.

I thought back to the interview I'd seen earlier with Vellus. "On the tru-cast," I whispered to myself. This could totally work. "Sasha, on the tru-cast—he wasn't wearing an anti-jacker helmet!"

"That's right!" Ava said. "Otherwise, how would they pick up his thought waves for the interview?"

"We'll have to track him until he gets near." My voice rushed to match the racing of my heart, which hammered double time with the adrenaline and the excitement. "We'll shimmy around the perimeter until we're close enough to jack, then wait for the moment to make our move."

"Okay," Sasha said, clearly sold on my hastily put together plan. "But you get to explain this to Julian when we get back. He'll have my head."

I grinned. "He'll pin a medal on you when you come back with Vellus's mind in your pocket."

Sasha shook his head. He glanced back at the alley we had just come from, then looked at Ava, concern drawing down his face. I knew that look too well from all the times I'd seen it on Julian—Sasha was worried about Ava doing an op so close to a perimeter crawling with Guardsmen.

"We could send Ava back," I said, trying not to have our plan derail before it got started.

"You'll do no such thing," Ava said. "You need me to track

him until he gets within your range." She brushed her hands free of the last traces of alley dirt, then slid next to Sasha and stared up into his dark eyes. "Besides, I want to be there when you scribe the worst jacker-hater on the planet."

Sasha lips parted like they wanted to say something, but the words were lost. He had one of those looks he reserved just for her, as if she was the only thing standing between him and desolation. He pulled her into a brief, fierce kiss that knifed through me before I could look away.

It wasn't just the normal embarrassment that averted my eyes and heated my face, but a cruel kind of jealousy. Of both of them, for what they had. Or rather what they didn't, and I did—a whistling hole in my chest that I tried to fill with missions and training and a singular focus on killing Kestrel.

Sasha whispered in Ava's ear. I sucked in air, trying to breathe through the pain and focus on the mission. Sasha caught my eye and waved his dart gun down the street, deeper into Jackertown and farther from the Guardsmen. He pulled Ava along, their hands clasped between them, and I trailed after.

Sasha led us to a shuttered brownstone, taking us up to the third floor where we could keep a lookout for any sudden incursions by the Guardsmen. Ava mentally cast out and found Vellus's entourage on her own, then tracked them as they slowly wound their way toward Jackertown.

Sasha leaned against one wall, next to a cracked window, intermittently peering down at the street through thin tatters of drapes. I paced the wooden floor in the center of the room, far enough from the window to avoid attracting attention. My entire body was strung with tension, and I was beginning to regret hastily chowing down the sandwiches Ava had forced us to eat before we left.

Ava called out Vellus's movements from her corner by the stairs. Apparently his entourage had a few stops to make along the way. Was Vellus doing photo ops with the demens now? There wasn't much else between downtown Chicago and Jackertown.

Sasha watched me from his spot next to the window.

"You need to call Julian," he said. "Or I will."

His words grated on my tight-strung nerves, but I managed not to snarl at him. He was probably right. Vellus would be here soon. If we were successful, no one would know he had been scribed. A transformed Vellus could dream up a plausible reason to call off the siege, and who knew what else he could do for us. But if we had to resort to a physical assault or were caught... well, I didn't want Julian to see it first on a tru-cast. I snatched the short comm from Sasha's outstretched hand and jacked into the mindware interface, buzzing Julian.

"Kira!" He didn't sound very calm. Not a good sign.

"Hey, we've acquired the target." I avoided using Vellus's name. The National Guard probably couldn't crack Julian's encrypted short comm system, but I didn't want to take any chances.

"Good. Just give us a location and time and we'll send a team."

"Um, the location is here and the time is now, so we're proceeding."

"What?" Definitely not calm. "Kira you promised! I want—"

"Sorry, gotta go do an op!" I said cheerfully into the short comm and mentally nudged it off. Sasha shook his head slowly as I handed the small black device back to him.

"What?" I said. "It's not like any explanation on my part was going to make him any happier."

Sasha pocketed the short comm, rubbed both hands over his face, then peered out the window again. Letting it go was a wise choice on his part. My nerves were hyped as it was—I didn't need to worry about Julian's excessive protectiveness right now.

"He's getting closer," Ava said. Since everyone in Vellus's party was helmeted, we wouldn't know his precise final destination until he was nearly there. "There's also a team of unhelmeted reporters gathering along the perimeter near Cermak Road. They're setting up to do an interview, and Vellus is definitely heading their way."

"Cermak Road?" I tried to visualize the ten-square-mile footprint of Jackertown. I'd patrolled the section near Cermak a few times, and it was one of the least populated areas. "That's at least a half mile from here."

"Maybe you can boost me that far?" Sasha asked, obviously reluctant to move from our little safe haven.

"Your range with enhancement is only a hundred feet, Sasha," I said as I hurried to the stairs. "I can boost you to about

59

twice that, maybe, if we sync. I'm not sure we can even make that work. We need to get closer."

My hand skimmed the worn-smooth railing as I took the stairs two at a time. Ava and Sasha pounded the creaky wooden steps behind me, but I was out the door at street level long before them. I cast out, searching for the reporters Ava had sensed, but they were still out of my reach, so I waited for Ava to catch up and lead the way. We stuck to the main streets—half a mile wasn't far, but we needed to move quickly.

Ava had to close her eyes every once in a while to focus. "Vellus's party has reached the reporters. They're moving around slowly now, so I think they've left their vehicles."

My reach finally locked onto the reporters, and I ran faster, not looking back to see if Sasha and Ava were keeping up. I kicked aside a rusty metal can in my way, instantly regretting the ricochet sound it made as it tumbled down the broken sidewalk. The Guardsmen didn't need any more reason to step over the line into Jackertown. I kept one eye on the ground as I ran.

I scanned the perimeter, but the Guardsmen all stood more or less stationary at their posts. Vellus's team included a dozen helmets, and there were four reporters without protection. I brushed their minds to search for information about the interview, surging up a mix of wild grass-and-flower mindscents. They were planning a segment with the shield fence construction in the background and were already setting up shots. We zigged down a street and ran parallel to Cermak Road. One block more... I searched for an alley to cut over to Cermak, but even so, we would need a place to hide. We couldn't just stroll up the street to get close enough to jack.

"There!" I pointed to a center alley that cut between the three-story brick buildings. A back door stood open, half falling off its hinges. We could creep right up to Cermak through the shop. I motioned Ava and Sasha to sprint, and we squeezed through the half-open door just as a Guardsman strolled past the alley opening.

The chill of Chicago winter gave way to a stuffy warmth inside. The air was stale and thick and smelled of grease. As we worked our way to the front, we passed through a room with half-assembled bicycle frames and wheels hanging from the ceiling, like a demens collection of dismembered bicycle parts. I stepped around the greasy boxes that littered the floor and we slipped into the main showroom. All the fully assembled bicycles had long since been cleaned out, leaving the room barren. Empty hooks lingered where goods once hung on the walls, and an ancient register sat open on a counter covered with decades of dust. The windows weren't papered over, so we could see out through a thin layer of grime.

Through the corner window, I glimpsed Vellus's tall, lean form, far down the street, towering over a petite tru-cast journalist and several other people gathered around them. Suddenly, at the opposite end of the store, a single Guardsmen walked in front of the window. I grabbed a fistful of Sasha's jacket and pulled him down behind the counter. Ava quickly ducked with us. We held our breath, waiting for a sound or some indication that we had been seen, but there was nothing but silence and motes of dust drifting in the dim, filtered light.

I let myself breathe again and released Sasha. My reach told me the guard had moved on, no longer by the window, but he hadn't gone far. Vellus was close enough that Sasha should be able to scribe him, depending on how far I could enhance his reach between the sync and the adrenaline.

"Sasha," I whispered. "See if you can visually triangulate Vellus's position. We need to be ready the moment he takes his helmet off for the interview."

Sasha nodded, popped up for a quick look, then hunkered down next to me again. I did one quick sweep through the crowd. Vellus was still helmeted as far as I could tell.

"Ok, first I'll dose you with adrenaline, see if that boosts your reach enough. If not, we can try the syncing. Are you ready?"

Sasha nodded, his jaw set, waiting for me. I reached out to push into his mind, but he was seriously tensed up and reflexively shoved me back out.

"Sorry," he whispered. He closed his eyes and I saw him trying to relax. I tried again, this time slipping into his mind with no problem. I had only searched through Sasha's mind one time before, and his mental networks were more tangled than most jackers. It took almost a solid minute before I found the right thread. I followed it to his adrenaline centers and dosed him strongly. His breath caught as the chemicals coursed through his body. I felt him extending his mindfield out toward Vellus.

"Can you reach him?" I asked.

"I think so. At least, I can reach the reporter next to him, as well as the helmeted minds near her."

"Good." I followed him, trying not to distract him, and checked the minds around his reach. Ava focused on Sasha's mind more than the entourage on the street, which was fine. She wouldn't be much help in the jacking department, anyway, if things got tricky.

The reporters were getting ready for the interview and waiting for Senator Vellus to get off the phone. They were jittery, being so close to Jackertown and unhelmeted, but their thoughts likened it to being in a war zone. They mentally congratulated themselves on being so brave. Every few seconds, the cameraman checked the barrier that was the backdrop for the interview, as if he expected a mongrel herd of jackers to spring over at any moment. The reporters' thoughts showed they expected Vellus to take off his helmet. I prayed their boom mics weren't the kind that recorded sound.

The lead tru-cast reporter approached Vellus once he was off the phone. "I'm so glad you agreed to do an interview with us today, Senator." Her solicitude made me want to gag.

He was still wearing the helmet, so I heard his spoken words through her thoughts. "Always a pleasure, Ms. Reed."

"I'm afraid we're not set up for sound today," she said. "Would you mind terribly if you removed your helmet? If it's a security concern, we can shoot some scenes of the construction here and then move to a more secure location for the interview."

No, no, no. Take it off. Take it off. As if my thought chants

63

would do anything. If the journalist kept giving him a way out, I would jack her to insist he remove it. I didn't care if my jack was picked up on the boom mics. By the time anyone figured it out, we would be long gone—and besides, they were on the edge of Jackertown. No one would be surprised if she was jacked.

Senator Vellus said nothing for a moment. Then his smooth timber of spoken words rumbled in her mind, setting it at ease. "Not at all, Ms. Reed. We're perfectly secure here. In any event, I have mindguard security that can assist if we have any problems with nearby jackers."

"Yes, of course," she said.

Sasha tensed next to me. "Mindguards will know the senator was jacked, assuming I can even get in."

"I'll handle the mindguards," I whispered, popping my eyes open to look at Sasha. "When they take off their helmets, I'll catch them by surprise. Even if they realize Vellus was jacked, they'll expect him to recover. They won't suspect he's been turned, and if they find out, then Vellus will be discredited. Either way, it's better than things are now. But you need to do your thing *fast*."

"Understood," he said without opening his eyes. The dark skin of his face was flushed with the effects of the adrenaline rushing through his body.

I rapidly scanned the helmeted minds near Vellus, unsure which were his mindguards and which were regular security. My hand gripped the splintered edge of the counter, anchoring me while I crouched. I rocked slowly onto my toes and back to my heels again, trying to calm the tension in my body while I waited for the slightest movement of the helmets. After an agonizing spread of several seconds, one of the helmets moved up, then down. The mindguard immediately swept out toward Vellus, who remained helmeted.

I held back from attacking the mindguard. If I alerted him too soon, before Vellus had removed his helmet, I might not distract him long enough for Sasha to do his work. I tracked his mindfield, dodging as he scanned the perimeter, looking for nearby jacker minds. I wasn't sure of his reach, so I held my breath while he searched. Suddenly, Vellus's helmet moved. I slammed my mindfield into the mindguard's head. His mindbarrier wasn't very hard, but he was strong enough to immediately fling me out again. He cast out, searching for me. I drew back to the limits of his reach, then surged forward again before he could find the three of us huddled in the abandoned bicycle shop. I baited him, wrestled with him, tried to keep him engaged in a cat-and-mouse dance long enough for Sasha to scribe Vellus, all the while praying the mindguard wouldn't pinpoint our location and come after us physically.

"Sasha!" I heard Ava cry, and he slumped into me, knocking me back into the thin wooden wall of the register desk. Only my grip on the counter's edge kept me from falling with him. He convulsed on the floor, his arm flailing against me and his eyes rolling back in his head.

What the...?

I grabbed Sasha's shoulders and tried to hold him down, but the seizure stopped of its own accord, leaving him splayed out like a limp doll. A light sheen of sweat on his forehead reflected the dim light from the windows outside. Ava's terror-stricken face froze me for a moment, then I remembered Vellus. I flung my mind back out, but crashed into the mindguard, who was now sweeping around Vellus's mind to fend off the attacking jackers—namely me. I dodged his sweep and dove in. All I needed was a second or two and I would take Vellus down the old-fashioned way: by stopping his heart cold in his chest. Forget subtlety. Julian would just have to forgive me for killing the state's leading anti-jacker politician at the edge of Jackertown. But I only snatched the barest whisper of contact with Vellus's mind before my reach was cut off by a helmet dropping firmly over his head.

No!

I slammed my fist into my knee, a white-hot heat boiling through me. So close, and I *lost* him. Sasha's whole body shuddered, and a moan seemed to be shaken out by it. His eyes slitted open and he struggled to get up from the floor. I helped him up to sitting, grabbing hold of his shoulders and peering close to his face.

"What happened?" I asked, my voice harsher than I expected. Ava frowned at me and I rocked away from him, my face running hot. "Are you okay?" I asked belatedly.

Sasha wiped the back of his hand across his mouth, and I saw it tremble. "I don't know what happened. One moment I was reaching for his mind, the next I was on the floor."

"Did the mindguard push you out?" I asked, trying to keep

my voice gentle. I didn't cast my mind out again, for fear of leading the mindguard straight to us.

"I don't think so," Sasha said. "I don't remember. I just suddenly found myself on the floor feeling this... horrible feeling..." He drew his hand across his forehead like it still lingered in his mind and he was trying to rub it away.

I looked to Ava.

She just shook her head. "All I know is that something awful attacked him. I lost contact with him as soon as it happened."

I nodded and put a hand on Sasha's shoulder. It was still shaking underneath his ultralite.

"It's not your fault, Sasha." Bitterly, I knew exactly whose fault it was and who would be taking the full blame for this failed operation. "They must have had a second mindguard that attacked you while I was distracted with the first mindguard. Someone with wicked skills we haven't seen before."

I took a deep breath and sat back on my heels, my shoulders drooping. "Meanwhile, we need to get out of here before the mindguards find us and haul us all into Vellus's Detention Center." I gave Sasha my hand, helping him up into a crouch but staying below the counter level so we wouldn't be seen. We crept, slowed by Sasha's unsteady legs, back into the bicycle graveyard that comprised the back of the shop.

I didn't even want to think about how angry Julian would be when we got back.

Chapter SIX

J ulian's shouts on the short comm were muffled by Sasha smashing it against his ear, but it was clear from the taut muscles in Sasha's face that he was getting a massive verbal lashing. I sent apologetic looks his way, but he wasn't paying attention to me. When the call ended, the set of his jaw and the dark look in his eyes stopped the words in my throat. Ava's soft blue eyes were wide, her gaze flitting between Sasha and the cracked concrete sidewalk in front of us, avoiding me altogether. The streets felt even emptier than when we had set out on our mission. I folded my arms over my ultralite and huddled against the cold as the three of us hustled toward JFA headquarters.

I had disobeyed a direct order from Julian. I had endangered Sasha and Ava by taking them on an unauthorized mission. I had engaged the perimeter, just like Julian told me not to. And, worst of all, we had failed. All would have been forgiven if we had returned to headquarters having defeated the enemy before he could box us in. Now we had nothing to show for my flagrant violation of Julian's orders.

I had messed up. Bad.

The jitters in my stomach stepped up to a full jitter riot when we reached the crumbling red-brick building that was the JFA headquarters and pulled open the shiny black, bulletproof door. Hinckley was flopped on the weathered couch, eating a sandwich, but he just shook his head slowly and refused to look our way. Several of Hinckley's military men sat in clusters at the battered kitchen tables, but no one was talking. They kept their heads ducked, and I couldn't tell if they were mindlinked to discuss my failed mission or if they were simply rendered into embarrassed silence by our presence.

I didn't link in to find out. I didn't want to hear what they were thinking.

Sasha slid his arm around Ava and pulled her over to lean against the kitchen sink for an intimate mindlinked conversation. I hesitated, having assumed they would at least come with me to face Julian. I squared my shoulders, ready to take responsibility for the failed mission alone. The faces at the kitchen table ignored me as I strode by.

An angry rumble of voices floated in past the racks. I followed the sound, winding through the ancient machinery that used to manufacture doors but now sat silent. I passed a few bunks filled with younger recruits playing holographic games on their phones.

None of them would look at me, either.

It must be even worse than I thought. I'd disobeyed Julian's

Susan Kaye Quinn

direct order, something I'd never seen anyone else do. What would he do? Yell at me? I couldn't imagine him scribing someone for disobeying an order. Usually, when someone was irredeemable in Jackertown, he kicked them out, banishing them forever. The jitter riot in my stomach froze up.

Was Julian going to send me away? Was that why no one would look me in the eye?

A haze clouded my vision, and my toe stubbed a box of machine parts sticking out from a rack, sending me tumbling forward. I caught myself on the edge of the spindly frame, the cool metal biting into my hand but keeping me upright.

I had to force my feet to start moving again. The voices were coming from near the privacy rooms Sasha had built along the east wall. There was no mental barrier to the privacy rooms, just an unspoken agreement that no one jacked through those walls unless they were invited. It was part of the respect built into Julian's new jacker society. A society that he might soon be banishing me from.

I stumbled my way forward and eventually found Julian and Anna arguing in the thin corridor between the industrial machinery and the privacy rooms. I crept up on them, unsure if Julian knew I was there. Anna's arms were crossed, her hands clenched into fists as well. She saw me, then looked away.

No, no, no. The frozen ball of fear in my stomach melted into a puddle of dread that pooled at the bottom.

"Now is the time, Julian," Anna said, kicking up the intensity of her voice. "It's our best option. Probably our only option."

"No." Julian's voice rose to meet her pitch. "It's reckless and dangerous. Not unlike today, except we will probably lose our best assets in the process."

"There are always going to be risks," Anna said, tempering her voice and unfolding her arms. "You know that. Sasha knows it. Kira knows it, too. It's part of what we're doing, and everyone is willing to put themselves on the line for the JFA. You have to let her try."

They were talking about me. I meant every word when I told Anna I would do whatever Julian asked of me as long as it didn't endanger my family. Which was probably what Anna had in mind: sending me back to recruit my dad to infiltrate Vellus's defenses and take him down that way. Or maybe she had thought of something new.

"Let me try what?" I asked, my voice soft.

Julian whipped his head around. His face was a rigid mask. "I'll speak with you in a moment."

Oh no.

My mouth hung open.

Julian turned his back on me as if I weren't even there. He wasn't going to send me off to recruit my dad, he was going to plain send me away. Of course. How could he trust me now, after I blatantly disobeyed a direct order from him? My chest squeezed with the realization. It became hard to breathe. Where would I go? I couldn't go home—I had left there in order to keep my family safe in the first place. I sent a wild look to Anna, wishing like crazy I could link past her impenetrable mindbarrier.

I begged her with my eyes. *Please, Anna. Don't let him send me away.*

But she was engaged in a staring contest with Julian. "It's now or never with Vellus."

"The worst thing we could do right now," Julian said, "is try to take on Vellus directly. He knows we just tried to jack him. He was assaulted at the perimeter of Jackertown! It's a public relations nightmare. And we didn't even manage to scribe him. Now all of us look far more dangerous, and the assault just gave him more reason to crack down on us."

I didn't think my stomach could sink any lower, but there was a basement it hadn't discovered yet, and it slithered into that. I hadn't just failed in the mission to scribe Vellus, I had made things worse. Now the public would support Vellus as he quarantined us from the world. I had made it easier for him to cut us off, the very thing Julian said we weren't ready for.

No wonder he was so angry.

Anna clenched her hands at her side as if she was losing her patience with the argument and was considering using her fists to beat some sense into Julian. "No matter what happened today, Vellus would still finish erecting the barrier. I'm sure his future plans are worse than just a siege. He needs to be neutralized, not coddled, before he turns all of Jackertown into a prison. This isn't a PR war, Julian. You need to let Kira go to her father and see what he can do, quickly. Before Vellus suspects her father might be helping us and we lose that avenue of attack altogether. If we can scribe Vellus, he would be extremely useful to us, but failing that, eliminating him has to be an option as well."

I badly wanted to jump in but held myself back. It was one thing to take Sasha and Ava on an unauthorized mission. If we got caught, well, that was part of being in the revolution, like Anna said. But my dad... any mission to take out Vellus had a high likelihood of failure, and Vellus would do much worse to my dad than simply put him in jail.

Besides, my dad needed to be home, protecting my mom and Xander, the changeling we'd rescued but who was more like a little brother to me now. Things were getting worse every day for jackers and the people who loved them. I was the revolutionary, not my dad. If anything, I should go on a covert op, by myself, to get Vellus. Could I possibly convince Julian to let me do that when I had just disobeyed a direct order?

"I don't want her anywhere near Vellus," Julian said, dashing my hopes. "If he gets his hands on her, it will demoralize everyone. You know he'll force her to go on the tru-casts, and that will set the movement back, not only with our own people and jackers still at large, but with the public as well."

"The public is not on our side!" Anna said. "We are at war, Julian. When are you going to face that?"

"I know that!" Julian shouted back, his face darkening. "There are just some risks that aren't worth taking."

Anna's fingers slowly uncurled from her tightly closed fists, and somehow that seemed more dangerous than when they were clenched. "You need to get your priorities straight."

Julian closed his eyes, took a breath, then opened them again. "We'll come up with a plan to counter Vellus's moves. Later." Then he turned to me, his face inscrutable. "Can I have a word with you in private?" He swept out his arm toward one of the privacy rooms. I tried to catch Anna's eye, to get her support, but she was busy sending angry glares down the hallway away from us. And avoiding my gaze again.

I swallowed and marched through the open door to the privacy room. It was empty except for a couch and a couple of chairs with a blanket draped over the back. It smelled like a coat of paint had been put on recently, making it jarringly fresh compared to the rest of the decrepit factory. A portable heater in the center wafted puffs of air that brushed my face and made me uncomfortably warm in my ultralite.

I didn't bother taking it off, not sure how long Julian would let me stay. Once the door shut soundly behind us, I turned to him. "Julian, I'm sorry—"

He cut me off by wrapping his arms around me. His hug nearly lifted me off the ground, my toes just barely touching the tiled floor. My arms ended up around his neck, although I wasn't sure what to do with them there. Confusion did a whirling-dervish dance in my head.

His face was buried in my hair, and I felt him draw in a breath. "Don't ever do that to me again."

Right when my brain figured out that Julian wasn't mad at me, that he was worried instead, he relaxed his grip and eased me back to the floor. I scrambled for something to say, how I hadn't meant to worry him, how I was just trying to complete the mission—

Then he kissed me.

His lips pressed gently to mine, soft and warm. Before I could think, something surged up inside me, lifting me up and welding my lips to his, as if they weren't already pressed together. His hands on my back crushed me to him, and a small moan rumbled in his throat, vibrating through me as well. The feeling rushed my body, flooding every small dip and turn, gushing and unstoppable. The hole that perpetually sat in my chest like an empty grave overfilled with it, and the whistling wind inside me fell silent.

My body stilled.

Julian froze. As my brain caught up with what my body was doing, he slowly untangled his lips from mine and relaxed his fever-tight grip on me. I teetered, then pushed back from him, my hands lifting free from his shoulders. My legs wobbled like the world had gone on tilt and forgotten to tell me. Julian was breathing hard and his face was flushed. The shock on my face crashed into the unmistakable half-lidded hurt in his eyes. Then it bounced back to slice me through the heart.

Julian turned his back on me and pressed the back of his hand to his mouth. I took a half step toward him, then stopped.

What just happened?

My mind grabbed at the pieces, trying desperately to put them together. Julian worried about me the way Sasha did about Ava. He was angry because I had put myself in danger. All those times he leaned close, all the soft looks and whispers and orders for me not to go on dangerous missions... *Julian is in love with me.*

I had no idea what to do with that.

The feel of his lips was still imprinted on mine, but the hole in my heart didn't have room for those kinds of feelings. It simply swallowed them like a black hole of emotion, one that I fed constantly with ops and training and anything that would dull the aching. But that hadn't stopped me from kissing Julian back like... like I was hungry for it. Beyond hungry. Starving. Was it still that instinctual love, the one he had planted so long ago, that made me respond without thinking?

I didn't know. I didn't know if it was real, or fake, or what—it was all tangled up in my head. More importantly, I had somehow missed that, somewhere along the way, it had become real for Julian. He sucked in a sharp breath and turned back to me. His face had no expression save the carefully controlled look that I had seen a dozen times before when he had to sit in judgment of a fellow jacker.

Tears jumped to my eyes and my chest seized up. *Please, no.*

"Anna is right," Julian said, his voice flat. "I need to..." His eyelid twitched like the words were causing him pain. "I need to get my priorities straight." He sucked air in between his teeth. "We need to neutralize Vellus. We need to buy time. We have to use every resource that we have. Your father has access to him. We need you to try to stop Vellus." His words were choppy bits that he spit out, one at a time, each one a blow that knocked my world a little more out of alignment.

Julian wasn't sending me away, he was sending me on a mission. The only one that I didn't want to do. One that *Julian* didn't want me to do, because apparently he was in love with me, something I had just figured out ten seconds ago. And yet he was asking me to do it anyway, because it was what the JFA needed.

There was no way I could say no.

"Is that an order?" My voice was barely a whisper. It would be easier for me to do if he ordered me. His face showed a crack in the rigid mask he had put on, but it disappeared quickly. In that moment, I hated myself for asking.

"No," he said. "I would never... no. You can say no. You should say—"

"Julian." It was as much a gasp as a word. "Anna's right, he has to be stopped. I'll do it."

His shoulders stiffened, and his mouth drew into a tight line. He nodded once, sharply, then strode past me, leaving me in the privacy room with the door wide open.

Just like the hole in my heart.

Chapter SEVEN

I shifted on the rough wooden chair, bringing out another creak that made me cringe. The chair was devoid of a comfortable spot, despite my efforts to find one. How did Julian spend an entire chat-cast in it without going crazy? I stared into the tiny round eye of the camera, ignoring Hinckley's scraggly face behind it, determined to finish what I started, no matter how much it made me squirm.

"I'm sorry... well, I'm just sorry for being such an idiot," I said into the camera.

Hinckley paused, then lowered the slim silver device. "Is that it?"

I grimaced. "Was there something else you wanted me to say?"

He held up his hands in surrender. "Hey, this is your recording. I was just asking if you were done."

I nodded, closing my eyes and trying to ratchet down the tension in my body. This mission was likely a one-way operation.

If we were caught, it would be bad enough for Sasha and worse for my dad, but the real danger was to the JFA—Julian was right that Vellus would put me in front of the cameras. Which is why I went straight from the privacy room to the JFA's cast room.

But that wasn't why a fluttery panic was beating inside my chest.

Julian loves me.

The charming, charismatic leader of the revolution wanted more than a Friend-in-Chief. More, when all I had to give was a whistling hole in my heart. I gave what little I could to the camera and the chat-cast that Julian had spent four months trying to persuade me to do. I had mumbled a few things about the revolution, about Julian, about how jackers needed to stick together. Things that I had been thinking all along, but never said out loud, at least not to Julian.

It was all I had.

I took a deep breath to calm the panic and opened my eyes. Hinckley had pulled the memory disk from the camera and held it out between his long, stringy fingers. "This is the whole thing."

I didn't take the small, black square disk from Hinckley's outstretched hand. "You hold on to it."

His eyebrows hiked up. "I thought you'd want to, you know, give it to Julian personally."

I slid off the uncomfortable chair and peered up into Hinckley's face. He was in his twenties, but his forehead was creased by seriousness. Or maybe his years of mindwork for the military had aged him early.

"The only way Julian's going to see that recording is if this mission blows up in our faces."

His somber look didn't change, but he nodded. "Then I'll have it for you when you return."

I gave him a grim smile, appreciating his confidence. "The next time you see me, I may be on a tru-cast saying things I would only say if Vellus had a gun to my head. If that happens, you give that recording to Julian. But not before."

"Understood." He pocketed the tiny chip in his camouflage pants.

I strode out of the JFA's chat-cast room, my body buzzing. I tried taking more deep breaths to calm myself and gather my wits. Between Julian kissing me and me spilling my guts on the chat-cast recording with Hinckley, I was adrift on a stormy sea of emotion with nothing to hold me down.

When I reached the kitchen, I ignored the glances and whispers from Hinckley's crew-cut men, still hanging out at the tables, and went straight for the cabinets. I rummaged through them, strapping on a miniature dart gun and a small-caliber pistol, one on each leg, plus a couple of extra med patches, a bulletproof vest, and a handheld, jacker-tuned Taser for good measure. I would have brought the butterflies—mobile attack Tasers just for jackers that Julian had lifted from the Feds and reverse-engineered—but the launch gun was bulky, and I was already weighed down too much. It was all probably unnecessary anyway. This had to be a stealth mission in order for Sasha to get close enough to Vellus to neutralize him. If we were shooting our way in—or out—it meant we had failed. And there was Julian's PR angle to consider: I might get a kill jack on Vellus, but getting away with it was a whole different story.

I glanced around for Sasha and found him back in the racks with Julian. They stood close together, far down the center row, but I still heard Julian's harsh tone. I wasn't sure if Sasha was getting instructions or chastisements, but they were words Julian probably meant for me. Only Sasha had to take them instead.

I splayed my hands on the pitted wood of the kitchen counter and closed my eyes, wishing I could control my emotions like I could my fast-twitch muscles or adrenaline. During my early explorations of my mind, I had found a trigger for dopamine, but it had left me in a freaky, jittery daze for hours. I would simply have to deal with the fact that I was an emotional mess.

Or use my coping mechanism of choice: ignore it.

I opened my eyes, pulled another pistol out of the cabinet, and tucked it in the back of my pants. Sasha had wandered to the front, finding Ava at the far edge of the kitchen area. He was holding her, whispering to her, their faces close. I looked away, ignoring the emotion that surged up through my fake outer calm.

I would wait for him outside.

I grabbed a white-hooded coat on the way out into the early afternoon sun, stepping through the door before I even zipped it, all in my haste to get out of the building. Only after I was outside, leaning against the frigid brick of the JFA entrance, did it occur to me that I hadn't said goodbye to anyone. The way they were avoiding my gaze when I first came in, it was probably just as well. And I had no clue what to say to Julian. With a twinge, I realized we hadn't actually said much of anything in the privacy room.

The streets were still empty, hushed by the specter of the Guard and the uncertainty of the future. I felt the pressure of a hundred eyes peering from behind curtains, a thousand minds anxiously waiting for the JFA to stop the threat that was hemming us in. I licked my lips, already chapped by the wind, and drummed my heel against the wall, ready to get on with doing my part.

After a few minutes, Sasha pushed open the door and strode into the wind, followed by Myrtle. I threw a questioning look to the diminutive woman who was the adopted grandma of most of Jackertown's changelings, but she didn't say anything, just shuffled next to me, out of the wind. Julian must think we needed his strongest jacker along on this mission, although I couldn't see why. We weren't likely to brute-force our way in. Still, I was glad she was here. Her lilac-soap smell reassured me even more than her nod and the wave of her fingerless hand-knitted gloves.

Sasha stood in his ultralite, no flak jacket or winter coat, with his arms crossed, staring down the street. The wind made his dark, curly hair dance along his forehead.

I couldn't stop myself from asking, "So, did Julian chew you out again?"

Sasha looked sideways at me, and I realized I was biting my lip. I stopped.

"He was giving me instructions," Sasha said carefully.

"For the op?"

"Not specifically." His dark eyes seemed full of warmth, not the hollowness they normally evoked. "He said not to come back without you."

I swallowed, my face heating up. "We're all going to come back from this," I managed to get out.

"That's what I told Ava, too." He went back to studying the street, but I cringed at his implication. That we all knew the danger, and that I had consoled Julian the way Sasha consoled Ava, by telling her the best possible outcome: that we would all come home. Only I hadn't even said goodbye.

"I made a deal with Julian, though," Sasha continued. "That while I was gone, he wouldn't send Ava on any missions."

"She's not going to like that," I said, trying to lighten my tone.

"I know." He half-smiled, which tore at me, then he turned to look at me again. "But Julian understands. He knows it kills me every time Ava puts herself in danger." He cleared his throat and returned his stare to the horizon. "I don't need the distraction, you know?"

Julian understands... so Sasha knew how Julian felt about me. Which meant Ava had to know, even thought she'd never said a thing. Did Anna know? With a sinking feeling, her words on the rooftop made sudden sense. *Julian's important... we can't have him distracted by things that aren't central to the cause. He needs to keep his focus.*

Did everyone know but me? Had I been in a cloud for the last four months? The answer to that was painfully obvious: yes, I had. A fog of emotional wreckage caused by losing Raf. The hole in my life wasn't only the pain of having my love ripped literally out of his mind. It was the empty space where he used to be. The boy who understood me, even when I didn't understand myself. When he lost that, something came unmoored, untethered, inside me.

There were holes in me too.

All those times when Julian leaned close, all those times I resisted thoughts of inappropriate hugs—was it just that instinctual love surging back? Or was it something more, and I'd just been oblivious to it as I'd been to Julian's feelings all along? I thought he was the leader of the revolution I had thrown my heart and soul into, to bury the pain of losing Raf.

Now... I wasn't sure what Julian was anymore.

"We should get moving, Kira," Myrtle said quietly by my side. I nodded and turned my face into the wind, letting the wintery breeze wipe clean my tangled thoughts of Julian and Raf. I needed to focus on the mission. Make sure that Sasha could keep his promise to Ava to come home.

I shaded my eyes and peered down the road. It was a good mile to the perimeter in that direction. "I'll have to get closer to see if the National Guard has blocked this street."

"They have—I had Ava check." Sasha gestured down the street with his chin. "There are fewer Guards a block over from the main street than anywhere else. That's probably the best place to try to breach the blockade."

"Right," I said, glancing at Myrtle. "You up for a road trip, Myrtle?"

She pulled her stuffed winter coat tighter around her, looking like a tiny puff marshmallow. "Lead the way."

We marched down the street, shiny with the late-afternoon sun, until I could mentally reach the perimeter. The National Guardsmen were easy to find, tiny floating spots impenetrable to my reach. There was a string of them, spaced evenly as far as my reach could go. They thinned out a couple of blocks to the north. We cut down a side alleyway that crept up on the perimeter.

At the end of the alley, we peeked around the corner, then pulled back. There were four along this strip of street—one close on the south end and three toward the north end. They all had large, semiautomatic weapons, urban military fatigues, and of course anti-mindjacking helmets. At least the fencing hadn't reached this stretch of perimeter yet.

Sasha frowned. "I don't like the size of their guns. Or our odds on this, Kira."

"We need a distraction," I agreed. I cast my mind out, roaming over both sides of the street. A group of changelings had stolen out to the steps of their brownstone apartment two streets over. I'd like to think the Guardsmen wouldn't shoot a bunch of kids, but I was completely unwilling to find out if I was wrong on that.

My reach showed three demens clustered a block away, on the far side of the street, outside of Jackertown. The demens normally didn't gather together, not liking the peppermint-flavored madness of each other's thought waves any more than normal mindreaders did. The sudden sting of their mindscents on the back of my tongue made me choke. I muffled my cough with my hand to avoid attracting the attention of the Guards and pulled out of the demens' heads for a moment to recover.

The demens were living up to their name, fighting over a battered box like it was a treasure chest. It was just the kind of disturbance we were looking for. Only we needed it moved one block to the west and south.

"One distraction coming up," I said to Sasha and Myrtle. "North end of the street. Be ready to run." I braced my hand against the cold cement wall as I jacked back into the dizzying thoughts of the demens. One of them had managed to wrest the box from the other two. I jacked him to take off with his booty toward the Guardsmen two blocks away. His fellow demens sprinted after him in hot pursuit. I pulled out of his head as soon as I dared, hoping the jack would hold. Now that he was being chased, he ran faster of his own accord, and I simply nudged him in the right direction.

I hoped the Guardsmen wouldn't shoot him.

The lead demens sprinted out of the alley, stumbled, and fell on top of his box. Three of the four Guardsmen swung their rifles in his direction. The fourth—the one nearest to our alleyway hideout—kept his gun pointed at the ground, watching. Tripping may have saved the demens his life. The Guards hesitated once he was sprawled on the ground. Then the other two demens burst out onto the street and piled on the downed guy, who held on to his flattened box like his life depended on it.

The Guards' guns went slack as they slowly drifted toward the demens. They must have been given orders to keep jackers in, not keep the demens out.

"It's not working," Sasha said in a hushed voice. He was right. The fourth Guardsmen would see us if we tried to cross, and his buddies would leave the demens in a heartbeat to come after us. The Guardsmen's laughter rolled down the street as they watched the spectacle.

"Wait." I plunged into the spinning madness of two demens at once. They leaped up and lunged for two separate Guardsmen. The third Guardsmen joined the first two in beating back the demens with their fists and the butts of their guns. The fourth Guard tensed, raising his rifle but holding his ground.

I pounded my fist against the cement wall. I needed something else. *Fast.* I closed my eyes, breathing in and out—ten, nine, down the elevator, find the thread. *Focus, Kira!*

"What are you doing?" I heard Myrtle's gruff voice, but I ignored her.

There was no time to wait for every muscle in my body to flip to fast-twitch. Just my legs, then. I only needed a quick burst of speed, and I couldn't afford the blowback anyway—we still had to get to the suburbs and execute the rest of the op. The switch zinged through my legs, and I didn't wait to open my eyes before I started running. I flung my mind out to find the blank spot of the Guardsman's anti-jacker helmet and honed in like a missile.

My eyes opened right before I hit him. We fell in what seemed

87

like slow motion, and something scraped along my arm. Before the momentum carried me away from him, I hooked my fingers through the cage of his anti-jacker helmet, wrenching his head back and pulling him with me as we skidded across the gravelly pavement. He was stunned, but he flailed against my hold, trying to find his dropped gun. I twisted my fast-twitch legs on the pavement and braced my sneakers against his helmet and chest, grabbing with both hands under his chin for his helmet strap. He stopped reaching for the gun and grasped at my hands, but he was too late. The strap came loose and the helmet slid off. I jacked him unconscious before he could think to call out to his fellow Guardsmen.

They were still busy with the demens down the street.

Fortunately Sasha had figured out what I was doing. He and Myrtle were already on the other side of the perimeter. I rolled away from the limp body of the Guardsman and tried to scramble to my feet, but the mini-blowback had already struck. Somehow I got up, but it was like walking on strings of spaghetti. I stumbled for the alley where Sasha and Myrtle had taken cover as shouts came from the Guardsmen down the street. Sasha caught me, and with him under one arm and tiny Myrtle under the other, we hobbled down the alley.

We turned down one street, crossed over, and ducked in another alley. My legs screamed in protest. I ignored them. Another street, then two. I reached back, but we'd put enough distance between us and the Guardsmen that they were out of my range.

Relief washed through me when we ducked into an abandoned building to hide. Sasha pulled out his phone to hail an autocab. He had Julian's special frequency that tapped in to the autocab network and overrode the normal programming that prevented them from coming within a mile of Jackertown. If we were lucky, it would get here before the Guardsmen could search all the empty buildings between us.

I slumped to the rotted wooden floor and leaned against a musty and heavily patched wall. The shakes had set in, so I clasped my hands together, determined to fight them off by the time we got to the suburbs. I just hoped my dad would be willing to help us. I dug my phone from the leg pocket of my cargo pants. The trembling in my hand made it nearly jump out of my grasp. I jacked in to scrit a message to Xander.

What's new in the suburbs?

I hoped he didn't have his phone turned off. I hadn't spoken to my dad or mom since I left. I wasn't sure what I was going to say now, but calling my dad on the phone to recruit him to scribe his ex-boss wasn't the right approach. A face-to-face chat was pretty much mandatory for that. Hopefully, Xander could smooth the way for me.

Hey! the scrit came back from Xander. *Long time no scrit, big sis. Need some help in J-town? Got my J-card ready to go.*

Xander calling me big sis made my insides twist. He shouldn't want to be a revolutionary—he was only a kid. At least my real brother, Seamus, was safely tucked away with his fellow reader cadets at West Point. I badly missed our scrits, but I had stopped sending them when I left home, for the same reason I hadn't spoken to my dad for months: to keep him as far from what I was doing as possible.

J-card? I scrit to Xander. *Didn't know you were a member.*

J-card=tag, he scrit. *You're the JFA girl. Supposed to know these things.*

I didn't know what he was talking about, but I needed to cut to business. *Is dad home?* I scrit. *Have important business w/ him.*

Er, not home.

When will he be back?

We're all not home, he scrit. *At the testing station.*

I gripped the phone with both hands and mentally nudged in the next message. *What. Are. You. Doing. There?*

Not a choice. Get the notice, go in. Otherwise the Chi-town jack cops come for you. Bad.

Dad's there with you?

Mom, Dad, me, he scrit. *I'm done. Mom's still inside.*

My vision telescoped down so that I could only see the words floating on my phone. *Mom's still inside.* I curled up a fist and pressed it against my mouth. Panic threatened to choke me.

Myrtle noticed. "You okay?"

I waved her off, focusing on the phone. *How could Dad...* I stopped before sending the scrit. How could my dad take my mom down there? He was supposed to be protecting her! I erased the words and focused on the phone, anger clouding my thoughts.

After a moment, Xander sent another scrit. *Don't worry. She's a reader. She'll test out. No reason to keep her. She'll be fine.*

His attempts to reassure me only ratcheted the tension higher in my body. Sometimes people came back out of the testing stations, sometimes not. She was a reader, but they might make a mistake. Who knew what went on in there? My dad should have worked a deal with Vellus. Or fled. Or gotten Mr. Trullite's help. The last thing he should have done was taken my mom and Xander down there willingly.

Which testing station? I finally managed to scrit.

What? Xander scrit. *Why?*

Coming to get you.

No! Bad move.

Which testing station?

Too dangerous, he scrit. *Crawling with jack police. Things bad now. Worse since you left.*

Since I left? The anger boiling inside me ate away at my stomach. Had my leaving made things worse for my family instead of better?

Testing station. Tell me.

Washington station, he scrit. *Don't tell Dad I told you. Will kill me.*

Be there soon.

However badly my dad was handling things by taking my mom to the testing center, I was going to make it worse by recruiting him to go after Vellus. My dad and I might not come back from that mission, and that would leave Xander to protect my mom. He was a jacker, but he was only thirteen.

I swallowed and clenched my hands against the fading shakes that still rumbled through my body. When I told Julian I would do the mission, I knew it would come down to this. And I would follow through.

But first, I would make sure my mom got home safe.

Chapter EIGHT

The autocab dropped us off in a part of the city that reminded me of Jackertown, minus the jackers: run-down, clearly taken over by the demens for the last few decades, but now reclaimed by Vellus for his testing station. My winter coat had taken a thrashing from its encounter with the pavement, so I left it in the autocab. I didn't want my parents to think the JFA kept me in tatters, and the ultralite and flak jacket should keep me warm. My legs were mostly functional now, so I gently pushed Sasha away and walked carefully into an alleyway that was caked with grime and stank of old grease. I only stumbled once, a crack in the pavement making me wobble. The three of us—me, Myrtle, and Sasha—passed an overturned dumpster. I edged up to the corner so I could peek around to survey the testing station.

A steady stream of people came and went from the crumbling, red-bricked building, squat and plain. The original name, *Markus Community Clinic*, remained as a ghostly outline, the letters long removed. A small screen flashed the words *Washington Testing Station* in angry orange-and-black above the door, alternating with a biohazard symbol. As if jackers were some kind of communicable disease.

Two guards in full riot gear with CJPD stamped across their chests stood at the entrance. The Chicago Jack Police officers had anti-jacker helmets as well as rifles to back up the threat of putting down anyone who got out of line. The jack police wore holstered dart guns in case they decided not to actually kill the pale, shaking citizens who were timidly passing by them on their way into the station.

I couldn't help curling my lip in disgust.

My mental reach showed they were the extent of the security—a fairly small force, given the number of jackers who would pass through the testing-station doors. A mindwave disruptor field wrapped the station, so there was no telling what was inside. The idea of my mom in there made me queasy.

"Are you sure your dad is here?" Sasha asked while peeking around the corner with me.

I pulled out of view of the jack police. "I'm sure. Xander said they were still waiting for my mom. I don't know how long the testing takes, but that was only fifteen minutes ago. I'll let him know we're here."

I slipped my phone out of my pocket, nudged it awake, and scrit a message giving Xander directions to our alleyway across the street.

Don't tell Dad I'm here, I finished the scrit. *Just come to the alley.* My dad would flip out when he saw me, and it would not be mesh to fight in front of the guards.

He's not going to be happy with me, Xander scrit back.

Don't worry, I scrit. *He'll be busy yelling at me.*

Sasha stepped closer. "What's your plan here, Kira?" His dark eyes had lost their earlier warmth and were now all business. Which was what I needed to be too, in order for this mission to have any chance of working.

"When my dad comes out," I said, "we can discuss the options. I think the best plan is for my dad to make an appointment with Vellus to bring me in. Claim I've had a change of heart or something. Make it somewhere public, so you can hide nearby, close enough to scribe after I've enhanced you. We'll have to find a way to get Vellus unhelmeted, but we'll cross that hurdle when we get to it."

Sasha glanced in the direction of the testing station. A teenager helped an older man as he hobbled down the sidewalk toward the doors. The boy was probably his grandson, considering the gentle touch he used on the old man's arm to steady him. Yeah, the two of them were definitely a threat to society that needed to be tested.

"What if Vellus doesn't go for it?" Sasha asked, pulling my attention back to the alley.

"Then we find out where he is and go after him in a straight-up assault. We have to stop him before he leaves Chicago or ambush him en route to Springfield. It will be nearly impossible to get to him once he's back in the capitol." Not only was it much more fortified in Springfield, but the last time I was in Vellus's office, I'd felt like a fly in his carefully laid trap. I had no desire to return there.

Myrtle shuffled toward us. "I'm not much use to you, Kira, unless the Jack Police take off those helmets."

"We'll need you for any mindguards who might try to stop us." I was channeling Anna now, with her perpetual military strategizing. "We don't know who Vellus has for mindguards these days, but someone had crazy skills when we made the attempt on him earlier. My dad might have better intel on that. If you had been with us before, I suspect we would have been able to stop Vellus then."

Myrtle nodded, but Sasha looked uncertain, like he still wasn't quite sure what had gone wrong with our previous mission. I didn't know either, but it showed that we had to be prepared for any contingency.

I peeked at the test station again, in time to see my dad striding out, his arm wrapped protectively around my mom and shielding her from the uninterested gaze of the CJPD guards. My mom, dad, and Xander were all dressed for a stroll through the fall leaves with jeans, boots, and light winter jackets. They didn't seem like much of a threat, which I guessed was good, considering where they were. My heart beat a little faster, a turmoil of emotions revving it up: relief to see my mom okay; happiness that my dad was at least trying to protect her, even if he brought her here; anxiety as his long legs carried him quickly across the street, heading straight for our hideaway. I couldn't imagine what Xander had told him, but I hadn't felt my dad mentally surge us yet.

I retreated around the corner. Whatever confrontation we were going to have, we didn't want to catch the notice of the CJPD.

Xander must have skipped ahead because he rounded the corner first. He didn't have to reach up to give me a hug, like he had the last time I saw him. Had his birthday passed? Was he fourteen now? He was almost eye to eye with me when he pulled back, his smile bright.

My smile was automatic, but it died when I saw the bright red J inked on his cheek. His pale face flushed, making blotches around the stamped red tattoo, and my anger boiled to a tipping point. The last thing he should be is embarrassed. They had marked him, as if he were an animal, branded and categorized.

"Xander—"

He pulled away from me. "I'm fine. Told you. Got my J-card now. Lots of jackers have them."

My fists curled. I wanted to hit something.

He scanned me up and down, nodding his approval at my bulletproof jacket. "I see you're all mesh down there in Jackertown. What's it like? Have you guys invented some new secret weapons to fight the readers' anti-jacker tech?"

He must not have been watching the news.

"Vellus has sent the National Guard in to surround Jackertown."

His eyebrows hiked up. "Whoa, really? When?"

97

"Just this morning."

He reached out a gangly hand to nudge my shoulder. "That didn't stop you from busting out, though, did it?"

My mom and dad came around the corner, and the look on my dad's face went from stormy to Category Five hurricane when he saw me. I wanted to say something, but I couldn't break my gaze from the angry red J on his cheek. Any ties he had to Vellus must not exempt him from being branded a jacker.

My mom broke free from under my dad's arm and hurried over to hug me. Her wispy brown hair had more streaks of gray than I remembered, and it floated in a cloud that embraced me along with her arms. I unclenched my fists to hug her and fought through the tears that threatened to leak out of my eyes. She winced and pulled away, rubbing her shoulder like it was sore.

My gaze was glued to the spot where her hand gripped her jacket. "What did they do to you?" I had to force the words out through my teeth.

"They just took my DNA for the test." She was still rubbing her arm.

That didn't sound right at all. "Haven't they ever heard of a saliva sample?" Just one more reason why my dad shouldn't have come down here.

"They said they needed to take blood."

Which didn't make sense either.

She dropped her hand. "I'm fine, really, Kira."

I blinked back angry tears and pressed my lips tightly together to keep from blurting out accusations at my dad. Neither would persuade him to help us.

My mom glanced at Xander, standing on my right, and we both knew he was busted. Then she gently took hold of my shoulders and looked me in the eyes. "Kira, why did you risk coming down here? I'm fine, sweetie. You didn't need to come get me."

I swallowed, unable to speak for a moment. I hadn't even known they were at the testing station, much less had I come for her. I was here to recruit my dad on a ridiculously dangerous mission, one that would make my mom sick with worry. Guilt was a dagger through my gut.

My dad kept silent, his gaze flicking between Sasha, Myrtle, and me. His face was slowly turning purple under the shadow of yesterday's forgotten shave. I could link in to hear his thoughts, but it was better to do this out in the open.

"Mom," I said, then cleared my throat to make my voice stronger. "I'm glad you're okay. I knew Dad would take care of you. That's not why I'm here. I need to talk to him."

My mom released my shoulders. "What is this about?"

My dad edged closer to her, putting his hand on her shoulder again, and I drew in a breath. This was going to be harder than I thought.

"I don't suppose you've got Vellus's phone number handy?" I asked my dad. His face lost some of its color. My mom looked rapidly back and forth between my dad and me.

"What does she mean, Patrick?" my mom asked.

My dad didn't look at her, just held my gaze steady. "She means she wants me to kill the senator."

My eyebrows flew up. "No!" I said. My dad narrowed his eyes. "Well, maybe," I conceded. "He's fencing in Jackertown so he can put us under siege. We need to stop him, right now, and..." I hesitated, not quite sure how to phrase it.

"And you want me be the one to do it."

"We want you to help us get close to him," Sasha spoke up from behind me. "I would much prefer a minute or two with the senator to actually killing him. He'll be much more useful to us that way."

My dad nodded slowly, and I hoped that nod meant he would help us. He had seen Sasha's ability up close and personal when Sasha scribed Molloy, the jacker who turned my boyfriend Raf's memories into Swiss cheese.

"Can you get us close to Vellus?" I asked my dad. "We only need a small window of time, and no one has to get killed." At least I hoped no one would get killed. That would be the best possible outcome out of this. The worst was... bad.

"I don't like the sound of this," my mom said, peering up into my dad's face.

My dad still didn't look at her. "I'm sure he'll want to see you, Kira." He ran a hand through his hair, brown like mine, but cut short like Hinckley's men. "But I can't say that I like the idea."

"We know he's in town now, or at least he was earlier today."

"I'm sure he would make a special stop to see you. Our house has been under surveillance since you left." He glanced at

Xander. "It's a good thing you didn't go there first. I don't want any of this coming home."

His clear blue eyes held mine. I hadn't seen him in months, but I understood his unspoken words. This mission had to stay far away from my mom and Xander. On that, at least, we were in complete agreement.

"You can talk in code all you like, but I know what's going on," Xander said, giving me a look that was far too knowledge-able for his fourteen years. "I've been listening to Julian on the chat-casts. The day is here, exactly like Julian said it would be. We have to stand up for our right to exist or people like Vellus will destroy us."

Hearing Xander quote Julian made a slither of fear crawl up my back. His synth tattoo burned red against the anger flaming his cheeks. Xander should be at home, watching out for my mom, not getting his J-card. He certainly didn't belong in Julian's JFA.

"Whatever it is that you're planning," Xander continued, "you still need someone to watch out for your mom." He stood a little taller. "I can do that."

I glanced at my dad and he seemed to think so too. An uncomfortable weight pressed on my chest, but I didn't have the luxury of thinking of Xander as just a kid anymore.

"Okay," I said. "Your part of this mission is to get Mom back home."

Xander nodded too quickly. "Once she's safe, I'll come join you and Julian and the JFA."

"No!" my dad and I both said at the same time.

Xander shrugged, like us saying "no" didn't mean much to him. How long had he been planning to run off to join the JFA? My chest squeezed tighter. Was he doing this because of me? I didn't know which was worse: Xander in the suburbs, marked as a jacker, or having him on the front lines, behind Vellus's barricade. Neither one was good.

"There are changelings in Jackertown who can do a lot more than babysit a reader," Myrtle said, giving Xander a nod of approval. "But if Kira and her dad are going to help the JFA, Xander, they need to know that you're at home, keeping everyone safe."

"She's right," my dad said to Xander. "I'm only going to be able to do this if I know you're looking out for your mom, not running off to the JFA."

Xander nodded his agreement. He looked disappointed, but not by much. Which worried me.

"Promise me, Xander," I said. Then I cringed, because it felt like an odd echo of what Julian had said, right before I disobeyed his direct order and went after Vellus on my own.

Before Xander could answer, my dad's face suddenly went on high alert. His gaze had been captured by something over my shoulder, down the alleyway. I flung my mind out behind me and ran smack into a trio of anti-jacker helmets. All of us pivoted as one toward them.

Three figures, one in the lead and two flanking him, marched steadily toward us, dressed in drab olive-and-brown camouflage. Their black boots and anti-jacker helmets looked military, but they weren't any uniform I recognized, not even the black riot gear of the CJPD. But they had black guns pointed at our heads and skintight masks under their helmets.

Fronters.

Stupid young men proving how tough they were by hunting jackers. Stupid young men with guns.

I stepped in front of my mom to protect her. Three of them. Six of us, but one was a reader and one was a kid. I was armed, and I was pretty sure Sasha and my dad were packing, maybe Myrtle, too. We might be able to take them.

I flung my arm back, pushing my mom to the side of the alley until we were flush against the rough brick wall. As soon as I moved, Sasha, Xander, Myrtle, and my dad all scattered. I tucked up my leg to retrieve my dart gun and fired at the lead Fronter, the sound of their dart guns already popping the air as they shot at us. Xander went down by my feet, and Myrtle crouched over him, firing on the Fronters with a tiny gun gripped in her hand-knit gloves. I resisted the urge to go to them and kept shooting while the Fronters took cover behind the dumpster. Sasha zigzagged down the alley, getting closer to them. My dad flung himself against the wall in front of me, and I nearly shot him as he went by.

I cursed inwardly but realized that now he could cover my mom.

I quickly linked a thought to him, *Stay with Mom!* and pulled out before I could hear his response.

Halfway down the alley, Sasha was already down, but I saw

what he was trying to do. He had been heading for the dumpster, to get into their blind spot, then maybe go over the top to get into close range, where he could get a hand on their helmets. All three Fronters were still behind the dumpster; even if I couldn't get them all, I might be able to give enough distraction for my dad and Myrtle to sweep in and take the rest. I started to push off the wall, but my dad collapsed in front of me, sliding down the crumbling brick. I hesitated, not wanting to leave my mom. Something bit into my shoulder, sending racing streaks of pain down to my fingers. A dart stuck out of the arm of my ultralite. I fumbled to tug it out, but my hands weren't working.

My mom cried out as I fell into her. I dove into my mind, ramping up my already pounding heart and searching for the trigger for my adrenaline, but darkness chased after me. I tried to push on it, but it buried me under an avalanche of horror, pressing on me with realization of what was happening.

We were caught.

Chapter NINE

Something was tapping my face. Roughly, more like slap-ping. It hurt.

I opened my eyes and cringed, hunching up my shoulders to protect my sore cheek. One of the Fronters crouched in front of me, his hand pulled back, ready to slap me again. How long had he been hitting me? The stinging told me he'd done it more than once or twice.

He didn't hit me again, just stared from behind his skintight black mask. I couldn't see his eyes, but the way his features moved under the Second Skin made me think he was smiling. Or possibly leering.

"What's your name, beautiful?" His voice had the halting, thick sound of most readers, uneven from a lack of use, and it sent chills down to my toes. I looked away, trying to gather my wits and assess the situation.

It looked pretty bad.

I was leaned up against a rough wooden post that dug into

my back. Bindings bit into my wrists, which were tied behind me, but when I moved, I found they were free of the post. The floor was cold concrete underneath me. Myrtle slumped by my side, still passed out from the tranq dart they's shot her with. My dad lay across a crack in the floor next to Myrtle, his hands and feet bound, also passed out.

Another Fronter stood behind Mr. Hitter, his arms crossed over his camouflage jacket and his face unmoving under his black mask and anti-jacker helmet. Even though his face was covered, his stare made me shiver. I had a hard time focusing past the two Fronters. Behind them, dim squares of light patch-worked the floor between dozens of bare shelving racks. The air was musty and choking, as if every living thing had left long ago and taken the oxygen with them. The Fronters had brought us to some kind of abandoned warehouse, probably not far from the testing station, judging by how everyone was still passed out and they had to slap me awake.

But why?

An electric sparking sound and a muffled cry snapped my attention to my left. I blinked rapidly and Sasha came into focus, tied to another wooden post like mine, his body con-vulsing as the third Fronter held a Taser to him. The Fronter paused, then zapped him again. The current coursed through Sasha's body, and mine twitched in response, every hair stand-ing out in horror. The Staring Fronter tapped the shoulder of Mr. Hitter and jerked his thumb toward the Fronter who was torturing Sasha.

Mr. Hitter barked out, "Hey! We're just supposed to bag and drag."

Bag and drag. They had already "bagged" us, but where were they "dragging" us to?

The electric arcing cut off, leaving a faint smell of singed air in its wake. "Yeah, yeah," the third Fronter complained. "Just having some fun here before we take 'em in to the DC." He shrugged and stepped back, taking his Taser with him. The DC... the *Detention Center*.

Sasha slumped, held upright only by the rope tying him to the post. His dark, curly hair fell into his face, the rest of him deadly still. I hastily reached out to brush his mind. He was alive, just stunned to unconsciousness. My throat closed up, unsure if I should try to wake him. At least he wasn't moaning anymore.

My heart squeezed when I saw a large red J inked on his cheek.

Jackers who were captured by Fronters simply disappeared, never to be seen again. I had assumed they were killed, but maybe not. Maybe the Fronters were working with Vellus's Detention Center, rounding up jackers and dropping them there for incarceration. Which was better than outright killing, but that meant the Fronters and Vellus were somehow connected.

Staring Boy turned his mask-covered eyes back to me. His knuckles turned white as he clenched his hands, folded into his arms. Whoever he was, I had a feeling he would rather use the Taser on me than Sasha.

The bitter taste of fear and hatred stewed in my throat, pooling saliva in my mouth.

The Hitter still crouched in front of me, inspecting me. I spit my fear-fueled excess saliva straight into his face. He hit me again, sending a blinding wave of pain across my face. My cheek was on fire, like it was stung by a hundred angry ants. My assailant reached up between his helmet guard and the black mask, trying to wipe away the spit, but only managing to smear it. A crazy grin broke out across my face.

Mr. Hitter made a sound of disgust, then stood up and took a step back. I reined in the mania that was telling me to roll after him and bite his ankles. I needed to keep calm and find a way out of this. I blinked a couple of times and shook my head. It stayed fuzzy. I stepped up my heart rate to fight off the residual tranquilizer from the dart.

As my vision cleared, I realized all of a sudden that someone was missing. I jerked my head around, straining to see. Relief and fear grabbed equally at my throat when I didn't see my mom or Xander anywhere.

"What have you done with them?" I asked, my voice still raspy from the sedative. "What did you do with the reader and the boy?"

Mr. Hitter tilted his head and chuckled. "Had to throw the kid back. The DC won't take 'em that young, but don't worry. Sooner or later he'll join you there."

So they let Xander go. "What about the reader?" I asked, my voice stronger this time, but he didn't say anything more.

I sent up a fervent prayer that my mom was okay. Fronters loathed jackers, but they held readers in the highest esteem. I told myself they had no reason to hurt a reader like my mom, even if she was caught with jackers. They would think they had rescued her. Especially since she had just been to the testing station and was proven innocent of being a jacker. Whatever mark the test left on her shoulder, the lack of a red J on her cheek should be proof enough for the Fronters.

If wishes were granted on the strength of wanting them, my mom and Xander would be back home safe already.

Staring Boy's face was still unmoving, not even a blink underneath the fabric.

Mr. Hitter turned to him. "You want this one? You can have her. She's a spitter."

Staring Boy didn't say anything, but his knuckles cracked as he clenched his fist tighter. Mr. Hitter seemed to notice the tension rippling through Staring Boy's body as well.

"Hey," Mr. Hitter said, batting Staring Boy's chest with the back of his hand. "You want some privacy for this one?" He was leering again, and his words sent fear gushing into an icy pool in my stomach.

Staring Boy turned sharply to Mr. Hitter and shoved him in the shoulder. Not overly hard, but enough to take Mr. Hitter by surprise.

"Whoa!" he protested, throwing up his hands. "What's got you all riled up?" Then he looked back at me, peering closer this time. He pulled his phone out of his pocket and snapped a picture of me. Then he examined the image, or maybe something else, on his phone.

"No way," he said. "It's *her*."

I swallowed through the tightness in my throat. They knew who I was. This was, in no way, a good thing. Mr. Hitter turned to the Fronter by the post where Sasha was hung. "Hey, come check this out! You're never going to guess who we bagged."

Staring Boy's hands dropped to his side. His chest rose and fell, small puffs of air inflating his skintight mask where it stretched over his mouth, now slightly parted. This sharpened the fear in me even more. With my dad and Myrtle passed out and Sasha tied up, the only hope was me somehow getting us out of this. But it looked like Staring Boy had an issue with me.

Which meant he might have a special party planned just for me.

A quick check of my ankles and the back of my pants showed the Fronters had taken all my weapons. Of course. Maybe if I surged up a crazy amount of adrenaline, plus my fast-twitch muscles, I could leap up and catch them off guard. Run at them, or maybe simply run away. That was it: I needed to run. I could come back with reinforcements. Or at least weapons. It made me sick to think of leaving, but getting dragged to the Detention Center wouldn't help either. If I even made it that far.

Myrtle, lying next to me, let out a low moan. Maybe she was waking. I wasn't sure if that was a good thing or a bad thing. Her jacking skills were extraordinary, but they meant nothing as long as the Fronters had their helmets on. Then she was just a frail old woman.

I brushed her granite-like mindbarrier, hoping like crazy she would let me in. *Myrtle, it's me!*

Kira? She stirred, her face grinding into the dirty floor, but her mindbarrier relaxed a little, letting me in. She was struggling to open her eyes.

Play possum, Myrtle! I have a plan! I linked it so hard and fast that she reflexively pushed me out again. But she got the message because her body relaxed into the floor.

I closed my eyes, trying to quell the hitched breathing that was taking over my lungs. I didn't know if I could take Myrtle with me, but playing dead would keep her from being abused, at least for a while. Running was still our best hope.

I needed to focus, ignore the drumbeat sound of blood pounding in my ears and the shuffling of footsteps. Dive deep into my mind, go down the elevator. I amped up my adrenaline along the way, and the heat of it coursed through my system, readying my body for the run of its life. I dug down deeper, finding the thread, following the pathway, and hoping I could get away before the blowback hit. The Fronters' voices fell around my ears. I tried to ignore them, but they beat their way into my consciousness, slowing me down.

"Wow," one said. "It really is her."

"Are you going to just tag and drag her?" another one asked. "She's on the Most Wanted list, like the other two..."

"That's the protocol," the first one said. "But hey, man, I can understand if you'd like to, you know, do something a little different here."

"Yeah," one chuckled. "Maybe show her a good time, huh? A little payback for what she did?"

There was a scuffle on the floor in front of me. "Okay! Okay. I was just joking."

My body trembled with the adrenaline overload. The shaking of my body and the pounding of their words were distracting me. The Fronters were silent for a moment, and I kept following the thread to the center where my fast-twitch muscles were controlled. A couple of more seconds...

"We'll tag her just like the rest," Staring Boy said. "You take care of the old woman. Leave Kira to me." His smooth and practiced voice saying my name made my heart stutter and ripped my focus out of my head.

My eyes popped open, and I gasped in a breath.

"Raf?"

Chapter TEN

Staring Boy whipped his head to me, and I knew it was Raf, even though I couldn't see his face. Same build, same tall, trim soccer physique. A single dark curl of hair poking from beneath his mask, right at the nape of his neck.

All feeling drained into the deep pit in my chest. Adrenaline still sang through my body, crying out for me to kick, scream, run—something—but all will to move had emptied out once Raf's voice jerked me from the depths of my mind. His face was obscured by the skintight mask, but his jaw visibly worked underneath it.

"How..." I said. "Why..." The words were a jumble in my mouth and in my brain. "How did you find me?" I finally spat out.

That seemed to unleash whatever invisible force was holding him back.

"Find you!" He dropped to one knee, leaning forward and curling a fist. I stared at it, wondering if he was planning on hitting me with it. I was too dumbfounded by that thought to do or say anything.

"I never wanted to find you!" He was so close that his words reached me on huffs of air. "If I never saw you again in my entire life, it would be too soon!"

I watched his mouth move under the taut fabric of the mask. It mesmerized me. The words washed over me like a hundred shards of glass that were somehow painless, even while they sliced me to ribbons. I would feel the cuts later.

Raf's memories—his *life*—was a Swiss cheese of randomness, all because of me. It made sense for him to hate me, given all the lies his parents had told him, but to join a hate group?

A small voice inside me said, *You should have known this would happen. After what you did to him.*

But it was so far from the boy I loved—who I *still* loved, even though that boy didn't exist anymore—that my brain couldn't process it.

Next to us, Mr. Hitter had pinned Myrtle to the floor, his beefy knee punching deep into her stomach. Her legs kicked, landing nothing but air. He covered her mouth with one enormous hand. My heart clenched, wondering if Myrtle could even breathe. He twisted her head to one side and pressed his other hand flush against her cheek. I couldn't see if there was a synth-tattoo film under his palm, but I was sure that was what he was doing.

She's on the Most Wanted list... I thought the Fronters' attacks and the testing station summons were random, but apparently the Fronters and Vellus were working together with a list of some kind. And how did Fronters get hold of government-issued jacker tattoos? You couldn't get those at the local synth-parlor; they had special anti-counterfeiting measures built in.

Even though Myrtle struggled, the Fronter held her head still for the thirty-second transfer. She made no sound, just glared hatred at her attacker.

This was what Raf had become?

Molloy had taken all Raf's memories of me, but he hadn't re-written Raf the way Sasha could. Somewhere under the Second Skin mask was the boy I grew up with. Raf's mask blew in and out with his labored breathing, his face near mine. Blood and adrenaline pounded through my body, but there was only one thing that was important to me. And it wasn't running away.

"I don't blame you," I said, nodding, "for never wanting to see me again. That's why..." My voice cracked. "That's why I left, so you wouldn't accidentally run into me."

Raf leaned back, his breath hitching a little, then a scowl bunched the fabric on his forehead.

"If you weren't looking for me..." My voice faded. Was it just random? Was the universe simply that cruel to me? It wouldn't surprise me, if that's all it were.

"We were looking for him." Raf jerked his head toward my father. The third Fronter hooked his hands under my dad's arms and dragged him toward the far end of the warehouse. My throat closed up, watching my dad's boots bump against a shelving rack as the Fronter pulled him out of sight.

I swung back to face Raf. "Were you trying to get back at me by going after my family?" I didn't want to believe he would take it that far.

Raf rocked back on his heels, still squatting in front of me. That's when I noticed he had a tattoo film clenched in his hand. A bright red J was stamped across the clear sheet.

"And how did you know?" I asked, my voice gaining strength. "How did you know that my dad would be at the clinic?"

He didn't answer me. A moan from Myrtle drew our focus. The Fronter who had tagged her was done. He rose and lumbered over to Sasha. The third Fronter had returned, without my dad, and together they worked to take Sasha down from the post. They were going to drag him away, like my dad. *To the DC.*

Raf waited until they were busy, then whispered to me. "The name Moore came up. We weren't going to take them in to the DC. I just... I just wanted some answers."

"Answers?" So Vellus hadn't sent Raf after my family; Raf had done it for his own reasons.

"Why?" Raf demanded. "Why did you do this to me? Was it some kind of sick joke to you?"

"I didn't jack you, Raf. I never would—"

"You punched holes in my mind!" His voice had turned from whisper to hiss. "There are whole pieces of my life that are missing now!"

The pieces that had me in them.

"I didn't do it, Raf, I swear to you." I blinked to clear the blurriness, but that only rolled the tears down my cheeks. Raf turned away, disgusted. "But maybe I should have." That made him swing back. "Maybe if I had jacked you to forget about me, you wouldn't have had this." I gestured with my chin to Myrtle, who had recovered well enough to work her way up to sitting. "All of this wouldn't have happened to you. They attacked you because of me. They took out the pieces that... that had me in them. I'm sorry you were caught in the middle, Raf. I'm so sorry."

My shoulders sagged, the truth draining any remaining fight out of me. I was bitterly, painfully sorry; but sorry didn't cover the giant black-hole-sized amount of pain and regret that I carried around in my chest. I had never had a chance to say it before. But what Raf was doing now... it had to be stopped. I couldn't let this be who he had become. Who I had turned him into.

He pulled back and stared at me, that unblinking stare from before. Then he slowly reached up and pulled the mask down, uncovering his face and gathering the fabric under his chin.

"I want you to see me," he said. "I want you to see who finally tagged you for what you are."

He had the same deep chocolate-brown eyes that I loved, but they were dulled, like a film of forgetfulness had been drawn across them. They were the eyes of an old man who has lost something precious but can no longer remember what.

That's when I felt the cuts, like small surgical strikes on my heart.

I didn't flinch as he leaned forward, tattoo in hand. If it weren't for the anti-jacker helmet, I could have plunged into his mind, but I already knew what was there from all the times he had let me in so willingly. I looked into his eyes and spoke the truth to them.

"This isn't you," I whispered. He was close now. The others were too far to hear, carrying Sasha away. Even Myrtle would have had to strain to hear us.

He raised the tattoo. "Yes, it is," he said between his teeth. "You don't know me."

"No, Raf," I said. "You have it backward. You don't remember me. But I know you."

He faltered, looking more than a little freaked out by that statement. I kept my voice low. "You're a good person, Raf. The best." I pushed the words out like they were a force field that could stop his hand, which still hovered near my cheek. "You're kind and decent and good. You did things for me—you helped me—when I needed it most. You were the one person who understood what it was like for me to be so... different. Who accepted me and looked past all of it. That part of you, the part with the open heart, is still inside you, Raf. That part doesn't go away, no matter what you remember or don't. It's part of who you are." I swallowed down the dryness in my throat, and it didn't escape my notice that Raf had frozen in place, his hand hovering in the empty air between us.

"This," I flicked my gaze to the tattoo, "this isn't who you are, Raf. If I could change what happened to you, I would. In an instant. I would give anything—anything—to erase it. Just because I can't undo what's happened, please... don't throw away the good and decent part of you, Raf. The part that I loved."

I gasped, not intending to say that last part and wishing all of a sudden that I could pull the words back in, keep them inside me like the air I held trapped in my lungs.

Raf's hand literally wavered in the air, swinging closer and farther from my cheek, emotions flitting across his face with it. In one quick motion, he peeled away the thin plastic film that covered the tattoo. I closed my eyes and waited for the stinging that would come when the tattoo's acid etched into my skin. Waited for the rough feel of his hands grasping my head and holding me still while he marked me. I couldn't help thinking of the tattoo he'd put on our wrists, matching hearts when we were in love, pretending the world wouldn't notice and would let us stay that way. That tattoo had faded. I told myself this one would too, even if it would mark my heart forever, just as the first one had.

After several seconds of waiting, I realized nothing was happening.

I opened my eyes. Raf's hand had dropped and the tattoo lay on the floor. I glanced at it, then met his stare, trembling and wondering what he was thinking. Before I could say anything, Raf reached behind his back and drew something out. A silver knife blade glinted dull yellow from the late afternoon sun that fell through the high windows of the warehouse.

I sucked in a breath, but he was too fast. Before I could pull back, he had put his arms around me and grabbed my wrists. In a painful tug that cut into my skin, the bindings fell free. Raf stepped quickly back, rising up to his full height and staring down at me. I still sat on the floor, but now with free hands. I marveled at them, then looked up at him, speechless.

He scuffled over to Myrtle and cut her bindings too, then sheathed the knife behind him again.

"I don't ever want to see you again," Raf said, staring at me with a wide-eyed look, like he wasn't quite sure I hadn't jacked him into letting us go. Or that he was doing the right thing. But he was doing it nonetheless.

I nodded, unable to form words.

He turned and walked in the direction the other Fronters had dragged my father and Sasha. I didn't hesitate. I leaped up, grabbed Myrtle's hand, and yanked her small frame to standing. We ran in the opposite direction, weaving through empty shelves, searching for the back of the warehouse, stumbling over stray boxes left strewn on the floor. I prayed we would find a back door and that Raf wouldn't change his mind before we could get away.

A dull gray metal door beckoned, half-covered by a stack of cardboard boxes. We shoved them out of the way and pushed the door open, running blindly into the afternoon light. I heard angry shouts behind us, but I didn't waste time looking back.

Chapter ELEVEN

We kept running until the Fronters were out of my reach and we couldn't hear their angry shouts any longer. Then I stepped down the pace, letting Myrtle catch her breath. We steered clear of the demens floating around the abandoned brownstones and decaying storefronts. The wintery wind blew lonely down the street, lifting scattered dead leaves into the air for company. The Fronters had taken my flak jacket, so I only had my ultralite, and the dying afternoon sun didn't warm the air in the slightest.

My quarter-mile sweep didn't reach the testing station, but I recognized the nearby buildings from our autocab ride in. We weren't far from Jackertown. The tactical piece of my mind kept track of the relative position of Fronters' hideout. Maybe Julian could send a strike team later, in case they kidnapped more jackers. I wished we could call for backup now, before my dad and Sasha ended up in the DC, but the Fronters had taken my phone as well.

Eventually, my reach found several National Guardsmen patrolling the half-constructed barricade. As we approached, we feigned that Myrtle was in dire need of jacker medical attention that could only be found in Jackertown. She was shaking from the residual tranq dart, which made her pretty convincing. The Guardsman were more intent on stopping and searching an inbound truck delivering groceries. The truck got turned back, but we were let through with a warning: they had orders not to let anyone back out again.

Like we didn't know that.

I was desperate to call my mom or Xander, praying they were safe. Emotions roiled through me as we wove through the Jackertown streets and approached the JFA headquarters. We had failed so badly, I didn't know how I was going to face anyone there.

I swung open the heavy door to HQ and tensed in anticipation of seeing Julian again, but there was only Anna and a smattering of JFA recruits milling in the central kitchen area. Myrtle coughed and shrugged off her jacket. The J still blazed red on her cheek, but her whole face was unevenly splotched. She didn't look well, probably because of the trauma of being branded like cattle.

Anna stalked over to us. "What happened to you?" she asked Myrtle, about as subtle as a hand grenade.

"I'm fine," Myrtle said, but I could tell she wasn't, not really. I gestured that she should go sit on the couch. My anger threatened to boil up out of me and explode on Anna.

"Fronters captured us," I said quietly to Anna, trying to deflect her attention from Myrtle gingerly settling in on the couch. Unwelcome tears sprang up, and I coughed to cover them, wiping my face while turned away.

"What?" There was no sympathy in Anna's voice. More like, *how could you manage to get captured by Fronters?* "Where is Sasha?" She looked to the door, which was already shut against the Chicago winter winds.

"The Fronters have him," I said, my voice choking up. "And my dad, too. I think they've taken them to the Detention Center."

Anna pressed a fist to her forehead and turned from me as if she didn't have words for how massively I had messed up. I was barely holding things together as it was—I didn't need her dressing me down.

Then I saw Ava.

She hovered at the periphery of the kitchen, holding on to the edge of the counter like it was a life preserver. On the best of days, Ava was thin, pale, and wispy. Today, she looked like she was about to float away. I stepped toward her to hug her or something, then stopped. I had managed to get her boyfriend captured, Tasered, branded, and hauled off to the DC. Any words I might have were empty and stuck in my throat.

"Is he...?" Ava asked, her voice as light as a feather. "Did they...?"

"He's alive," I rushed out. I would sooner have been branded myself than tell her the man she loved had been strapped to a post and tortured. "They took him to the Detention Center, but I promise you, we'll get him out. I promise, Ava." I wanted to hug her, to erase the tormented look on her face, but I couldn't. I was shaking too badly myself.

Anna reined in her anger enough to whip back and face me. "You need to tell Julian this. I don't want him to hear it from me."

I swallowed and nodded.

"He's on the roof," Anna said, more quietly this time, the heat evaporating from her voice.

I avoided Ava's gaze as I swiped a spare phone off the kitchen counter and headed toward the back. My boots clanged heavily on the metal steps of the stairwell to the roof, the echoes bouncing off the concrete silo to pound on my ears. I jacked into the phone and sent a call to my mom first, but it went straight to message. So did Xander's. Maybe the Fronters had taken their phones too. I hadn't sensed either of them near the Fronters' hideout. Could they have managed to find an autocab, without phones and in the no-man's-land that autocabs were programmed to avoid? That seemed very unlikely. They had to be wandering around, trying to get back home after Raf and the other Fronters had released them.

Raf's last words had lifted me in a perverse way. *I never want to see you again.* It wasn't so much the words as the way he said them. Without the hatred. Without the anger. Somehow they reached straight into the black hole of my heart and showed how empty it was. I had spent the last four months trying to fill that hole with other things, not realizing it wasn't right for anyone to walk around with empty spaces inside them.

I understood why Raf had gone after my dad. *To get answers,* he had said.

To fill up the holes again.

The irony wasn't lost on me: I could change the chemistry of my brain, cause my muscles to alter their form, ramp my heart rate up and down, but I couldn't heal my own heart.

I paused, my hand on the chilled doorknob at the top of the stairs. I had to face Julian, having failed in a mission he never wanted to send me on. Having lost not only Sasha, but also my dad and any chance of getting Vellus. And I wasn't even sure if Julian wanted to talk to me.

I took a deep breath and eased open the door, the blustery wind fighting me for it. The setting sun had painted the sky blood orange, and plasma lights had started to wink on throughout Jackertown, though it wasn't quite dark yet.

Julian sat cross-legged at the corner of the building, right at the precipice, like he was meditating. He faced away from me and surveyed the broken brick and boarded-up landscape that was Jackertown. I had been whisper silent when I opened the door, but I could tell by the way Julian's back turned ramrod straight that he had sensed me.

He didn't turn around.

I didn't reach out—no one volunteered to link in to Julian's mind, if they could help it. But at this moment, as my boots crunched the graveled surface of the rooftop, stepping slowly heel-to-toe up to him, I wished that he would hold back his automatic defense mechanism so that I could link in to his mind, and he could read my thoughts.

Just so I wouldn't have to say them out loud.

When I had crossed half the roof, only a dozen feet between us, his voice made me freeze: it was as biting as the wind on my damp face. "I haven't seen you on the tru-casts. Or any news about Vellus having a sudden change of heart. Did your father tell you no?"

I didn't say anything, just closed the distance between us and stood behind him. He still hadn't faced me.

"You know," he said, "I can reach a hundred minds from here. Sense their instincts, their most basic drives. The things that make them love or hate or protect. It's a sea of primal emotion that I can reach out and shape with a thought. And I can reach thousands more with my words on the short comms and chat-casts." He stopped. "But I can never reach you, even when you're just a few feet away."

Words burst out of my throat like sob. "We were captured by Fronters."

Julian's head whipped to the side, then he pivoted out of his meditation pose and stood in one smooth motion. His hands reached for me, gently taking hold of my shoulders. He looked me over, head to toe, like he expected to find a bullet hole somewhere between my ultralite and cargo pants.

His gaze finally traveled back up to mine. "Are you okay?" His voice was soft, and he was so close... the same gush of emotion swept through me as when he had kissed me before. My body sang with his touch.

"I'm fine." My voice betrayed me by squeaking. "But the Fronters tagged Sasha and took him and my dad to the Detention Center. One of the Fronters let Myrtle and me go..." I couldn't bring myself to say it was Raf. "I couldn't stop them, Julian. I was tied up, and poor Myrtle... I couldn't stop them, and..." The words were coming out in gasps now. "And I lost our chance to get Vellus, and my mom and Xander are missing, and I'm sorry..."

Julian's hands moved up, warm on my face. "Shh. Shh. It's okay. It'll be all right." His words washed over and soothed me. He had that holding-back look that I had misunderstood so many times before... but I couldn't let him kiss me. The rush through my body wanted it, but with the crazy mix of emotions rolling through my chest, I couldn't be sure it was real. Not just an instinct. Not just my body responding to his brilliant blue eyes and gentle touch. I hadn't even sorted out the first time, but it was real for him: he deserved the same from me.

I took a half step back. The wind carried away the heat and intensity building between us.

His hands dropped to his sides, his shoulders falling with them. "You're never going to forgive me, are you?"

I blinked. "What?"

He sucked in a breath. "You're never going to forgive me for what happened to your boyfriend. To... Raf." He stumbled over Raf's name, as if he didn't want to say it out loud. "It's because you love him, isn't it? I mean, you really did love him, and you can't forgive me for not saving him in time."

My lips opened and closed, the words they were trying to form swirling in my mind. How could I explain that seeing Raf had made me realize how empty I was? The pain in Julian's eyes was making it difficult for me to speak.

"I don't blame you for Raf," I finally choked out. "That was all Molloy, and he paid for it. I can't..." I searched for words but all I found was pain. "I just... there's something wrong with me, Julian. I'm... broken." The word escaped me, carried on pain wrenched from deep inside. Julian's hands flew back to my face, gently cupping my cheeks.

He ducked his head to whisper, "Let me fix it."

The words surged up a crazy thought, a demens kind of hope. Maybe he could reach through our linked thoughts, like he had when we were being held in Kestrel's prison, and heal this wound inside me that I couldn't seem to seal up.

I peered up at him, his face close. "Can you fix me? Like you did before? If I linked in to your mind..."

Julian shrank back, pain flashing across his face and slicing me through the heart.

"That's not what I meant."

"You wouldn't have to..." I stopped. *You wouldn't have to make me fall in love with you.* I couldn't say that out loud and simply thinking it was making me dizzy. "You could just... just fix the part that's not working." This wasn't coming out right, and every word seemed to stab into Julian, which wasn't what I wanted at all.

"It wouldn't be real, Kira." His voice was back to the icy

coldness that matched the wind. "You don't understand. It's all connected and I couldn't just... you would be different. I'm not sure that you would be able to love someone again. Not for real." He paused, then softened. "But I guess... I could make the pain stop. Is that what you want me to do?"

Guilt twisted me so hard my chest physically caved in. I knew he was still tormented by the one time he had permanently altered someone's instincts. My simply asking hurt him—how much more would it hurt for him to actually reach into my instincts and change me? Yet he would do it, or at least try, if I wanted. It made me realize how messed up I was, that I would even consider having Julian handle away my pain.

I straightened, trying to regain some of my shredded dignity. "No, I... I shouldn't have asked." I gave a rueful half laugh. "You would think I could fix myself, right? With all my crazy mind powers." I waved my hand in the air, trying to joke it off, but it came out weak. My shoulders slumped. "I'm a mess, Julian. Trust me, you don't want to be mixed up in it."

"You're not a mess." His voice was warm again. Patient. Understanding. My heart squeezed with the familiarity of it. It was how Raf used to talk to me.

"Well, there's no question that I've messed things up pretty good," I said, desperately trying to change the topic away from my pathetic emotional state. "Vellus is still in his right mind, I've managed to lose one of our best assets, and you don't even want to see Myrtle's face." An image of Myrtle, bent under the Fronter's knee, surged up and buried my attempt at lightheartedness. "They need you downstairs to come clean up my mess. They need you to lead them, encourage them, like you always do. To help them find a new plan of how to deal with Vellus, now that I've failed."

"You know," he said, peering at my hanging head, "it was always you who should be leading them, not me. From the beginning, I've known that was true."

Even now, Julian wanted me to step up and stand by his side. His judgment was clouded, obviously, by the feelings he had for me, but it was tremendously sweet. Still, he wasn't thinking it through.

"I can't even keep the people I love safe, Julian," I said. "My dad is in the Detention Center, which is bad enough, but my mom and Xander are also lost somewhere. The Fronters released them, but I can't reach my mom on her phone." I paused to clear the closing up of my throat. "I couldn't lead them out of a paper bag. I never meant for any of this to happen. All I've ever wanted was to keep them safe."

"I know," he said, gently. "Which is precisely why it should have been you leading us all along."

I frowned, shaking my head. He wasn't even making sense now. And he had a kind of glow about him that seemed at odds with the direness of our situation.

"I need you by my side, Kira." It was a simple statement, and I flashed back to when he had said it before, at the Mediation Center. "Right now the JFA needs us both," he continued. "Besides, I've been thinking. There may be a way we can stop Vellus and get everyone safely back as well. Including your family."

My eyebrows rose. How did this boy always manage to find hope in the darkest of situations?

He smiled down at me. "Are you with me?"

There was no question in my heart. Whatever idea Julian had, I was in one hundred percent.

I mustered a small smile. "I'm standing on your freezing-cold roof, aren't I?"

He grinned, grabbed my hand, and towed me toward the stairwell.

Chapter TWELVE

This whole revolutionary thing," Ava said, "has a certain odor that I didn't expect."

Odor was a generous term. The tunnel stank of mildew and countless small dead things. After a night of fitful sleep and a rash of tactical planning early this morning, I was now marching alongside Ava through a thirty-foot-high sewage tunnel a couple of hundred feet below Jackertown. Our helmet lamps cast beams that were quickly swallowed by the inky darkness, barely reaching the crew ahead of us: Julian, Myrtle, Hinckley, and seven of Hinckley's military jackers. Technically the tunnel wasn't for sewage, just storm runoff. This far underground, the earth warmed the bedrock walls and kept the trickle of water that ran along the bottom from freezing.

But that didn't help with the smell.

"You could go back." I snuck a sideways look at Ava so I wouldn't flash her with my helmet-mounted light, but her face was too shadowed to read. "It's not too late. Sasha's going to be really upset if he finds out you went on a mission without him."

"Would you stay home?" She took something from the pocket of her cargo pants and bound her long blond hair at the back of her combat helmet. "If you were in my position, wouldn't you do anything you could to bring home the man you loved?"

It wasn't a fair question. Ava knew all I'd done to try to save Raf. "It's not the same. Sasha made Julian promise. You know how he feels about his promises."

"I know," Ava said lightly as if this barely concerned her. "He should have checked with me first."

I shook my head but smiled under the cover of dark, then glanced up, shining my lamp on the roughhewn rock above us. Up ahead in the vast darkness of the tunnel, an access portal would lead to the surface somewhere beyond the perimeter of Jackertown. Julian said the portal might be marked by emergency lighting, but we couldn't count on it. I kept checking for a hole in the ceiling, hoping we hadn't missed it by mistake.

"Can you reach the station yet?" I asked Ava.

She slowed but kept walking. "We're almost to the perimeter shield. A little farther and I'll be able to survey the station." The target of our mission—the Hawthorne Water Pumping Station—was only a mile outside the perimeter. Which was outside my reach, but Ava should have no problem once we were past the shield.

I nodded and picked up the pace to join Julian. He trailed behind Hinckley and his men, their helmet lights bobbing and collectively illuminating the mist that clung to the walls and drifted along the floor. Over Anna's objections, Julian had insisted on joining the mission. She had stayed behind to maintain chain-of-command, sending Hinckley in her place. He had suggested leaving a copy of my chat-cast recording with Anna; I agreed, although the idea of her watching it made me squirm almost as much as when I made it.

"Hey," I said to Julian when I reached him. "Ava says she'll be able to give us surveillance soon."

"Excellent," he said. "We're making good time, which will give us room to plan once we get a read on the station."

Julian's plan was simple and dangerous: take over the water pumping station, hold it hostage, and negotiate with Vellus to release the JFA prisoners at the Detention Center including my dad and Sasha and anyone else illegally detained there. My mom and Xander were still missing—I'd already asked Ava to search Jackertown, but they weren't inside the perimeter. Once my dad was free, we would look for my mom and Xander together.

Julian dropped his voice so it didn't echo in the tunnel. "I wish you could have talked Ava out of coming."

"I'm not exactly the poster girl for that discussion," I said. "I wish you had told Myrtle to stay behind; she's in no shape for this."

"*Touché*," he said. "Except that Myrtle is vital to the mission."

Myrtle had recovered somewhat from the trauma with the Fronters, but Anna and I both thought she should have stayed behind. Julian had won that fight, too, saying Myrtle was key to the PR part of the mission. Which I still didn't understand.

"What odds do you put on Vellus agreeing to turn over the prisoners?" I stepped sideways to avoid a patch of slimy green moss on the floor. Julian did the same and then we met back in the middle.

"The mere fact that we escaped his perimeter fence will give Vellus pause," Julian said. "We won't need to assassinate or scribe him if we can blunt the effect of his actions. Jackers are still coming from all over the country to Jackertown, even with the barricade up. We're entrenched and we have strength in numbers—Vellus hasn't resorted to military assault because quarantining us is a much better play with the public. This isn't only about Jackertown, Kira, or even Illinois. The entire country is watching what happens here. If we can take the station with a minimum of casualties..." I raised my eyebrows, but it was too dark for him to see. "...then we'll be more sympathetic in the public eye. We need to win the hearts of mindreaders if we're going to survive long enough to make it to the tipping point."

"The tipping point?"

"The point where mindreaders have to accept us. Jackers don't have to be the majority—although that day will come as well—we just need a majority of mindreaders to believe that locking up jackers in the Detention Center is unacceptable. That's why you're one of my most powerful weapons, Kira."

"Me?" I smirked. "You mean you don't keep me around for my charm, good looks, and freaky ability to run faster than a cheetah?"

He grinned. "Those are rather attractive features as well." Then he got serious. "The reason Vellus wants you is the same reason I don't want you anywhere near him. You are still the original sympathetic face of the jackers. People remember you rescuing those changelings, Kira, a brilliant piece of PR that I couldn't have dreamed up on my best day."

"Yeah," I said. "PR. That's absolutely what I was thinking at the time."

"I know it's not." Even in the dark, I could see him roll his eyes. "But in one act, you did something I've been struggling to do ever since."

"What's that?" I asked, not following him entirely.

"You humanized jackers." He paused, holding back from saying something more, which piqued my curiosity. Julian was rarely stymied for words. His helmet light made a steady spot on the back of Hinckley's head ahead of us. "You made us seem human," he said quietly, "but you were more than that. I watched the tru-cast like everyone else that day. You were brave and selfless and full of the determination that those changelings had a right to exist. You were willing to do everything and anything to bring them home." He dipped his head and peeked a sideways look at me. "You inspired me, Kira. At a time when I really needed it. And that was before I even knew you."

The weight of his words held my breath captive in my chest. "And now," I said softly, "you know what a mess I really am."

"And now," he said, looking straight forward again, "you make it very difficult for me to be objective in my duties."

I didn't know what to say to that.

He smiled into the dark. "But, once upon a time, a girl on a tru-cast showed me that some causes are worth risking everything for.

And I wasn't the only one. She showed it to the entire world. It's the very opposite of what Vellus says we are. He wants to dehumanize us, lock us up, make us appear too dangerous to set free. And as long as the public believes that is acceptable, we are fighting a losing battle. Which is why it's important for us to secure the water station—but with minimum casualties. Especially if we're going to threaten to cut off the water supply to the suburbs."

I let out the breath I was holding, glad we were back in safe territory again. "I'm thinking water-terrorism isn't making us sympathetic to anyone." I was half-joking, but I could just imagine the reaction of Raf's family to jackers turning off their water. Mama Santos would have a fit.

"Which is why," Julian said, "a grandma who was recently tagged by Fronters is the perfect person to make demands."

Myrtle would make a compelling spokesperson, I had to admit. Plus, shutting off the water wouldn't really endanger anyone in the suburbs. It would be inconvenient, but they had other ways of getting water. After all, they didn't have the National Guard surrounding them with a fence.

"I'm not sure we'll have time to make demands," I said. "It won't take long for Vellus to redeploy the National Guardsmen from Jackertown to Hawthorne. We're just not that far away."

"Once we have control of the water station," Julian said, "we'll be expecting their counterattack. Like the power station, the water station is practically a bunker, so it won't be easy for them." He paused to let me step over a pooled clump of slime. "Vellus won't want an extended military battle in the middle of

Chicago. Even if he doesn't agree to all our demands, we need to hold the water station. It doesn't just feed water to the suburbs, but to Jackertown as well. It's like the power station—we won't last through a siege without it."

"So we're not just bargaining for the prisoners."

"No, this is about fighting to survive." He tipped his head toward me but kept the light from shining in my eyes. "But you've always known those were the stakes, haven't you?"

I nodded. Vellus's move to quarantine us in our own homes was confirmation of everything Julian had been predicting: Vellus planned to eliminate us. While we were still few in number, he could quarantine us, and if we died of malnutrition or thirst or disease, Vellus could claim he hadn't actually killed anyone.

It was completely evil, but also slightly genius. Which was a pretty fair description of Vellus.

One of the head lamps in front of us shone up on the ceiling, spotlighting the access portal. A vertical tunnel had been carved in the rock, and a very long ladder climbed up through it. My tactical mind protested the idea of climbing up that hole one at a time. If anyone was expecting us at the top, it would be easy to pick us off. I reached up to the surface, but there was no one there. The water station was still out of my reach.

Ava caught up to us. "There's a building with a disruptor shield topside and about a half mile to the south."

"That's Hawthorne." Julian had one foot on the first ladder rung when Ava fluttered a hand to stop him.

"Wait," she said. "There are guards posted outside the

pumping station. Two with anti-jacker helmets. I can barely sense them moving against the stationary background of the shield."

"That seems like a lot of security for a water station," I said.

Julian frowned. "They must have realized it's a critical water-supply point for Jackertown. Or maybe they beefed up security after we took the electrical station? Hard to say. Maybe they were planning on cutting off the water to Jackertown even sooner than I thought." He started climbing the ladder. "We need to get eyes up top."

I wished he had let someone else go first. I tucked in behind him, and we all single-filed up the ladder. I couldn't sense any blank spots of anti-jacker helmets in the range of my reach, just a few demens floating around topside. We were still deep in the no-man's-land of the city. When we reached the top, we spilled out of the hole in the ground like spiders crawling out of a drain, all black-garbed and heavily armed. The ultralites and bulletproof vests kept us warm against the crisp morning air, but the bright winter sunshine made me squint.

We trotted forward in a crouched run. I pulled to the front of the group with Hinckley, and Julian fell to the back with Ava. The streets were wide and the buildings low, a few stories high, without the narrow alleyways and hiding spots of Jackertown. Sneaking up on the water station might be a problem. While we were still a block away, I flung my hand out to catch Hinckley in the chest, stopping him and our entire entourage.

I brushed Hinckley's mind. I didn't expect our voices to carry down the block, but I wasn't taking any chances. *Take two of your men for reconnaissance.* Hinckley nodded and motioned to two of his hulking military jackers.

Dart guns only, I linked a parting thought to him. *Julian's orders.*

Hinckley frowned but didn't protest. Their thick black boots made no sound as they crept forward. Behind us, Julian appeared to be having a mind-link conversation with Myrtle, probably going over her role once we were inside. I didn't like it—she looked more shriveled than normal, the oversized flak jacket hanging loose around her body—but I could see Julian's point about her being a sympathetic face.

I brushed Myrtle's rocklike mindbarrier, wanting to join the conversation. Even though she relaxed her mindbarrier, I still had to shove hard to make it through. Her lilac mindscent was almost overpowering.

What do you make of these guards out in front of the pumping station? I asked her. I could never sense Julian in someone else's mind, but they should both know the question was directed at him.

I don't want you using your fast-twitch ability this time, Kira. Julian's voice echoed in Myrtle's mind. *It may take time to secure the plant. I don't want your blowback to hit in the middle of the battle.*

He had a point there.

Hinckley returned and the set of his jaw didn't bode well. As he linked in, Myrtle bore the party in her head fairly well.

It's not looking good, boss, Hinckley thought. *There are at least four guards around the perimeter—we haven't covered the back—and fencing in addition to the shield. The front gate is the only way in.*

There have to be more inside, too, I thought. *Why are they defending this thing like it's the Pentagon?*

Julian's hand rubbed his chin. *They must have known we were coming.*

How could they? I asked. *We just thought up this plan yesterday.*

Julian shook his head. *Maybe they don't want a repeat of the power station embarrassment.*

I nodded. Maybe.

In any event, Hinckley's thoughts rang in Myrtle's mind, *that makes this a lot more tactically challenging. Unless you lift the no-casualties restriction, Julian. I have a few munitions Jameson is itching to try.*

Jameson—the name was familiar. I didn't personally know all Hinckley's troops, but I remembered Jameson breaking down the door of the power station.

Not that I wouldn't enjoy seeing Jameson use his explosives skills, Julian thought with a smirk, *but that's not going to work for the politics of the situation. Taking the plant is only the first step. We need to keep our objective in mind: getting the prisoners out of the Detention Center. Plus, I don't want to blow up Jackertown's water supply.*

Hinckley nodded, but he looked like Julian's restrictions had put him in a box one size too small.

Maybe I can help, I linked in.

Kira. Julian crossed his arms over his black flak jacket. *I told you, I don't want—*

I held up my hand to cut him off. *You'll like this plan, Julian. I'll be on the support team this time. You, on the other hand, will probably need to be on the assault force. Which isn't the best of plans, but...* I counted heads in our group. *We might not have enough people otherwise.*

Julian grinned. *And your plan is?*

I tipped my head to Hinckley. *Our dart guns are effective at three hundred feet, right?* He nodded. *The buildings surrounding the station—are they within that range?*

He pushed an image into Myrtle's mind so we could all see. It was the layout of the buildings surrounding the water pumping station that he and his team had just reconnoitered.

The buildings are within range of our dart guns, Hinckley thought, *but even if we take out the standing guards all at once, we'll still have to penetrate the station itself. They'll pick us off one at a time as we come through the gate.* He glanced at Julian. *And those are not dart rifles they're carrying.*

If you had suppressive fire, I thought, *and some kind of shield, you could storm the gate all the way to the building. You won't have time to blow the door, but what about the windows on the ground floor?*

Hinckley hiked up his eyebrows. *Suppressive fire? As in shooting at them, so they don't shoot at us? With dart guns?*

They don't need to know that we're firing darts, I thought.

If we simultaneously discharge weapons into the roof, they'll think we're using live rounds. At the least, they'll be unsure. You take the assault team in through the windows, and we'll cover you with suppression from the rooftops.

Hinckley was nodding now. *We'll have to time it tight,* he thought, but his eyebrows had resumed their normal scowly position. *Going through the windows is tricky—we'll be silhouetted against the window frame, easy targets.*

You can throw a smoke bomb for visual confusion, I thought, *but you're right. The timing has to be precise. If I'm up high on a building where I can reach everyone, I can mentally coordinate the attack. Once you penetrate the building, the shield will cut me off, but the station is small enough to be within your reach. You should be able to manage a room-by-room search on your own.*

I turned to Julian. *Minimum casualties, dart guns all the way.* When Julian nodded his approval, I turned back to Hinckley. *You need to scout out several good sniper locations first, front and back. We only get one shot at this.*

Hinckley pulled out of Myrtle's head and lumbered off to gather his team and tell them the plan.

Julian's grin stretched so wide it threatened to break his face. *Maybe I do like having you on ops after all.*

Myrtle shook her head and rolled her eyes.

I shrugged like it was obvious all along. *I tried to tell you.*

I had to fight a grin as I turned to join Hinckley and his men.

Chapter THIRTEEN

Hinckley had his people in position, huddled flat against the wall of an abandoned truck depot just south of the water plant. The five of them—Hinckley, three of his brawniest ex-military jackers, plus Julian—were around the corner, out of sight of the patrolling guards. I would rather have had Julian on a rooftop, doing sniper duty like Myrtle and Ava, but he wasn't the best of shots. He would serve the mission better on the ground, even if the front line wasn't the best place to put the leader of the revolution.

If Anna knew, she would kill me.

I linked in to the minds of the assault team but hesitated with Julian. He had promised to pull back his automatic horror-show defense mechanism to let me link in, and it was necessary for the mission. Still, it gave me pause. Linking in to his mind would give him access to my instincts—that was how he had handled me before—but that wasn't the source of my hesitation. Our rooftop discussion, when I had hurt him and embarrassed myself, kept tipping into my thoughts and making me cringe. Not my finest hour. When I linked in now, would he be able to read me? Not my thoughts, but my instincts? For some reason, that made me nervous. But we had a mission to do, so I took a deep breath and cleared out those feelings.

Then I linked in to Julian's mind, something I had vowed never to do again.

Ready there, Revolution Boy? My thoughts bounced around in his head.

Revolution Boy? Is that what you call me in your thoughts? His mind was like an empty room, and his thoughts sounded strange, as if he was projecting them through a static-filled megaphone. And there was no mindscent. Which meant the "thoughts" I heard were no more his true thoughts than the ones I carefully chose and linked into his head.

That buffer was comforting.

I call you many things in my thoughts, I linked to him, *none of which I'll be repeating during a mission. Unless you mess up.* Julian couldn't see my wry smile, given I was a couple of hundred feet away, lying prone on the cold, gravel roof of an abandoned auto-repair shop. But he probably heard it in my thoughts.

I peeked over the low concrete lip of the roof's edge, using a televiewer to get a visual on the patrolling guards and the fenced-in station across the street. The six snipers—four of Hinckley's men, Myrtle, and Ava—were in position as well, strategically placed on rooftops and third-story floors around the perimeter of the pumping station. They each had a guard in their sights. I held a steady link with all six, even the ones near the back. The shield wrapped tightly around the building and blocked my reach inside, but through the images in the minds of our snipers, I saw all six guards.

I was the only one with a vantage of every part of the battle-field. I was the center point and the control. Ava could have been our coordinator, but I was able to jack as well as link, which would come in handy if anything went sideways. Everyone was focused on their part of the mission, waiting for my signal to begin.

Ready for go, Operation Water Tower? I linked to each of the snipers simultaneously. Six *ready to gos* returned to me.

You know, Julian's thoughts intruded on my check-in with the snipers. *I might die today. You should probably tell me the rest of your pet names for me before I go into battle and die a war hero.*

Will you kindly shut up? I linked back. *I'm trying to run an op here.*

Yes, ma'am, he thought. Was that sarcasm in his thoughts? It was hard to tell with all the echoes. I resisted the urge to come up with another snappy comeback. I really did need to focus.

Instead, I linked, *Ready for go, Operation Water Tower?* to Hinckley and his team of four, including Julian.

Five *ready to gos* came back, including Julian's tinny reply.

The guards held their shiny black rifles in a position I now recognized as "ready to shoot without having to think about it."

I couldn't peek behind their anti-jacker helmets, but their body language didn't indicate any awareness of the dart guns aimed at a soft tissue part not protected by their flak jackets. Or the assault team poised at the corner.

Surprise would be our most important weapon.

Hinckley had scavenged an old metal door from a nearby building to use as a shield. I didn't know if it would stop a bullet, but that was all there would be between Julian and the armed guards inside. At least we had brought flak jackets and helmets. I prayed their makeshift shield would get them to the building in one piece.

I took a deep, steadying breath and issued the command to both teams. *Go.*

Simultaneous small pops sounded across the street like children's balloons bursting in the distance, something you would have missed if you hadn't been listening for it. The three front guards dropped as a single unit to the ground, the only sound their large, metallic guns clattering on the sidewalk beneath them. I saw the rear guards fall through the sniper's eyes. At the same moment, Hinckley's assault team surged forward on silent, shuffling boots, a black-clad centipede with a flat metal head and ten legs quickly covering the space between their hidey-hole and the fence. They flowed over the fallen body of the guard stationed there and burst through the gate.

Muffled sounds came from inside the building, and one of the vertically slit windows that lined the front of the pumping station smashed outward. A rain of bullets targeted the assault team, pinging off their metal shield.

Suppression Fire! I linked to the snipers. The three forward snipers sent a hail of darts to the open window. At the same time, the three rear snipers, who had repositioned and switched to live munitions, pounded the roof with bullets, adding an impressive sound to cover the pop-whoosh of the dart guns.

The assault team headed for the gray metal door that was the entrance to the water pumping station. *Hold fire and move!* I linked to the snipers, partly to keep our team from going down under friendly dart fire and partly to give the snipers time to shuffle their position. I wanted the gunmen inside the building to be targeting the empty space where our sniper team used to be. As soon as the suppression fire stopped, the row of tall front windows spewed glass onto the lawn, the gunmen inside returning fire.

The assault team had reached the front door and pressed flat against it, huddling under their metal shield. They folded into a crouching centipede as the glass flew around them.

My mental map of the newly positioned snipers showed the gunmen were aiming wrong, plus my snipers were crouched behind protective brick and concrete. I'd never been so glad for the solid Chicago architecture of the twentieth century as I was now.

The gunmen inside the pumping station hesitated and I commanded, *Suppression fire!* Bullets pounded the roof again, cracking the air with their shots, now coming from new forward positions on the roofs. Inside, figures flung themselves back from the windows, but I couldn't tell how many had been hit by sniper darts. I knew how difficult it was to hit anything moving with a dart pistol, much less a moving target inside a building hundreds of feet away. My hand itched for my own gun, but I held steady, gripping the rough casing of the televiewer. My fingers were numb from clutching it so hard.

Ready for smoke bomb, I linked to the assault team. They crept toward the blown-out window nearest the door. I noticed a tiny movement at the edge of the window—a rifle muzzle tucked in the corner. If the assault team got too close to the window, they'd be point-blank in front of the gunman.

I sent the image to Hinckley. He passed the shield to Jameson behind him and crouched under the level of the window, creeping up to it. I directed the snipers to hold fire so they wouldn't accidentally hit Hinckley, but instructed the roof brigade to keep firing. I knew what Hinckley was thinking, and I didn't exactly like it, but I wasn't going to tell him to stop, either. I guided him with my vantage point, zooming the televiewer in to get him a good visual on the rifle and where the gunman likely was, right inside the window. Guided by my thought-image, Hinckley quickly reached past the broken glass, grabbed the barrel of the gun and hauled the surprised gunman out through the window. The gunman made it halfway, snagging on the jagged glass around the frame, before he must have realized what was happening and let go of the gun. It sailed across the grass and Hinckley yanked the gunman's anti-jacker helmet off in one quick tug. Hinckley jacked him, and the gunman went limp, draped across the window frame.

Which only alerted the remaining gunmen inside that the assault team had arrived.

Smoke bomb! I linked to Jameson, who quickly lobbed the grenade over the inert body of the gunman. A beat or two passed, then a flash inside the water station told me it had detonated. A cloud billowed and rose to the ceiling, burgeoning toward the windows. The assault team pulled down their masks, covering their eyes and noses with a clear membrane that would filter out the smoke and keep them from choking. Once they were past the disruptor field, they would be able to sense the anti-jacker helmets even if they were blinded by smoke.

The gunmen inside had to know things were going badly for them now, and gunfire started up again inside the building, even with the suppression overhead. Jameson threw the metal shield to the ground, and the entire assault team swarmed the windows. They crawled up and over like snakes slipping into the building, covered by the smoke and their low-profile entrance through the windows. I held my breath, praying hard that they made it through without catching a bullet on the way. Once they were inside, my link with their minds was painfully cut off by the disruptor shield, and it made me physically cringe with the force of it. They had disappeared into the smoke, and my breath caught in my throat as I ordered everyone else to cease fire and wait.

Wait.

Wait.

Wait for the shield to come down so I would know what had happened. Wait and strain for a sound, any sound, to tell me what was going on inside. Wait to find out if he was hurt.

What was I thinking? How could I send him in there? What an incredibly, stupendously stupid idea, sending Julian in with the assault team. Every linked mind on the rooftops watched and waited with me. Just as my breaths were starting to come short and panicky and I thought my head might explode from the ten-sion, the shield came down. A breath burst out of me, and I flung my mind into the station, searching, searching for Julian.

I ran into a mental horror show that made me scream from the rooftop. My mind reflexively jerked back, my body shudder-ing with the shock of it.

Julian. His defenses were up, not allowing me into his mind. *He's alive.*

I slumped, thunking my head against the rough lip of the concrete rooftop. I let the dizziness of my pounding heart wash over me, pulsing relief through my body in waves, beating the thought again and again. *He's alive. He's alive.* I waited until I pulled myself together, then linked to the six jacker snipers who were anxiously waiting to hear.

We've taken the station.

Chapter FOURTEEN

E ven before I reached the door of the water pumping station, I linked back to everyone still conscious. All except Julian, who kept his defenses up while he wandered around upstairs. Which made sense—now that the assault was over, there was no need for us to communicate that way. But for some reason, it bothered me. Before, I was nervous about linking in to his mind; now I wished he would let me in, just so I could see he was okay.

The sniper team had brought in the patrol guards, still knocked out from the dart guns, and lined them up along the back wall of the first floor. The assault team had quickly cleared the building, sweeping through the lower level with the shattered windows, a second-floor control room with a few offices, and an overlook on the third floor that peered into a cavernous room in the back. It had pumps and large, L-shaped tubes that pushed water to the giant blue tank behind the pumping station. At least that was what I had gathered from the thoughts and images ricocheting through the minds of the jackers who secured each room.

The smoke still lay heavy on the floor. The whitish-gray mist curled up to the bodies and swirled as the living walked by, tingeing the air with the smell of burnt chemicals.

One of Hinckley's men wrestled with an upturned table to block one of the shattered windows. The station guard that Hinckley had pulled through the window was laid out next to the other readers, who all had darts sticking out from their arms or necks or other exposed parts. The guard's shirt was sliced open from his encounter with the jagged glass, and blood seeped into the starched blue of his uniform, turning it an ugly purple. A quick link in to his head showed he was alive. Hinckley stepped back to let Ava have access to him. The white first-aid kit she used must have come from the station because I didn't recognize it. She tended the man's wounds with bandages and med patches.

Next to the unconscious guard lay one of Hinckley's jackers. I'd missed him in my initial post-mission sweep. I linked in to his mind, but I recognized his face at the same time I realized why I missed him before: Jameson's mind was empty now. Vacant. I should have known he was dead by the bullet hole through his helmet and the still-spreading pool of blood underneath him.

My gaze was drawn to the squareness of his jaw and the light blue of his eyes, now staring unseeing at the ceiling. The leftover smoke lapped at his fingers.

I brushed Hinckley's mind and he let me in. *I'm sorry.* I couldn't think of what else to say.

He was a good man. Hinckley's normally crisp mindscent

was heavy with a bitter aftertaste. He didn't speak out loud or turn to me and kept his arms folded as he watched Ava tend to the mindreader. There was no outward sign that either of us had said anything.

I bent down to Jameson and lightly touched his eyelids, closing them. His skin was still warm. The bullet hole had punched in his helmet and the pool of blood reminded me way too much of Simon lying on the desert floor. It felt horribly wrong that I hadn't properly noticed the color of Jameson's eyes before. My brain fuzzed out trying to think about what to do next. How could we arrange a funeral when we were in the middle of an operation? I wondered if he had someone back home, like Ava, who would be nervously pacing and waiting for him to return. At least Ava still had hope of getting Sasha back.

But only if our mission succeeded.

I slowly stood up and Julian had appeared by my side. He was saying something, but the sound was empty of meaning, like my ears were blocked.

"What?" I blinked rapidly, trying to clear my head. Sound and meaning rushed back into the world.

Julian tilted his head toward a stairwell at the far end of the room. "I have something I need to show you." His right hand gripped his left shoulder, with his arm dangling at his side. He had a look of serious urgency, motioning with his head to the stairwell again.

I stared at his hand clutching his ultralite. "Are you hurt?" I asked, my throat tight.

He barely looked at his arm. "No, I'm fine," he said. "But I need you up in the control room."

I nodded and strode toward the stairwell, Julian following close behind. I glanced back as I started up the stairs. His face was pinched. Was it pain? Or worry? It was hard to tell. I reached ahead to the control room, but there was nothing amiss there, just a member of the assault team coming through on his way back from checking the pumps. He passed us at the top of the stairs. Light brown hair, dark brown eyes. He was probably twenty-five, with the muscular build of the ex-military men Hinckley had recruited. It suddenly seemed important for me to notice. I brushed his mind and his name popped up. *Michael.* He padded downstairs without a look back.

I swallowed the dryness in my throat. Julian stepped ahead of me into the control room. One side was lined with offices, doors ajar. The other was dominated by a wall of screens. About half showed pictures of the station while the rest were filled with charts and data. A couple of chairs faced the screens, and a small tabletop held interface keyboards, but it appeared that most of the controls had mindware interfaces. A trio of offices behind us had windows, and Myrtle was already there, interfacing with a chat-cast box on the screen. She must be casting out the message Julian had prepared, listing the JFA's demands: 1) a JFA representative on hand to monitor all water-station activities, 2) assurances from the City of Chicago that water service would continue uninterrupted to Jackertown, and most importantly, 3) release of all jackers held without due process at the Detention

Center, including those illegally turned in by the Reader's First Front.

"This is important, Kira." Julian's strained voice pulled my gaze back. He had mentally pulled up a map of the water tunnels and pipes throughout the Chicago New Metro area. It looked like blue spaghetti to me and I gave Julian a concerned look.

"Please tell me you don't want me to run this thing."

He smiled, but it was more of a wince. "I do not want you to run this thing."

My shoulders relaxed a bit, and I leaned against one of the chairs.

"However," he said, lapsing into his professor voice, "I do need you to understand it." He mentally commanded the map to zoom in on the lakefront. "Chicago New Metro pulls its water from Lake Michigan, then sends it through this network to a series of pumping stations like the one we're in now."

He paused for a breath and shifted his grip on his arm, then mentally nudged the map to show Jackertown. "This station pumps water to both Jackertown and a portion of the suburbs near the city." He swiped that away and brought up a control panel. "Additional chlorine is added here at the pumping station, and this is the router for sending the freshly chlorinated water to the tank, then out to either the suburbs," he said, highlighting one control switch, "or to Jackertown." He highlighted a second switch. "Normally, both channels are green, which means water is flowing to both. It's controlled by the mindware interface, but there's also a manual control." He tilted his head to a gray metal panel next to the screens. "That's in case of emergencies, but it can also be used to override the mindware interface."

"Why are you showing me all this?" I was afraid he really did want me to run the controls after all.

"Because if anything happens to me, I need you to understand how to work the controls and shut off the water supply to the suburbs if necessary. And how to keep Jackertown's water supply safe."

"Nothing's going to happen to you, Julian." I heard the tremble in my voice and couldn't keep my gaze from straying to where he clutched his arm. A small, bright red drop oozed between his fingers and ran down them, hugging the hills and valleys of his knuckles.

"Julian!" I sucked in a breath. "You're bleeding!"

His face tightened. "I'm fine." He looked into my eyes, capturing me with that intense gaze of his. "Tell me you understand the controls."

"I understand the controls," I hastily repeated back, then pried his hand free from his arm. I gasped. An enormous gash had been torn out of his ultralite. There was nothing but a bloody mess underneath—I couldn't tell which part was Julian's flesh and which was the jacket.

"God, Julian!" I yelled at him. "Why are you standing here telling me about water controls when you're bleeding half to death!"

"It's important." He had a faint smile, but I finally noticed the thin sheen of sweat on his forehead.

I cast around wildly for a first-aid kit. The main control room didn't have one, but one of the offices did, hanging on the wall. The white aluminum box looked to be a hundred years old, rusted out at the corners, but it was the same size as the one Ava had used downstairs. I grabbed Julian's good arm and towed him into the office, gently pushing him to sit on the edge of a pitted gray-metal desk. I yanked the box off its hooks and prayed the contents weren't as ancient as the box itself.

I set the kit down next to Julian and worked on prying open the rusted latch.

"Take off your jacket," I said, not looking at him while I struggled to get a nail under the metal latch. Finally, it popped open, and I was relieved to see modern medical supplies inside: a tiny silver gas canister labeled *anti-bacterial* that I hoped was still in date, a couple of dozen packets of gauze and sterile wipes, and an assortment of medical tapes and glues, plus a laser-suture gun that made my hands shake simply looking at it.

Julian sucked in a breath as he shrugged off his flak jacket. When he unzipped his ultralite, I got a better look at his injury. Whatever bullet had grazed him must have been big or possibly the shooter was close, because it had taken a chunk of Julian's arm with it. He eased off the tattered ultralite and let it fall to the desk behind him. His garish wound was tangled up with the shirt material underneath, which was soaked all the way down to his wrist, turning his white shirt crimson red.

My hands fluttered as I reached for him, like they had that long ago time when I accidentally knocked out Raf and he lay unconscious on the floor. My throat closed up—not because of the wound, but what it meant. Julian had been *shot*. If the bullet had been a little higher and to the left, he would be lying next to Jameson on the ground floor with a hole through his head.

What had I been thinking, sending him in with the assault team? *Stupid, stupid!*

I forced air back into my lungs and clenched and unclenched my hands, trying to stop the ridiculous fluttering. My first-aid training kicked in. I searched the box for scissors to cut away the fabric tangled with his wound. There was nothing.

"You'll need to take off your shirt, too." My voice was surprisingly flat, almost calm sounding, even though my heart was rushing blood through my ears like a freight train. I avoided Julian's eyes. I couldn't hold it together if I looked at him. While he fumbled with one hand at the buttons, I searched the kit for gloves, but there were none of those either. I ripped open a packet of sterile wipes and scrubbed my hands until the skin turned pink and raw. Then I sprayed the fronts and backs with puffs from the anti-bacterial canister, trying not to use it all on my hands because I would need it for Julian's gunshot wound.

Gunshot wound. I tried not to dwell on that thought or else my hands would start shaking again.

Julian was taking too long, and I finally looked at him, concentrating on the buttons of his shirt. They were those fancy magnetic latches that you had to twist and unlock, which required two hands. His one good hand tugged at the top button with an extreme ineffectiveness that just ramped up my nerves.

Only Julian would wear a boardroom-ready shirt on an op.

"Stop it." I pushed aside his hand. "At that rate, you're going to bleed to death before you get that thing off." I grabbed the bottom half of the button in one hand and twisted the top to the unlock position with the other, then pulled the two halves apart. I moved rapidly through the buttons, focusing tightly on each one and trying hard not to brush the bare skin that was revealed by each unbuttoned step, but I felt the warmth of his skin on my fingertips. I tried not to notice that his chest was very well-muscled for someone who spent his time on chat-casts, not training. Heat rose up in my cheeks anyway.

"If I'd known getting shot would result in you undressing me," Julian said, "I would have arranged something with Hinckley much sooner."

"Shut up." His words turned the heat in my cheeks into a fevered inferno. I sensed his smirk even as I avoided looking at his face. I tore through the last two buttons and hastily tugged his shirt back over his shoulders, trying to get it off without looking him in the eye, but I couldn't miss the sharp intake of air, and the way his face twisted in pain.

"Sorry!" I gasped. "Sorry, sorry." I moved more slowly, carefully working his shirt down over the gaping red of the wound. I tore open several antiseptic packets and wiped the edges clean so I could see it more clearly.

The wound was wide but not so deep that it would need interior sutures. Thank heavens I could leave the suture gun in the box. The bleeding had slowed, but it still seeped from the edges. I thoroughly sprayed it with puffs from the antiseptic canister, then pressed two sterile gauze squares over the whole gash, holding for a few seconds. He winced and the warm brown skin of his face paled. My heart squeezed, and I almost let up the pressure.

Long before I was a jacker, I had dreamed of becoming a doctor. Of being someone who could heal people. That dream died when I ended up a zero, someone no one could trust. Maybe it had always been an impossible dream if the sight of a grazing gunshot wound made me want to burst into tears. Or maybe it wasn't the wound, but the patient. Maybe if Julian were a stranger who I was charged with patching up... maybe if him sitting next to me, bare-chested, didn't bother me quite so much... maybe a flesh wound wouldn't turn my hands into a shaking mess. I tried to imagine Julian as one of those ectomorphic dummies we tended in first-aid class, but failed utterly.

The idea of Julian being hurt made something wither inside of me.

I pulled the bandage away—it wasn't as bloodied as I feared it might be. I puffed the wound again with antiseptic and then ripped open two of the largest medical suture tapes.

"This might hurt a little," I breathed out, the words stabbing me like the wound was inside me instead of grazing Julian's shoulder. I pressed one end of the tape to the undamaged skin below, then gently eased the wound closed, pressing the tape firmly to the skin above. Julian gritted his teeth, but a small sound of pain still escaped him and sliced into me. I quickly applied a second suture tape, overlapping slightly with the first to seal it completely.

What I needed was anesthetic—a general pain-killer would be best, but a local anesthetic might work if it was strong enough. I rifled through the box, bypassing a couple of aspirins, and came up with two med patches at the bottom. I quickly peeled the films off and pressed them both to his bare skin below the sutures. They looked more like local anesthetic, but the pain rippling across his face eased, making the tension in my body step down a notch.

I dropped my hands and Julian peered down at the bandage, inspecting it. "You'd make a fair field medic, keeper," he said softly, then turned to smile at me. "I might have to get wounded more often."

"No!" The intensity of my voice made his smile flee. I gave in to the tug that drew my body closer to him. He was leaned against the edge of the desk, low enough that we were nearly eye to eye. Was my need to be close an automatic response left over from when he'd handled me long ago? I didn't know or care. The panic clawing at my throat wasn't because the revolution might be in danger of losing its leader.

"Don't you dare get hurt again." I slowly, very intentionally, put my hand to his cheek, my fingertips brushing the soft bristles that had sprung up since we last talked close on the roof, what seemed like days ago but was only last night.

"A small part of me dies," I whispered, like it was a secret, "when the people I love get hurt."

My body stilled, saying those words. Calmed. There was a rightness to telling him, like a truth that had needed saying, only I had tried so long not to say it, even to myself.

His eyebrows lifted, but I didn't say anything more, just let my words soak in.

The shock still paralyzed his face as I leaned forward to lightly kiss him. His lips were chilled, with no shirt and the trauma of being injured, but by the second kiss, they had warmed and he kissed me back, his lips moving against mine. Emotion welled up in me, flooding the hole in my chest with a pure light that blotted out the grave, obliterating it and lifting me up.

I had a light-headed need to touch him, hold him, have him pressed against me, as if he were my anchor and without a grip on him, I might float away in this lightness of being. My hands roamed the smooth, bare skin and solid muscles of his shoulders, staying clear of his bandage. I ran them along his back, urgently seeking some place to hold on to him without hurting him. His good hand slipped under the back of my flak jacket, bunching my ultralite and crushing me to him, like he needed the contact as much as I did. We breathed each other in, all skin and hands and his mouth on mine.

"Julian?" a voice called from the doorway, rough and deep, but with no apology in it. I jerked free of our kiss, vaguely recognizing the voice as belonging to Hinckley. Julian's arm was a locked iron band around the small of my back, not letting me pull free. His startling blue eyes blazed at me. I stopped trying to pull away and eased back into him, our faces close enough that I could feel his too-quick breath. I touched the heated skin of his cheek with my fingertips. A smile fought through the intensity on his face. Its brief appearance faded before he turned his head to Hinckley, who was waiting patiently by the door.

"What?" Julian asked, his voice low and breathy. It sent a thrill through me that was completely irrational, as if I had never heard him speak before. But it was different here, trapped willingly in his arms, feeling his voice rumble through my hand where it had come to rest lightly on his chest.

"We've heard back from Vellus," Hinckley said, no embarrassment in his voice, as if finding us in a heated embrace in a back office was completely expected. "He wants Kira. Says you have to send her as an emissary or he won't negotiate terms."

I had a surge of vertigo, as if I should push away from Julian, yet at the same time feeling like he was the only thing holding me up.

After all this time of trying to find Vellus, he had found me instead.

Chapter FIFTEEN

Julian's arm locked even tighter around my lower back. "Well, we're not going to hand Kira over to Senator Vellus no matter how much he would like her to come negotiate terms." He stated that as an indisputable fact.

Hinckley didn't seem at all surprised by Julian's words. "Understood. What will our response be?"

Julian sighed and dropped his gaze, studying the scuffed and dirty floor next to us. "Give us a moment, please."

Hinckley ducked back out, heading to the office where Myrtle was doing the chat-cast, which was also probably where the contact from Vellus had come in.

"Julian—" I said.

"Don't worry." He gently pulled me closer, kissing me lightly on the cheek before pulling back to look me in the eyes. "We'll send someone else to negotiate. He doesn't get to dictate terms, not while we have the station."

"How does he know I'm here?"

"Lucky guess." Julian ran his hand up and down my arm like he couldn't get enough of touching me. I didn't exactly mind. "He's wanted to trap you for a long time, ever since you evaded him before. I'm sure he's just fishing."

"Why do we have to send anyone?" I asked. "I don't like the idea of delivering someone into Vellus's hands. He already has too many of our people." My dad. Sasha. Hundreds of jackers whose names I didn't know but who had people who loved them, wondering if they would ever come home. Wondering if they were already dead.

"Agreed," said Julian, a shine in his eyes. "I'll get on the chat-cast myself. This negotiation is just start—"

Several rapid-fire pops drowned out Julian, and we both jerked in surprise. He dropped his hold on me and pushed up from the table. A dozen more pops, louder this time, rattled the windows that lined the office. Julian bolted from the room with me right behind, bringing his flak jacket.

Hinckley had already reached the stairs and took two at a time. More gunfire rang out. Julian paused while I slid the flak jacket on him, then pivoted and ran to the office where Myrtle was. Her thin hands gripped the edge of the table where she sat. She focused intensely on the monitor, controlling a dozen chat-cast windows via the mindware interface. A live image of the water pumping station popped up. National Guardsmen ran low and crouched behind makeshift barricades they carried, shorter and heavier versions of the fence they had erected around Jackertown.

"What's going on?" Julian asked her. "Who's shooting?"

"Not us," Myrtle said. "As far as I can tell, it's the Guard, trying to keep us from firing on their people while they set up a perimeter around us."

Julian leaned forward, his hand turning white as he held the edge of the monitor. "Where is this image coming from?"

"There are news people out there, Julian," Myrtle said. "This is the local tru-cast."

Julian fisted his hand and pressed it onto the table top. Then he slammed his fist, making the screen jump slightly. I knew he'd expected this to happen, but not so quickly.

I mentally reached out and brushed Hinckley's mind. It took him a moment, but he let me in.

Are we prepared for the Guardsmen? I asked. Through his eyes I saw three snipers holding positions at the windows, behind the upturned tables that blocked them, and Hinckley helping a fourth get the last window covered. Ava and the rest of Hinckley's crew dragged the limp mindreaders to a small office in the back, safe from any stray bullets. Whatever fire the Guardsmen had directed at us hadn't injured anyone so far.

As long as they don't actually attack us, we'll be fine, came Hinckley's wry thoughts.

I zipped my focus back to the room with Myrtle and Julian. "They're reinforcing downstairs, but Hinckley thinks they're not quite ready."

Julian strode out to the control room and examined the monitors. "Myrtle," he called. "Can you re-route these cameras to show more exterior angles? I need to know how many troops they have and where they are."

"On it, boss." Myrtle scurried out to the control room to manipulate the screens, and Julian returned to the office to examine the scrolling chat-casts.

I flung my mind out to the area surrounding the water pumping station. Now that the shield was down, I could access everything for over a quarter mile in every direction. I closed my eyes and skimmed the anti-jacker helmets the troops were wearing. There were so *many* of them.

"Julian, there are dozens of troops. Mostly at the front of the station, but they're pulling around the rear as well." I lifted my scan up, searching the sniper points we had so recently occupied ourselves. "They have snipers finding perches in the buildings next door as well." If there were reporters mixed in with the Guardsmen, they must be wearing helmets too because I couldn't find anyone unhelmeted within my reach.

I opened my eyes. Julian stared at the screen. We were lighting up the news on every tru-cast station, with snippets of Myrtle's demands scrolling in red lines across the bottom.

Then a video-call request popped up. The ID said *Police Negotiator*.

Julian put his hand to the small of my back and guided me around the desk. "You stay here, out of sight." He returned to the screen. "Don't say anything," he added, then mentally nudged the incoming call to accept.

I couldn't see the image that popped up, but the male voice on the line sounded older, like my dad. "This is Sergeant Lenny Lee of the Chicago New Metro Police Crisis Unit. Thank you for picking up. I'm here to listen to you and to make sure everyone stays safe."

The man's voice was calm and soothing.

"Sergeant Lee," Julian said. "I take it you're our negotiator today?"

"I am, Mr. Navarro," came the reply. "Can I assume that you're the one in charge of the water station right now?"

"Yes, you can assume that." I saw Julian fighting to keep the smirk off his face. Sergeant Lenny Lee might have years of experience dealing with crazed hostage takers and volatile crisis situations, but he had nothing on Julian's smooth confidence and clarity of purpose.

"It appears that you are injured, Mr. Navarro," Sgt. Lee said. "Can we send in some medical personnel to assist you? Is there anyone else who has been injured?"

The smile was rueful now, and not quite held in check. "Thank you for your concern, Sergeant Lee. My injuries are very minor, and I assure you that everyone is safe. We have no desire to see anyone hurt today. Our demands are simple. I assume you have been briefed on them already?"

"That's good to hear, that everyone is safe," Sgt. Lee said. "That's my paramount concern, Julian. May I call you, Julian? I don't intend any disrespect, sir."

"Julian is fine," he said, but the irritation was clear in his voice. "About our demands—"

"Yes, I've been briefed on your demands." Sgt. Lee's voice

kept the same measured pace in spite of cutting Julian off. "We have a team working on them right now. First, I need you to do something for me—"

Julian jumped in, his words speeding up even as Sgt. Lee's seemed to drag along. "I'm prepared to release hostages as a show of good faith. We have a dozen water-plant workers currently under sedation, and I have no intention of harming them. We can wake half of them and send them out. That is, if you can keep the National Guard from shooting them on their way."

"That's a great start, Julian." Sgt. Lee's praise sounded genuine, but his voice had the same calculated evenness of tone. "And certainly no one wants to fire any weapons in the future. That was a misunderstanding earlier, before I arrived, but the tactical officer here assures me that won't happen again."

"Good," Julian said.

"Since you're releasing some of the hostages—and I think that shows what a reasonable person you are here, Julian, very reasonable, and I appreciate that a great deal—could you do one more thing for me?"

"What is that?" Julian asked, wary.

"There's a girl named Kira Moore in the water plant with you." Julian's eyes went wide, but Sgt. Lee kept talking. "Her father is very concerned about her and would like her to come out. How about we keep her father from having to worry any longer by releasing her with the first set of hostages? That would go a long way in establishing good faith with everyone out here, I can assure you of that."

Julian didn't respond immediately, and I could almost see him measuring and discarding a dozen responses before he finally answered. "There's no one here by that name."

"Julian." Sergeant Lee's calm tone edged into patronizing, and I saw Julian grit his teeth in response. "I need you to be honest with me, Julian. I want to work with you to find a way out of this that's safe for everyone. We can only do that if we're being honest with each other, so I'll start by being honest with you—the water plant's surveillance footage shows that Ms. Moore is there inside the plant with you."

Julian flicked a look to me. He was trying to keep his face neutral, but this was news to both of us. I held a finger to my lips, so he wouldn't say anything, and mentally reached out to Myrtle in the control room.

I pushed hard to get her to let me in quickly. *Myrtle!* She reflexively shoved me out, then realized who I was and let me back in. *They've tapped in to the monitors on the outside! You need to shut them down!*

I'm trying, but I haven't located the controls for the cameras yet, Myrtle thought. *It might take me a minute.*

I reached downstairs to Hinckley. *Julian's started negotiations,* I linked the thought to him, *but they've tapped into cameras inside the plant. Can you disable them?*

I'll get someone on it right now.

I was drawn back into the room by Julian finally composing a reply to the police negotiator.

"If you can see Ms. Moore," he said, "you should be able to

171

see that she is not a hostage. I'm prepared to release the water plant workers, nothing more."

"I understand, Julian," the negotiator said in his smooth voice, "but Ms. Moore's father seems quite certain that she's being held against her will. You can imagine how worried he must be about her in this situation. I understand that Mr. Moore is friends with Senator Vellus, so I'm sure you can understand the pressure I'm under here, right? The senator wants to make sure that Kira is safe as well. She's underage, yes? Right now, no one's been hurt, and this is only a simple breaking and entering, but if you're keeping a minor against her will, well, that will complicate things."

Julian held my gaze while I motioned furiously for him to let me link in to his head. He gave an almost imperceptible nod.

Julian, my dad isn't saying any of this! I nearly gasped out loud, finally being able to communicate.

I know. His thoughts echoed around inside his head. *I can't say that your father understands the situation without compromising him. He has to be under Vellus's control right now.* Out loud he said, "You'll have to take my word for it, Sergeant Lee. Ms. Moore is not being held against her will."

Vellus probably has my dad at the Detention Center, I linked.

Exactly, Julian thought. *We'll get him out, just like all the rest.*

"You may be right, Mr. Navarro," Sergeant Lee continued from the screen. "I'll be honest with you, I have no idea what

Miss Moore's relationship is to you and your fellow mindjackers. I understand how things can get complicated. A young girl runs away from home, finds a new set of friends..."

"You don't know anything," Julian snapped.

Julian, no, I linked the thought to him. *Don't let him get to you because of me.*

Julian took a breath. "Ms. Moore is not a part of this negotiation."

"I'm just saying, I can understand how we might have gotten into this situation," Sergeant Lee said. "It's not your fault or hers. No one's really. But now we're in a bit of a sticky spot, yes? Her father is friends with the senator, and he's taken a special interest in ensuring her safety. We don't want that to complicate both of our goals. You want your demands met—which I'm currently looking in to how we can accomplish that for you—and I want to make sure we have a safe end to this crisis. How about this? Why don't you let her come out, and I'll personally guarantee her safety. She can be your lead negotiator on this side, to reassure you that we're negotiating in good faith. I understand Senator Vellus would like to have her take an active role in bringing this crisis to an end as well."

"I told you—"

Julian, no. He's right. If Vellus is sending the negotiator to get me out, he's not going to have a "team" working on our demands without it.

No, Julian thought, his face darkening. *I'm not giving you over to him.*

"Julian?" Sergeant Lee said. "Is everything okay? Are you all right?"

"I'm fine," Julian ground out between his teeth.

"Good," Sergeant Lee said. "I know things can get distracting during crises like these, but I need you to stick with me, okay? I can see that you're concerned about Miss Moore. I think we all want her to be safe. Like I said before, I personally guarantee no harm will come to her."

"I'll call you back." Julian shut down the call, and I hurried over to the other side of the monitor.

He grabbed hold of my shoulders and this time I think he truly was tempted to shake some sense into me. "Kira, it's a trap. You *know* this."

"I know."

"And once he has you... I'm never going to see you again. Do you understand *that*?"

I stared up into his pained blue eyes. "I'll go in, just like we planned before. You wanted someone to get close to Vellus. You wanted someone who could take him out. Well, guess what? I'm that person."

Julian shook his head, his face twisting, which I understood. Completely. But it didn't change the fact that a jacker was lying in a pool of his own blood downstairs. That my father and Sasha and a hundred other jackers were locked in Vellus's Detention Center. That this entire gamble of Julian's was going to implode before it got started. Someone had to stop Vellus, and he was asking for me. I wouldn't get another chance like this. And none of us were likely to walk out of this alive if I didn't take it.

"I'll pretend to give Vellus what he wants, get close, and then take him out."

"There's no way he'll believe you, Kira." Julian was trying to talk me out of it now, which told me I had already won.

"It doesn't matter if he believes me," I said, "as long as I can get close to him."

"There's no way he'll let you close enough to hurt him."

"I have a few skills Vellus doesn't know about," I said with a small smile. "He won't harm me as long as he thinks I'm going to give him the tru-cast he's wanted since he had me in his office before. And if I fail, well, you'll just have to come rescue me again."

"I told you," he said, and the tremble in his voice just about broke my heart on the spot, "I didn't want to do that anymore."

I pressed my fingers to his lips so he wouldn't say any more, then leaned close to him, as close as our two flak jackets would allow.

"There's a chat-cast I made." My voice was whispery, aching as the words leaked out of me. "Hinckley has it, and I gave a copy to Anna, too. If you see me on the tru-casts, saying things I would never say, you cast it out everywhere. The whole thing except for the last part."

Julian was shaking his head again.

"That part's just for you."

The soft whiskers of his cheek brushed against my fingertips.

I stopped the movement of his head by capturing his lips with mine and kissing him, hard. He held onto me so strongly I was afraid he wouldn't physically let me go. But when I pulled away, he slowly released me. I couldn't say anything else, so I left him standing in the office, a piece of my soul staying behind with him.

I linked in to Hinckley's mind as I hurried down the stairwell. *Wake up the plant workers, Hinckley. I'm walking them out.*

Chapter SIXTEEN

The Guardsman driving the armored transport didn't say a word the whole way to the Detention Center. His short buzz-cut hair disappeared under his anti-jacker helmet, and the rest of his body was swathed in combat gear: urban military fatigues, flak jacket, camouflage winter coat, a strapped-on communicator, and a pistol that he transferred to his left side for the drive.

Like he thought I'd grab it and shoot him.

I probably looked dangerous when I came out of the water station, fully armed and leading a stumbling brigade of half-awake water-station operators. I was quickly relieved of all my weapons. They even took my flak jacket and my ultralite so they could pat me down extra thoroughly. With only my black buttoned shirt and empty-pocketed cargo pants, I almost looked like a civilian. But I was still armed and dangerous, and the Guardsman seemed to know it.

He was taking me to see Vellus, and he didn't seem to think that was a good idea either.

We pulled up to the guard station at the front of the Detention Center named after the good senator. I mentally surged the blue-uniformed guard, who was sitting in his fortified-against-jackers box, then skimmed the disruptor shield along the twelve-foot-high concrete walls and barbed razor wire that circled the prison. Just to be sure there were no cracks in their security.

There weren't.

The large, gray concrete buildings of the DC loomed over the top of the razor wire. Apparently this was where I would meet Vellus. Either that, or it was all a lie, and they were simply taking me in without bothering with handcuffs.

The gate was comprised of a double-door system activated by the guard. A double-helix full-body scanner sat outside the heavy metal door, no doubt tuned to guns, explosives, and any kind of electronic device that might be construed as a weapon. A couple of employees without anti-jacker helmets approached the gate. A brief scan of their minds showed they worked in the kitchen. The guard checked their credentials, then spoke out loud to them through a speaker. They deposited their phones in a box that swallowed them up, and I lost contact with the workers as they passed, one at a time, over the threshold.

I climbed down the metal steps attached to the side of the Guardsman's armored transport. The air was crisp, and a faint ghost of my breath wisped out in front of me. The Guardsman hustled around the front of the vehicle, falling into step with me as we approached the guard shack. Hovering close to me, as if I might bolt.

He leaned down to the tiny speaker. "Kira Moore, here to meet with the senator." He pressed his badge with military insignia against the scanner. The guard only flicked a look our way, intent on verifying the information on the screens in front of him.

The Guardsman turned to me. "Are you carrying a phone, ma'am?"

"Yes."

"You'll have to leave it here, ma'am," he said with a completely straight face. As if he expected I would comply with no trouble. "Mindware enabled devices aren't allowed inside the DC."

Once I was inside, it wasn't like I would be calling for help—if I got out at all, I'd be talking or shooting my way out. Maybe sneaking out on a laundry cart. I fought off the grin that came with the gallows humor. I dug my phone out of my pocket and handed it to the Guardsman. He dropped it in the box.

The guard scowled at us through the glass of his concrete shack, then pressed a button on his console. "Step through the door." The gate swung open, waiting for me. I twitched, unable to suppress the reflex.

I was walking into a prison designed specifically for jackers.

I passed through the weapons detector without setting anything off, then stepped over the threshold of the gate. A slight electric buzz from passing through the disruptor shield made the hairs all over my body bristle out. I rubbed the back of my neck, smoothing the hairs down, but not soothing my nerves.

The metal door clicked and buzzed into place behind me. I mentally reached out, but I was hemmed in between the first and second gates, both of which were shielded. A boom mic hung overhead, the kind that picked up thought waves during tru-casts. I jacked into the mindware interface so that it would pick up my thoughts as well as my spoken words, but no one was talking to me. A prickling sweat broke out between my shoulder blades. I tried to keep my face calm.

After a stretch of seconds just long enough for my stomach to twist into a pretzel, the second door clicked. The sound made me jump, my nerves were strung so tight. There was someone waiting for me on the other side of the gate as it swung open, someone not in military fatigues or the starched, navy-blue uniforms of the prison guards.

Kestrel.

I saw the eyes first, piercing and blue. I didn't think; my body just reacted. I darted across the threshold, pulling my fist back and landing a punch before his hands were halfway to his face. My brain still hadn't engaged, being overrun by white-hot fury, but some part of it had aimed for his nose. My fist connected with his jaw instead, and my other hand grabbed a fist full of starched shirt and G-man blue jacket. He stumbled backward, but I clung to him.

Just as my brain clicked in enough to grab for his throat and plunge into his mind, he shoved me away. I lost my grip on his clothes and my footing as well, landing hard on the rough ce-ment of the prison yard. My head snapped back and whacked with a melon-on-concrete sound that dulled my hearing and made my vision warp. As I blinked to clear it, half a dozen guards descended on me, the sharp ends of their rifles pointed at my head. They all wore anti-jacker helmets. Kestrel waved them back, rubbing his chin and then spitting on the ground at my feet.

Warm satisfaction coursed through me when I saw red mottling the gooey saliva.

Kestrel took two steps closer until he was standing over me, composure regained. He had the same hollowed-out cheeks, the same look of stony dispassion, as always. As if I were a bug he didn't want to sully his shoes by stomping.

"Can't say I'm happy to see you either, *Kira*." He said my name like it was something foul in his mouth. "If it were up to me, you'd be locked in a cell, juiced up and forgotten, until you couldn't remember your own name." He sneered like he was picturing that happening. Trouble was, I could picture it too.

The guards had taken a step back, but their guns were still trained on me. As much satisfaction as punching Kestrel had given me—and I'm not sure I could have stopped myself, anyway, it was so automatic—I realized what an idiotic move that had been. I was supposedly here to negotiate for Julian, to gain the prisoners' release. I was here to pretend to give Vellus what he wanted so I could get close enough to kill him. I wouldn't be able to do any of that from a prison cell.

I swallowed and absently noticed my hand throbbing.

Kestrel looked disgusted with my lack of response. "Get up!"

Susan Kaye Quinn

He turned his back on me and marched toward the far end of the courtyard where the closest gray cube building loomed above us. The guards didn't take any chances, still tracking me with the business end of their guns. I pictured myself grabbing one of them and shooting Kestrel. It took every restraint I had not to try. I scrambled up from the ground to hurry after him.

Why was Kestrel here? Was he was pulling prisoners from the DC for experiments again? I thought we had shut him down with the raid a few months ago, but he certainly could have set up shop somewhere new. My heart pounded with that thought. My dad and Sasha were in here now.

"Too bad you're not in charge here, Kestrel," I said, keeping pace with his long stride and ignoring the forest of rifles pointed at my back. "And sorry to ruin your day by being unavailable for torture. I hope I'm not keeping you from rounding up some new changelings to torment."

"In spite of all the trouble you seem to cause wherever you go," Kestrel said with a sideways glare, "you're not keeping me from doing anything—I'm done with the experimental phase of my work."

I frowned, not expecting that response. He was done? What did that mean? "What are you going to do now?" I couldn't help asking. "Take up woodworking? If you're looking for a new hobby, I suggest—"

Kestrel stopped in his tracks right before we reached the door. He stared down at me. "Vellus seems to think you're useful to us, but I promise you, Kira, the moment you are not useful anymore I will have a personal appointment to meet with you."

I met his stare, imagining all the ways I would like to kill him. "I'm looking forward to that."

He flinched, just in the slightest, struggling mightily not to let it show. I still saw it.

He turned away and swiped his badge to open the door. I followed him in, our footsteps ringing on the metal stairs and the concrete-lined stairwell. Two of the courtyard guards followed, their heavy boots clanging the stairs even more loudly.

Kestrel was obviously working with Vellus. Of course, it had always been a possibility: they were both in the government, both working to destroy jackers. But why was Kestrel here *now*, at Vellus's Detention Center? If he truly was done with his experiments, he wasn't picking up new guinea pigs to take back to his lair. I had assumed Vellus wanted me because he still wanted the tru-cast interview. With Kestrel involved, I wasn't sure of anything.

My stomach was chewing holes in itself by the time we reached the top of the stairs. Kestrel swiped all four of us through a door and quickly strode through a large press area that overlooked a glassed-in room. It was shield protected but gave an excellent view of the interior of the prison. Two stories of metal-barred cells were crammed with thin, gray bunks: cages for jackers. Most of the cells were occupied by figures in pale-green jumpsuits. They were moving, so they weren't overly juiced up, but I was too far away to make out who they were.

Seeing the prisoners flashed me back to Kestrel's cells and his desert camp. I could almost taste the orange-spice tranq gas Kestrel had used there.

I bit my lip. My dad and Sasha were down here somewhere.

Too soon, we left the pressroom on the opposite side and wove through a series of doors that slid open with Kestrel's swiped badge. He clearly had the run of the place. We finally approached an office labeled *Warden,* and one of the guards took up a station at the door while the remaining guard stayed with Kestrel and me. The familiar tingle of a mindwave disruptor field buzzed my skin as we walked in.

The warden's receptionist's desk was empty just like the cushioned visitors' bench attached to the wall. Chemical smells from the seat mixed with the sharp scent of fresh paint, and pictures of Illinois cornfields gleamed green and gold on the walls. I reached toward the warden's door but ran smack into another shield.

The wall screen behind the desk flipped through views of the facility. I tried to plunge into the mindware interface of the nearby computer, but it was shut down without a remote-activation ability. I had hoped to find something about possible escape routes—or maybe laundry carts. But I needed to focus on how to kill Vellus. There probably wouldn't be much of a chance for escape afterward, anyway, assuming I survived the attempt.

The warden and Vellus strode out of the warden's office together, but Vellus strutted ahead like he owned the place. Which I supposed he did. I carefully controlled my reaction this time, having steeled myself for this since leaving Julian at the water pumping station. It was time to put on a performance, and there would be no dress rehearsal. It was improv all the way, and I had to be ready for the opportunity to take down the senator when it came.

Vellus's fashionably waved hair was smashed underneath an anti-jacker helmet that was gold-flecked and pretentious, just like him. The warden also had an anti-jacker helmet, but his was standard-issue black. He barely noticed me as he strolled out, telling the guard he was heading out for a lunch break. The secretary's screen showed it was twelve thirty pm.

Vellus towered over me, his lean, tailored suit rich and polished next to Kestrel's G-man coat and stiff-collared shirt. Unlike Kestrel's cruel eyes, Vellus's brown ones were deceptively warm. Vellus and I stared at each other as if one of us was a snake, finally having the bird in its sights, mesmerizing it with its slick, hissing voice. I had no intention of being the bird, but I put a little cower into my stance to let Vellus think he was the snake. That brought out Vellus's million-watt smile, the one he used on tru-casts and mindreading voters all over the state.

"So nice to see you again, Miss Moore." He stepped aside to clear a path to the warden's office and waited. I hesitated, then held my head up, the proud young revolutionary heading off to the gallows. I even put a stumble in my step, but mostly because I wanted to arrive at the warden's office an extra second or two ahead of Vellus.

It would give me time to search for a weapon to help him meet his maker.

Chapter SEVENTEEN

The warden's office door shut silently behind us, no menacing click to signal my imprisonment, but the guard posted outside and the disruptor-shielded walls promised I would stay as long as Vellus wanted. My extra second to look for a weapon was wasted: the warden's office was exceedingly spare. A heavy oak desk and an overstuffed leather chair dominated the center of the room, with an oil painting of the capitol hanging on the wall behind them and a plant too vibrant to be real filling one corner of the windowless office. A bank of screens lined the opposite wall, showing a mosaic of the Detention Center. I wished for a Warden of the Year award to bludgeon Vellus or a glass frame I could break and use to cut his neck, but there wasn't so much as a scribepad stylus to work with.

It was just me, Vellus, and Kestrel.

Vellus was big, six feet or more, and I couldn't take Kestrel physically, even without half a dozen armed guards to help him. Plus Kestrel was a jacker, and Vellus was helmeted. But

I had one ability those things were useless against. If I was fast enough, I could take Vellus by surprise—get him in a headlock and twist hard. A broken neck was almost always lethal. At least I hoped that was true.

It wasn't like I had practiced killing people with my bare hands.

But it would be tough to get into my hyped state with the two of them staring at me. I glared back at Kestrel, trying to check for a weapon under his G-man jacket in a not-too-obvious way. Even hyped on fast-twitch, it would be tricky if Kestrel was armed. Maybe I should draw him out first, see if he pulled a gun. Or I could relieve him of his weapon and use it on both of them.

That had a lot of appeal. Also a high probability of me getting shot by Kestrel or the guard outside before I could kill Vellus. While I was thinking through my limited options, Vellus leaned against the desk and folded his arms, studying me. For all the thinking that showed on his face, I wondered if he was weighing ways to kill me, too.

"I'm flattered you want me to be lead negotiator, Senator Vellus," I said in my most *I'm-the-snake* voice, just to throw him.

His eyes held nothing but mirth, not thrown in the slightest. "You're a much smarter young lady than that, Kira."

"Not smart enough to stay out of your reach," I said with mock-deference. Then I put some edge in my voice. "Regardless, I am here to negotiate. We're prepared to release the water-pumping plant undamaged and the rest of the plant workers unharmed if you meet the JFA's demands. It's really in your best interest to do this. You don't want all those mindreaders wondering why you can't keep grandma's water on."

"Oh, you're right about that." He held his hands out as if to ward off hordes of angry voters. "I fear the reaction of gray-haired ladies all over Chicago New Metro should I fail to keep their utilities properly functioning." Then he examined his finely manicured fingernails. "But, of course, I have no intention of giving in to your little revolutionary demands. That would look very bad, don't you think?"

"It's not a threat, Vellus," I said. "Julian will cut off the water."

"Ah, yes, Julian." He smirked, and a chill raced through me. "I wouldn't concern yourself with him anymore. Your time rattling around with his band of revolutionaries has only delayed the inevitable, but here we are, finally. The tru-casters are setting up in the pressroom, awaiting you." He examined the screen behind me, tapping his chin. "The young face of the mindjackers, liberated from the dangerous revolutionaries in Jackertown, come to the Detention Center to tell her tale of rescue and heroics. It will make for a fine tru-cast."

I knew the words I was supposed to say, but I couldn't seem to force them out of my mouth. I took a deep breath. I would say what I had to, pretend until the moment was right, then slip a stylus between his ribs, if only I could find one.

"I'm not doing any tru-casts," I said, "until you call off your National Guard from the water plant and Jackertown. Free the prisoners in the DC. Once everyone's free and safe, I'll do whatever you want."

Kestrel and Vellus both had a good laugh at that.

My face grew hot. Suddenly the situation felt like it was spinning away from me, like a grenade with the pin pulled.

"Kira, my dear, you're nowhere near that valuable to me." Vellus paused, apparently wiping tears of laughter from his eyes. "That water pumping plant," he said, sweeping his hand to the monitor behind me where the screen now showed an aerial view of the water station, "that is much more valuable, far too important to let your little friends play with it."

I stared at the image, my mind reeling. What did he mean, it was *more important*? He had just said he wasn't worried about grandma's water being cut off—

"However," Vellus said, pushing his anti-jacker helmet up from where it had slid forward, "your friends' demands gave me the perfect excuse to have them hand you over. I would much rather have you here, safe, in the warden's office."

He genuinely sounded as if my safety was of great concern to him. I stole a glance at Kestrel, who was enjoying a full smirk at my expense. The horrible feeling that I had missed something lodged in my throat.

Vellus smiled his unnaturally white teeth. "I thought we had reached an understanding in my office those many months ago. That our interests are so much more aligned than you realize. I thought you were the kind of girl who didn't like to see her friends get hurt. And yet, now, that's exactly what's going to happen. Frankly, I'm not sure how many of them will be alive by the end of the day."

His gaze flicked to the screen, and I slowly turned to look, my breath frozen in my chest. The aerial shot panned across the water plant as two double-rotor black helicopters descended on it. SWAT team members disgorged from the sides, rappelling down to the roof. They spread out like ants on a hot plate, skittering across the surface and looking for a place to burrow in. They disappeared and a moment later, a series of flashes went off inside the plant, shooting light out between the cracks around the boarded-up windows.

I flinched with each one like they were stabbing me.

Vellus didn't care about the hostages—I had only brought half of them out with me. There wouldn't be any negotiations. There was no audio on the screen, but I heard it in my mind. The shots ringing out, the screams of surprise and pain. My friends, dropping to the floor of the station, gaping in surprise at the holes bleeding in their chests.

Julian...

I was drowning in the need to stop it and the utter certainty that I couldn't.

Tears blurred my eyes. Vellus was murdering them. I swallowed, trying to picture Julian fighting off the SWAT team, protected by his bulletproof vest and the JFA militia he had with him, all of whom would give their lives for his. But all I could see was him lying in his own blood, like Simon in the desert.

"No..." The word was a gasp, suffocated by the thousand-pound weight on my chest. Julian was the heart of the revolution... my heart... and Vellus had just cut it out. Ava. Hinckley.

Myrtle. They were all in there, all dying. I left to try to save them and instead I was left watching while Vellus slaughtered them. The hole in my heart came raging back, only this time it spewed a volcano of anger.

I whirled on Vellus. "There were innocent people in there!" My fists were clenched and raised, as if I might strike him. I teetered on my toes. It took everything I had not to fling myself at Vellus and try choking him with my bare hands, like I had in my blind rage with Kestrel.

Vellus didn't move a muscle. "You should have thought of that before taking over the water station." His patronizing tone nearly made my head explode. "I wouldn't mind making you another casualty in the war, Kira. An anonymous one, of course. Can't have you being a martyr like your young friends here."

For a moment, I couldn't see Vellus through my haze of tears, then anger burned them off. It was an unbearable heat, lava boiling in my chest. I crushed it deep inside me, turning it into a diamond of hate that would sharpen my mind. I would use it to calculate the exact best way to kill Vellus.

With my bare hands was sounding more appealing all the time.

"But I'm glad you're here and not there, Kira," Vellus said. "We can achieve so much if we work together. Join me on the tru-cast, and let's put an end to this silly squabbling and waste of lives. What do you say, my dear?"

I'm going to kill you. "I say you've just created a martyr like you can't imagine."

Vellus would pay for that with his life. And if I died in the process... well, even if Hinckley was lost at the water plant, Anna had my chat-cast recording. She would use it and then Julian's death, my death, would count for something. That thought lifted me up.

"You can't stop us, Vellus," I said. "You can kill everyone in the water plant, but you can't kill us all."

"Your friends got themselves killed," Vellus said, the soft voice of the snake coming out. "They were awfully quick to hand you over, were they not? Perhaps they're not the friends you think they are."

I resisted the urge to snarl at him.

"I had hoped you would understand," Vellus continued. "Jackers and readers are in a silent war, and it's one jackers cannot win. I have been doing everything in my power to reassure people that the threat of jackers will be contained. Because what if it is not, Kira? Have you considered that?"

I simply stared at him. After I killed Vellus... what *was* the endgame for all this? Would it be an all-out war? We didn't have an army. We could barely run a guerilla campaign to take over a water pumping station.

If the readers declared a real war on us, we would all be dead.

Vellus must have seen the wavering on my face, because he was nodding now, which turned my stomach into a heaving storm of bile.

"Jackers should lay down their arms," Vellus said. "Come voluntarily out of Jackertown for testing and identification. You,

Kira, the young face of the jackers, can testify that they'll be treated well in the Detention Center. There doesn't need to be a wide-scale loss of life. You can assure jackers that it's the best path, that they will be treated humanely and allowed to live out their natural lives in peace."

I almost threw up on his shiny, custom-made shoes.

"You really are insane," I said, swallowing down the sourness stinging the back of my throat. "You can't possibly believe I would to tell jackers to volunteer themselves for lockup just so you and your buddy Kestrel can conduct your horrific mind-game experiments." Something tickled the back of my brain: *Kestrel said he was done with his experiments.* "What was the point of all that if you're just going to lock us away? Why don't you put bullets in people and be done with it?" I jabbed my finger at the monitor. "You don't seem to have any qualms about that."

Kestrel snorted behind me, and Vellus sighed like I was trying his patience. "I'm not the monster you seem to think," he said. "And Mr. Kestrel has simply been following orders, although he understands the importance of what we're doing, as well. I truly do not want to kill jackers—I don't need heaps of bodies on the tru-casts at the next election. I'm fighting for peace here, Kira. You want peace, do you not? Or have you only dreamed of war in your cloistered hideaway with your revolutionary friends?"

I shook my head. I wanted to shut out Vellus's words, but I couldn't.

"The bloodshed will escalate," Vellus continued. "As the number of jackers grows, the threat they pose becomes even more severe. The consequences will be dire, but you've already seen that, haven't you? In the camps and in Jackertown—a world filled with mindjackers is a world steeped in violence and anarchy. Is that how you want to live? You know this is where our country is headed if the jacker threat isn't contained."

No, no, no. I pressed the heels of my hands to my head, the fuzziness growing worse. *These are lies,* I told myself, *lies.* Julian was creating a better world. One where jackers could live and coexist in peace. *He would have made it happen.*

A chill ran to the pit of my stomach. I had just thought of Julian as if he were already dead. I dropped my hands and glared at Vellus. He needed to die *now*.

Bare hands would have to do.

Without turning around, I threw the full force of my mind at Kestrel, who was lurking behind me. I caught him off guard, managing to plunge deep into his head. Several images popped up, flashing before my mind's eye before he shoved me back out again.

The water plant. Me in a prison cell. Syringes.

But no gun.

Kestrel was fantasizing about locking me up, but he wasn't planning on shooting me. Maybe he was unarmed after all. Suddenly Kestrel grabbed my hair from behind and bent my head back.

"Do that again, and you will wish you hadn't." His voice in my ear sent shivers down my neck.

Vellus frowned. "Agent Kestrel. Please do not damage our young jacker revolutionary. We still have need of her."

Kestrel let me go with a small shove.

I rubbed the back of my head. "Thanks for calling off your lapdog," I said, mostly to see if I could provoke Kestrel again. He didn't make a move, but I heard his tightly controlled breathing behind me. His fantasies had probably taken a turn to the violent, but his first instinct wasn't to pull a gun. It might be possible to snap Vellus's neck before Kestrel could kill me.

"We do not have to be barbarians," Vellus said. "We do not need to mistreat jackers or conduct some kind of genocide. We can be more civilized than that."

"Yes, civilized," I said. "That's the word I was searching for when I was locked in Kestrel's cell."

"It doesn't have to be like that for you, Kira," Vellus said. "A world filled with jackers is a dangerous world for everyone, but not all of them have to live behind bars." He took a breath and adjusted his helmet. "It was never meant to be this way, but this is the world we live in now. Only a few people at the top will understand what must be done. You can be one of those people, Kira."

"No, I can't." I was done with pretending. "You can be one of those people. I'll be the kind that stops you."

Vellus's brown eyes lost their warmth. "I've given you more than one chance to join me in a real way. If I can't have your voluntary cooperation, I will take it in a different way. Mr. Kestrel tells me you're not very motivated by self-preservation, but I believe I have something you value more than yourself."

He glanced at Kestrel, and my stomach hollowed out as

Kestrel's shoes shuffled behind me toward the door. My window of opportunity was closing fast. If Kestrel had a gun after all, maybe I could simply grab it and shoot Vellus. I pivoted around, crouched and ready to spring at him, right as Kestrel opened the door.

There, shackled and held by the guard we had left in the reception room, was my dad.

Chapter **EIGHTEEN**

I was prepared to die trying to kill Vellus.

But I wasn't prepared to have my dad be a martyr too.

My dad shuffled forward into the warden's office, his wrists bound by the handcuffs. The red J on his cheek stood out sharply against his ashen skin. Dark circles haunted his blue eyes but they were alert, his gaze darting swift and sure around the room, measuring the guard, Vellus, and Kestrel, but avoiding me.

I linked in to his head. *Dad! Are you okay?* His familiar mindscent of fresh morning dew was laced with an acidic fear.

I'm fine, Kira, he thought, still not looking at me. *Whatever it is that Vellus wants, don't give it to him. He has no intention of letting us walk out of here alive.*

I hesitated. Should I tell him my plans? Kestrel could be in his mind at any time. *Vellus wants me to do the tru-cast,* I linked to my dad. *He would have a difficult time killing me after that.*

He would simply make you disappear, Kira. He finally

looked at me. *Believe me, he won't hesitate once he has what he wants from you. You'll just be a liability after that.*

He was probably right. Vellus had brought my dad here for one purpose: to convince me to do the tru-cast. Once I gave Vellus what he wanted, he would have no reason to keep me around. And my dad knew more dangerous secrets about Vellus than I ever would. It wasn't looking good for either of us.

Dad, do you know where Mom is? Maybe she had tried to come get him out of the DC.

His eyes went wide. *No, I woke up at the Detention Center with Sasha. I thought she had gotten away with you and Xander.* My dad must have been passed out the entire time.

The Fronters got us all. They let Mom and Xander go, but I don't know where they are. It gave me a small amount of comfort that Xander would be able to look out for my mom even if my dad and I didn't make it out.

"You can discuss things with your father later," Vellus said. "I'm done asking nicely, Kira. We have an appointment for a live tru-cast and I don't want to keep the reporter waiting." He pushed off from his desk and hovered over me. "Unless you would like to see your father join your friends as one of today's unfortunate mindjacker martyrs. One more body wouldn't surprise anyone."

"There's no need for that," I said as calmly as I could. "I'll do it. As long as you let us both go once we're done."

Vellus grinned a wide, wolfish smile. "Of course." He gave a nod to Kestrel. "You see, Agent Kestrel. I told you she could be reasonable once properly motivated."

Kestrel's face was impassive.

Vellus brushed past me and paused by the guard. "Please bring Miss Moore's father with us to the pressroom." He gave me a cold look. "A reminder of what you have to lose, to keep you properly motivated until we're through."

We followed Vellus out of the warden's office, tailed closely by the guard. A second guard joined us as we left the reception room. Our footsteps echoed through the halls as we wound our way toward the pressroom.

Vellus had said *we have an appointment.* He planned to be a part of the tru-cast, which meant he might remove his anti-jacker helmet. But taking it off wouldn't help me. Kestrel would be mindguarding Vellus, and there might be other mindguards in the tru-cast room as well. I glanced back at the guards and Kestrel behind us. The guards were both armed, one with a dart gun holstered on his hip, the other with a small-caliber pistol. Even in my hyped state, I would probably get shot before I had a chance to twist Vellus's neck. So I couldn't go directly for Vellus, but if I took out the guard with the gun, I could use his body for protection until I could shoot Vellus good and dead.

After that, it wouldn't matter what happened.

I would need a clear stretch of time to dive into my head. The interview would give me that, and if there ever were a place Vellus would let his guard down, it would be in the middle of his own maximum-security jacker prison, surrounded by armed guards while he was holding my father hostage right in front of my eyes.

The last thing he would expect would be an attack from me.

My dad mentally surged my impenetrable mindbarrier, a not-so-subtle signal that he wanted me to link in to his head. His thoughts whirled a storm of frustration that matched the tormented look on his face.

Kira, please! he thought. *Don't do this. We'll find a way out of this.*

I couldn't tell my dad what I had planned, and not only because Kestrel might slip into his head and foil the one chance I would have. My dad would know there was no way I could assassinate a senator on a live tru-cast and end up anywhere but prison. Or dead.

Dad, I have to do the tru-cast. My heart twisted. I really didn't want my last words to him to be a lie, but there wasn't much way around it. *I need you to get out and find Mom and Xander.* At least that much was the truth, although I couldn't see the prison releasing him after I killed Senator Vellus, especially given my dad was already a prisoner. I wasn't just dooming myself, I was taking him down with me. And lying to him in the process.

I love you, Dad. I sent all the emotion I could put into that statement without giving myself away.

He examined my face and for a moment, I was afraid he might have guessed. But his thoughts didn't show it. *Kira... you can't do this. Please don't do this. You don't understand the risk.*

Vellus says he'll let us go afterward. My heart seriously wasn't in this argument.

You know that's not true.

Just make sure you find Mom. I need you to take care of her. I smiled and pulled out of my dad's head. We had reached the threshold of the pressroom, and I couldn't bear to hear any more.

The tru-casters had outfitted the pressroom with an elevated platform by the window overlooking the prisoners' cages below. The tru-cast reporter perched on her chair, grasping her scribe-pad. She nearly fell off in her haste to get up when Senator Vellus strode into the room. I gagged at the way she smiled and rushed over to bow slightly to him. She wasn't wearing an anti-jacker helmet, and a boom-mic thread dangled above her chair along with two others.

My dad and the guard with the dart gun moved to the back of the room, my dad's hands straining the cuffs that bound them. Kestrel stayed by the door we just came through, and the second guard took up a position by the far door. He was the one I had to track because he had the real gun. The one that would hopefully put a bullet into Vellus and not into me.

The cameraman left his tripod camera to come look me over. He clearly knew who I was because he immediately spoke out loud, his voice unnaturally smooth for a mindreader.

"Is this what you're planning on wearing for the interview?" He seemed to take my buttoned shirt, cargo pants, and boots as a personal affront.

"Sorry, my luggage got lost at the check-in."

He clucked his tongue, as if I were a wayward urchin. "Well this isn't going to work, Senator," he said. "She's far too... rugged-looking."

Senator Vellus looked me up and down. "You're right. Kira, you look like you've been in a brawl. We should probably clean you up before the interview, maybe find you something softer, more feminine-looking to wear."

My nerves were strung way too tight for a debate about attire. "Well, I was just rescued from a band of revolutionary jackers," I said between my teeth. "One might expect me to be a little scraped up."

The cameraman cocked his head to one side, then took hold of my shoulders and surveyed me. I felt like a doll he was deciding how to dress. "It could work." He wasn't speaking to me, but to Vellus and the reporter. He ruffled his hand through my hair, leaving it mussed when he was done manhandling it. "Yes, she definitely has that 'just rescued' look." He reached for the buttons on my shirt. "Maybe a little more disheveled would work even better."

I smacked his hand away. He held it like a puppy I had just kicked, giving me a horrified look that I had the gall to hit him, flesh on flesh. I glared at him. There was no way he was unbuttoning my shirt for the tru-cast. I might end up dying in a few minutes in a hail of gunfire from Vellus's guards, but I wasn't going to do it with my shirt half-undone.

Vellus let out a low chuckle. "I think she's perfect the way she is." He guided me to the tru-cast chairs spotlighted in the middle of the room, his hand at the small of my back as if he were truly a caring senator tending to his young charge. His touch sent creepy shivers up my back, so I quickly moved away and climbed into my chair. The cameraman retreated to set up his lighting, moving it around and making minute adjustments.

I took a low, deep breath, focusing my mind. Outwardly, I probably looked like I was trying to settle my nerves for the big interview. Vellus eased into the seat next to mine, the smile wide and winning on his face.

"Now, I believe we have about ten minutes before the tru-cast is scheduled to begin," said Vellus. The reporter nodded her agreement. "We haven't had much time to review what you'll say," Vellus said to me, "but our lovely host will help us by guiding you with her questions, won't you, Ms. Trinkle?"

Ms. Trinkle. That was Ava's last name. That awareness jarred me out of my focus. She looked nothing like Ava, with dark eyes instead of blue, and long black hair instead of Ava's feather-light blond. The interviewer could pass for Sasha's sister. Sasha, who was now trapped in one of the jail cells below, a casualty of the fact that I wasn't here to rescue anyone but instead to assassinate Vellus. And distraction I couldn't afford to have.

Breathe in. Breathe out.

The tru-caster was speaking, but I was transfixed by Vellus taking off his anti-jacker helmet and running his hand through his somehow perfectly groomed hair. He set the helmet at his feet, and I tried very hard not to stare at it. The temptation to jack him was like a magnetic pull.

"Of course we'll want to hear all about your captivity," Vellus said to me when the tru-caster paused for a breath. "Tell us how ill-treated you were, how they were barbaric, even to their own kind..."

Breathe in. Breathe out. Down the elevator...

I dialed down the sensitivity of my hearing and focused on Vellus's lips as they moved, forming words that I no longer heard. My eyelids drooped, badly wanting to close, but I couldn't afford that luxury. I nodded my head, hoping it was well-timed for something that Vellus was saying. The spaghetti-mass of threads that tied my brain together splayed before me. I could study them for a hundred years and still not map it all out. But today, I only needed one thread...

Vellus's hand touched mine, cold fingers lying like a dead mouse on my skin. I jerked with the sensation, and it yanked me out of my head, flooding my ears with a rush of sound.

"Kira!" His stare was cold and insistent. "Are you sure you're all right?"

I sucked in a breath and cursed inside. "Sorry. Just a little... nervous."

His smile was back. "Of course." He nodded to the interviewer. "Very understandable, after all you've been through." He was completely in character now for the interview: the kind, caring senator looking after one of his citizens. "It was lucky we were able to get you out of the water pumping station along with the other hostages. Now that the station is safely back in the hands of the government, the workers can keep the water flowing to the suburbs."

His voice was sincere, but Vellus was lying about the water plant somehow, even though they didn't have their anti-jacker helmets on.

"Yes, it's good that we kept the water flowing." I couldn't tell if the sarcasm in my head bled through into my voice.

Vellus didn't miss a beat. "Right. Now, Ms. Trinkle, most people don't realize the importance of the water infrastructure for our great metro area..." Vellus chattered on, but I had stopped listening again.

The water station is much more important than you are, Kira.

Why did that nag at me?

In all my explorations of my mind, I had learned that the vast majority of its operations happened below the surface, like the tunnels we followed to get to the water station—buried far underground, but key to everything. Why were the hidden information wells of my mind nagging at me about the importance of the water station—

The cameraman reached for my face and I shrank back. He was only trying to powder my nose, probably to take the shine off under the tru-cast lights. I curled my lip, and he scampered off like a scared rabbit.

"I sponsored a bill last year, in fact," Vellus was saying, "that refurbished some of our least-efficient water plants, bringing them up to modern standards..."

The water station is much more important...

Why?

If Vellus cut off the water, there would be heaps of bodies, something he was trying to avoid. He wanted to weaken jackers, not kill them. My tru-cast was supposed to strike at jackers' will to resist so that they would turn themselves in voluntarily. Why was the water station more important than that?

"It's a good thing you were able to rescue Kira," Ms. Trinkle was saying. She glanced at the cameraman, who was motioning to her. "Looks like we have about five more minutes, Senator. Perhaps you could tell me more about these water station renovations..."

The water station...

The water.

It hit me like an electrical storm in my brain. My mouth dropped open. I coughed into my hand to cover it, hoping Vellus and the reporter hadn't noticed. I focused on my hands as my brain rapid-fired through it.

Vellus was using the water. Putting something in it, something that wouldn't kill jackers, just *weaken* them, like my tru-cast was intended to do. Make them easy to control. That was why the water station was so heavily guarded. He hadn't planned on us taking it at all. Vellus was guarding his access to the water supply that fed Jackertown, not to cut it off but to poison it.

But with what? *Kestrel's experiments.* They were done. He had figured out whatever medical thing he wanted to use to control us. Something to dull our brains, produce the dead spots I found in every changeling and jacker he had experimented on. Something that would reduce our ability to jack, make us docile, lifeless, unable to go on...

I flushed hot with the memory of contemplating my own

suicide while in Kestrel's care. Maybe it hadn't been my own weakness. Maybe Kestrel's serums not only weakened my ability to jack but my will to live. My face caught on fire as I imagined thousands of jackers drinking the water. Vellus wanted to make all of Jackertown into one giant padded cell so he could drive us crazy with drugs and imprisonment.

It was becoming hard to breathe.

It would undo everything Julian had tried to build, everything I believed in. I looked at my hands, limp in my lap. I could strangle Vellus. Or I could rev up into my hyped state, grab a gun, and shoot Vellus, only to die a moment later.

But I couldn't be sure that would stop it.

I knew—I could feel it deep inside—that Vellus's plan was in motion, and we had messed it up by taking the water station. That was why Vellus couldn't wait for the other hostages to be released, why he had to take the station back right away.

I could kill Vellus, but it wouldn't matter. I could refuse to do the tru-cast, but that wouldn't matter either. The weight of hopelessness pushed me deeper into my seat.

Ms. Trinkle cleared her throat. "Ms. Moore?" she said. "We're live in two minutes, honey."

Vellus had already won.

Chapter **NINETEEN**

The glare of the tru-cast lights was making me dizzy. My pulse beat a slow gong, ticking down the seconds until the interview.

It had been hopeless from the start. The moment I saved those changelings in the hospital, all those months ago, was the moment I doomed us all. I had ripped away the veil that was the only thing keeping us safe. All Julian's dreams of a better life for jackers never had a chance. Vellus's plan all along was to strangle that shining hope while it was still in the crib.

Julian.

I'd spent all that time mired in the black hole of my own despair when I could have been loving him. My heart swelled and cried tears I couldn't let reach my face. All that time, lost. The mint-green jumpsuits milled below us in their cells, waiting for a rescue that would never come. I wondered if they could see me up here in my glass box, betraying them.

Vellus's lips were moving again, but my ears were full of

the white noise of defeat. Would it matter if I killed him? The kindly politician with the winning smile, trying to help a young mindjacker, only to be killed by her. Vellus would become the martyr. The public would eat up that story with their morning cereal while Kestrel poisoned us with whatever he had cooked up in his genetics lab.

Kestrel eyed me from the door. He knew—had known all along—what the endgame was. He had captured his own kind and experimented on them to develop the poison Vellus would use to control us.

President Vellus. That's what my dad had said, and I could see it now. Vellus would be the man who solved the jacker problem without genocide. Who kept the mindjacker population docile, fenced in, and under control so mindreaders could sleep easy at night.

Jackers were doomed anyway—should I take Vellus's offer to be one of the few who didn't end up behind bars? Give up my foolish pride and finally, once and for all, save my family from the danger I had brought into their lives? Or should I kill Vellus and have the end come swift and final for me?

I reached down deep inside, not in my mind, but in my heart, to search for the answer. There was none. So I went with the hard diamond of hate cutting into my soul. Even if I couldn't stop Vellus's plans, I could at least make him pay for them.

Just as I came to this decision, a flicker of movement across the room grabbed my attention. In a blur, my dad lunged for the gun holstered on the guard next to him.

"No!" The word ripped from my throat. The guard grabbed for the dart gun. A pop-whoosh sound ripped the air. Vellus and the tru-caster ducked, but the dart hadn't found its target. I plunged into my dad's mind. Whatever crazy plan he had would only get him killed. Kestrel was already there, trying to jack my dad. I shoved Kestrel out. My dad kept wrestling with the guard. The dart gun waved in the air, but the guard's meaty hands were clamped over my dad's, keeping him from firing. The second guard, who had the real gun, inched forward. My dad's thoughts showed that was part of his plan. To remove himself as leverage for Vellus.

Tears sprung to my eyes. *Dad, stop!* I linked to him. Suddenly, my dad's mind whirled in confusion. He stopped fighting. The guard quickly shoved him to the floor, and my dad lay limp under his knee, blinking rapidly and wondering what could possibly have possessed him to want to attack the senator, the man he had risked his life mindguarding for years.

What the....? My eyes went wide. Someone was *handling* my dad.

Kestrel shoved back into my dad's head, now controlling him completely, but it was unnecessary. The first guard was cursing and sweating, but he had my dad fully under his control on the floor. The second guard still had his weapon out in case my dad lunged up from the floor again, but my dad wasn't going anywhere. He had already given up. It wasn't Kestrel who had handled him, and both guards had anti-jacker helmets. The only other people in the room were the tru-cast reporter, the cameraman, and... Vellus.

He was staring intently at my father. Anyone else might have thought it was a look of hatred or perhaps fear that froze his face into a mask of concentration. But I knew exactly what it was.

Vellus was handling him.

I quickly wrenched my gaze away from Vellus and stared at my hands in my lap.

Vellus was a jacker. A mindjacker. How could I possibly not have seen this until now?

His meteoric rise as a politician made complete sense if he was a handler. Just like Julian, he could slip into people's minds and control their instincts, creating that reflexive feeling of trust. They would never know they were being messed with. When Sasha and I had tried to take Vellus the first time, I thought there had been another mindguard, but there hadn't. It had been Vellus all along. When he was attacked, he was forced to defend himself, like now, when my dad had nearly shot him.

But how had Julian forced Vellus to release the prisoners last summer? Could one handler handle another? At the time, Vellus had accused me of jacking him, but if he was a handler himself, he had to know what had really happened.

A sudden doubt clouded over me. Before, at the Trib Tower, I had linked in to Vellus's mind and read his thoughts. He had appeared to be a normal mindreader.

I lifted my gaze from my twisting hands to peer at Vellus. He blinked a couple of times, took a deep breath, then put on a smile, turning back to the tru-caster with a word of reassurance and tossing a warning glare to me. I reached out and pushed through his mindbarrier. It was as soft as a changeling's, exactly like a mindreader's would be.

Are you all right, Senator? I linked to him. He slowly turned to me, and I met his gaze full on.

Thank you for your concern, Ms. Moore. His thoughts echoed in his head. *Perhaps you could convince your father to cooperate, at least until the tru-cast is finished?*

The echo was even stronger the second time, and I had the same feeling of being in a big empty room with his thoughts broadcast in from the outside. Exactly like Julian when he pulled back his defenses and allowed me into his mind.

And Vellus had no mindscent at all.

He turned back to the tru-cast reporter as if nothing had happened. He was back to pretending he was simply a mindreader.

Now I knew exactly what to do.

Chapter TWENTY

I didn't have to kill Vellus.

In fact, killing him was the last thing from my mind now. Instead, I would make him pay in the worst possible way: by forcing him to destroy all his own plans and dreams. A warm glow of satisfaction spread through me. It was the sure feeling you get when you know you've made the right choice—something you did on instinct alone, but if you had a thousand years to contemplate the possible outcomes, you would still do the same thing.

"We... we're almost ready to go live, Senator." The tru-cast reporter's eyes were still wide from the scuffle with my dad, which had lasted mere seconds before he was contained on the floor.

Subdued, like Vellus wanted to do to all jackers.

"I'm sorry for the drama, Ms. Trinkle," said Vellus. "I'm afraid Ms. Moore's father doesn't share her enthusiasm for seeing dangerous jackers restrained so that they can't threaten anyone else."

My dad stared at his shoes, the confused look still on his face. The guard stood next to him, a hand on my dad's shoulder in case he decided to make a move. Which of course he wouldn't. Then Vellus gave me a pointed look, waiting for me to respond. Waiting to see if I would carry through with the tru-cast.

"My father," I said in a confident voice, filled with the rightness of my decision, "doesn't understand the stakes like I do. We don't agree on many things, not least what I'm about to do here today. Which just means we should get on with it, don't you think?"

Vellus smiled broadly, and the tru-cast reporter nodded uncertainly. I linked to the boom mic over my head, then into Vellus's and the reporter's minds. Her first name popped up. *Sandy.* The mindware interface of the mic had a slight metallic taste, and the reporter's mindscent reminded me of lemon tea. It was light, but it was still there.

Vellus, of course, had no mindscent at all.

Sandy, I linked to her, making her aware that I was in her head. *I think we should do this by thought waves, don't you?*

Yes! At least, she linked, looking at the senator, *I thought that was the arrangement.*

Senator Vellus chimed in, his words still echoing like his head was an empty cavern. *That would be best. Most reassuring to your viewers, I would think.*

You don't mind me linking in to your mind, do you? I asked her.

Um, no, that's... fine. Sandy's thoughts had the same uneasy shifting that every mindreader had once they realized that mindjackers had to jack into their heads to read their thoughts. I resisted throwing a smirk at Vellus, who was doing precisely the same thing to her as he had with every mindreader he had ever known, only Sandy didn't know it. Like Julian, Vellus was just a linker—with the caveat of also being the most insidiously powerful kind of jacker, able to control your instincts, but completely without detection.

You see, jackers can't read minds, I explained to Sandy, enjoying how much my thoughts sounded like the professor-voice Julian used. *We have to physically reach into your mind to interface with your mindfield. Normally, I wouldn't do such a thing without asking, especially with a fellow mindjacker, who wouldn't care for that at all.* This time, I couldn't resist a small glance at Vellus. *Most mindreaders I know don't like it either. Are you sure this is all right with you?*

She stumbled over a flash of fear, then steeled herself with her journalistic nerves. A fleeting thought of how important this interview was helped her sit taller in her chair.

Absolutely, she thought. *No problem.*

Thank you. Then I turned inward to my own mind. Holding a conversation while slowly getting my body into its hyped state would be tricky. And I couldn't afford the blowback, so I would need to make my moves fast and minimal.

The calm stillness of my mind surprised me. It took no time at all to float down the elevator and slip into the depths as if I belonged there. I was a skilled explorer traveling a well-worn path.

Outwardly, I took a deep breath and let it out slow. *Are we live on this tru-cast, Ms. Trinkle?* I asked, just to make sure. It would be most effective that way.

She circled a finger in the air, signaling to the cameraman. *We will be momentarily.*

While she paused a beat, I dropped down to the mass of connections in my mind. Someday, if I lived through this, I was going to explore each and every one. That idea felt simultaneously impossible and wondrous with potential. My life was at a tipping point: the most important thing I would ever do would happen in the next minute or two. Anything after that would simply be a bonus, like presents when it wasn't your birthday. Or finding a boy to love when you only expected a hero.

I took another calming breath and gripped the edge of my seat. It probably looked like nervousness on the outside, but I was simply preparing to hide the jittery state that would soon overtake me. I searched for the thread and quickly found it, like an old friend in a crowd of strangers at the airport just waiting to pick me up and take me home.

And we're live, Ms. Trinkle thought. *Thank you so much for joining me today, Ms. Moore. I'm honored to have you in your first public appearance since your famous announcement to the world that revealed the mindjackers hidden among us.*

Breathe in, follow the thread. *The honor is mine,* I linked with complete sincerity. Vellus was staring at me. He shifted in his seat and crossed his legs. His mind was an echo chamber, hiding his true thoughts. But no matter.

Much has changed since you first helped those changelings at the military hospital, Sandy thought. *And I'd like to hear your thoughts on the status of mindjackers today, but first, can you tell us how it is that you, yourself, needed rescuing earlier today from a terrorist band of mindjackers who took over the Hawthorne Water Pumping Station?*

It's true that I was part of the mindjacker group who took over the station, I linked to her, Vellus, and millions of mindreaders via the boom mic. *The idea was to negotiate the release of mindjackers being held in Senator Vellus's Detention Center.*

Follow the thread to the end. Send the signal. The electric ping zipped through my body, flipping every muscle to fast-twitch. I would need all of them, not just my leg muscles.

Yes, we know, Sandy thought. *Those demands made by the jacker terrorists were cast everywhere.*

I knew that Kira wouldn't voluntarily be mixed up with those revolutionary mindjackers, Vellus cut in. *Which is why I helped to negotiate her release from the mindjacker group holding the station as quickly as I could.*

Muscles sang throughout my body as they converted over. I took another breath and let it out through my teeth, trying to make no sound. *I was glad to come out so that I could help negotiate terms. I wanted the crisis to have a safe ending for everyone involved.* I sounded like hostage negotiator Sergeant Lenny Lee now. Julian would be so proud of how well I dissembled in the service of the cause. I triggered a surge of adrenaline as I rose out of the depths of my mind, which only made my legs vibrate against the cushion of my seat.

And you brought out half the mindreader hostages with you! the reporter gushed. *You're a hero once again.*

I hoped she would take my shaky smile for humility. It was really all the muscles in my body, including my face, fully juiced and ready to move.

I'm not a hero, I linked. *Just trying to do the right thing. Trying to find a way to peace for jackers and mindreaders alike.*

Vellus frowned slightly. I had to grip the chair harder to keep my body from flying off. My fingers dug into the smooth fabric of the cushion.

I was very impressed, I continued, *that Senator Vellus was so concerned for the safety of all jackers and readers involved. I guess I shouldn't have been surprised. After all, Senator Vellus is a mindjacker.*

Um… what? Sandy asked as if she had misheard my thoughts. Which was funny all by itself, but I wasn't capable of smiling without it looking deranged. Vellus was caught in the shock of my thoughts but not yet reacting to them.

Senator Vellus is a mindjacker, I repeated, looking him straight in the eyes. *He's a special kind, called a handler, that can control your instincts for survival. It's a rare and powerful ability that's very difficult to detect. But he's really one of us, so it makes sense that he would be protective of mindjackers as well as mindreaders.*

Vellus's face went white, then red, then an odd kind of purple, almost like a chameleon hyped up on one of Julian's jacker adrenaline drugs. He sent out a booming wave of mental laughter. *That's very funny, Ms. Moore.* He turned a glinting smile on the reporter, who had lost all color in her face. *Of course I'm not a mindjacker.*

Well, you could get tested, I linked. *Don't you have testing centers now that take care of that sort of thing, Senator Vellus? A simple test would prove whether you were, or were not, a mindjacker.* Small tearing sounds came from the chair where my fingernails cut into the fabric.

Vellus gripped the arms of his own chair, turning back to the reporter. *I didn't agree to this interview to come here and be insulted,* he thought, as if it were her fault. She shrank into her chair. *This interview is over!* He was halfway out of his seat when the reporter signaled wildly to the cameraman to cut the tru-cast feed.

That was my cue.

I launched out of my chair and leaped off the elevated interview platform. I made it half way across the room in a single pent-up bound, my foot hitting the floor a quarter second later. My mind had already slowed down time so I could control my limbs as I hurtled toward the guard at the far door. I only got two steps before launching myself into the air again, leading with both boots forward. That landed a punch to the gut which slammed the guard into the wall and forced all the air from his body. I landed hard on my shoulder, but my muscles were taut like rubber bands so I bounced off the floor and managed to arch back onto my feet. I grabbed the gun from the stunned guard and unfastened the strap of his helmet at the same time, then shoved the helmet off his head. I jacked him unconscious before he started to slide down the wall.

I turned and pointed the gun at Kestrel.

Everyone else in the room, including Kestrel, was still reacting to my sudden movement and had lost track of where I was.

I fired. The sound of the shot exploded in the close confines of the pressroom. Kestrel flew backward, my aim dead-on.

I flung my mind into my dad's head, and as I had hoped, Kestrel's control had been broken and Vellus's concentration was disrupted by the gunfire and my sudden flight across the room. I couldn't wait for my dad to figure it out, so I jacked him to grab the holstered dart gun of the guard next to him, and with another round of unerring Moore aim, he shot Vellus.

The reporter screamed.

Vellus stared at the dart sticking out of his chest. Then he slumped in his seat, eyes glazed. I knocked out Sandy and her cameraman so I wouldn't have to worry about them. I trained my gun on the guard now struggling with my dad over the dart gun, but I couldn't get a good shot with them twisting and turning and slamming against the wall like one body with four arms and legs and the dart gun at the heart of it. My dad's hands were still bound and he was quickly sliding to the losing end of the fight.

I dropped my arm and ran at them instead, my legs stuttering.

I still arrived with enough speed to knock the guard pretty good with the anti-jacker helmet in my hand. It bounced off his own helmet and left him momentarily stunned. I stumbled to a stop, turned back, dropped my helmet, and grabbed his. The guard let go of my dad long enough to grab at his helmet with both hands, more terrified of losing it, apparently, than whatever my dad might do.

My dad shot him with the dart gun.

I stepped back as the guard slumped to the floor, the helmet still half-on and protecting his head from bouncing on the thin industrial carpeting of the pressroom.

My dad and I looked at each other over the guard's body. Disbelief burned in his eyes, and I thought maybe a little pride. In spite of the fact that I had just jacked him into shooting his boss. Or perhaps because of it.

But we were far from out of danger, much less out of the Detention Center.

Chapter TWENTY-ONE

Nice shooting," I said to my dad.

He smiled.

Then my body shook. The tremors had kicked in as soon as I stopped moving, but the blowback was still ramping up. I had run more than I had planned. I closed my eyes, diving back into my head to shift my muscles back to normal. The fast-twitch muscles flipped back to slow, giving an extra shimmy to the shakes. I pumped up my heart rate and dosed myself with a little more adrenaline to try to accelerate the process.

I opened my eyes again. My legs buzzed, and the floor of the pressroom seemed to tip. My knees buckled, and I tripped over the fallen guard at my feet. I caught myself with one hand on the wall and managed not to fall into my dad. He braced my shoulder with his bound hands as best he could. His gaze darted over me, looking for some injury. I wasn't hurt, but I prayed the blowback wouldn't get any worse.

"I'll be fine in a minute." I hoped it was true. I clenched my teeth together so they wouldn't chatter. My shoulder throbbed, but I ignored it.

Before, in Kestrel's cells, the tranq gas had kept Julian from handling, so in theory, Vellus being tranquilized should mean I could jack him like any other jacker and easier than most. If he was like Julian, underneath the crazy mind powers, he was just a linker and didn't have the ability to resist. But Vellus had been a handler for longer than Julian and was probably more practiced at it. And possibly more dangerous. If he had the same terror-inducing defensive ability, it would be in full form now that he was unconscious.

This was going to be tricky.

"What now?" My dad had tugged a tiny key from the guard's pocket to unlock his cuffs.

I gave him a tight smile. "Now we wake Vellus up."

His eyebrows flew up. "Why?" I could understand his reluctance.

"Because we have an appointment with Sasha." I jerked my chin toward the glass and the cells downstairs. "He is down there somewhere, right?"

My dad nodded. "We were sharing a cell."

I reached down with a shaky hand and tugged the guard's badge off his belt along with a comm-link clipped around his ear that was already squawking with chatter from the other guards, who must be losing their minds by now. With the guard's gear in one hand, and the gun in my other, I stumbled over to Vellus's body. He was slumped in his chair. I waved my dad over and motioned him to put his cuffs on Vellus.

"Let me do the jacking," I said. "You know Vellus is a jacker, right? I wasn't just saying that for a distraction. He was handling you like Julian did before."

My dad's jaw worked, and he glared at Vellus.

"It's okay, Dad. He's fooled a lot of people." I nodded to the dart gun in my dad's hand. "Better keep that ready, just in case." I held my gun pointed at Vellus as well. I'd already killed one man today, but I'd make it two if this scribing thing didn't work out. I glanced over at Kestrel's body, only to find it wasn't there. "What the...?"

"What is it?" My dad tensed and swept his dart gun toward the empty carpet where Kestrel should be.

"Where did Kestrel's body go?" I checked every corner of the room as if he could have resurrected himself like a zombie and crawled off.

"You must have just wounded him, Kira."

I shook my head. It wasn't possible. *I shot him.* I'd seen the bullet throw his body to the floor. My gaze finally fell on the half-open door behind where Kestrel's body should be, the one we had come through from the warden's office. My body trembled again, not with the blowback, but with a rage that made me physically shake.

My dad grabbed my arm, gently but firmly. "I know you want to go after him. But we have to worry about Vellus right now and how to get out of here."

I blinked a couple of times, then nodded and focused on the senator.

I suddenly realized Sasha had probably encountered Vellus's defenses, and the experience had thrown him into some kind of epileptic fit. I steeled myself, hoping not to get hit with whatever had left Sasha convulsing on the ground.

Vellus's mind held nothing but a juiced-up haze. I let loose a sigh of relief, then reached deeper to roughly jack him awake. I left the sedative swimming around the receptors in his brain. I didn't want him handling anyone, and he would have to be under the influence of the sedative for Sasha to do his work anyway.

Vellus moaned, groggily coming to. Vellus squinted up at me like he couldn't quite figure out what had happened. I pointed the gun at his forehead. That got his attention, but confusion still tumbled around his face.

"I will kill you without hesitation," I said.

That froze the confusion in place. I linked in to both his and my father's heads. *Or my father can jack you into compliance. It might be easier on you if you cooperate.*

My dad held his dart gun leveled at Vellus's belly with a stone-cold look that I was glad would never be directed at me. Vellus's mind had a scent now, like decaying leaves in the fall, bitter with fear, like any other person would be. We could jack Vellus if we needed to, but he would be a more convincing hostage if he was frightened out of his mind.

"Kira." He raised his cuffed hands, then lowered, then raised them again, his hands doing a jerky dance in front of him as if trying to conjure away the gun. "Kira, wait. I will do whatever you wish, but it doesn't need to be like this."

"Oh, I think that it does." A laugh bubbled up in my chest, but I held it in. It felt like manic nerves, but my hand was steady.

"Will you please point that somewhere else?"

"Nope." I moved the gun to point at Vellus's heart while carefully tracking the amount of sedative in his mind. "Put out your hand."

He eyed me warily as if I might bite him. Or possibly hand him a grenade and ask him to hold it. Which wasn't a bad idea. Finally he held out a hand, and I could see it shaking.

Pathetic.

I dropped the comm-link in his open palm. He bumbled, hooking it around his ear until it was close enough for the receptors to pick up.

A scuffle sounded beyond the door where Kestrel had slipped out. My dad grabbed Vellus by his trim, silky dress shirt and hauled him up out of the chair, putting his body between us and the door just as two guards in starched blue uniforms burst through the open space.

I shoved my gun into Vellus's side. "Stay back!" I shouted to the guards. They stuttered to a stop right inside the door, guns extended. "Call them off," I said to Vellus. "Or you're not going to make it out of this pressroom alive."

Vellus threw his cuffed hands out. "Don't shoot!"

My dad tugged on Vellus's arm and slowly backed toward the far door, opposite the guards and where we had come in.

"You don't have to do this, Kira," Vellus said, trying to find his footing as he moved with me and my dad backward toward the door. "We can work together. You're brave and strong and smart. I told you, I want someone like you on my side."

"Well, we do have something in common then," I said. "Because I want someone like you on my side, too." I couldn't resist grinning at Vellus's expense. I was sure he had no idea what was in store for him in Sasha's cell. "We're going for a little walk, Vellus. Call them on the com-link and tell your goons to let us through. I have a particular prisoner who I want free." Vellus's thoughts flashed to Julian, and my heart about ripped in two. I wanted desperately to know more, but his thoughts showed he hadn't heard anything back from the raid. And I couldn't let thoughts of Julian distract me.

We had reached the door, but it was shielded so we couldn't tell what was on the other side. My dad jabbed his gun so hard into Vellus's side that he cringed away from it.

"Call it in, Vellus!" my dad growled, his face close to Vellus's ear.

Vellus tapped the comm-link. "This... this is Senator Vellus. Clear the corridor. We're coming out."

My dad took the guard's badge from me, swiped it through, and peered through the cracked door. When he saw it was free, he held the door open. We marched Vellus down the hall, one of us on each side, his handcuffs stretched tight across his body. At the far end, a SWAT team of guards were huddled, blocking the way. I mentally reached forward. Not only did they have anti-jacker helmets, but they were hiding behind a bulkhead that supported a disruptor shield blocking the entire width of the hallway.

They weren't taking any chances with us. I ground my gun into Vellus's side.

"Tell them if they try anything, I can pull this trigger even with my dying breath."

"They're not going to try anything." But his voice was uncertain, and he seemed to be talking to the comm-link as much as me. "Command, let us through."

As we approached, the SWAT members at the end of the hall scrambled to clear the passage, backing up and away.

Vellus turned his head slightly to the side and dropped his voice. "Where do you think you can go, Kira? It's not like they'll let you leave the building like this."

"Right now, we're going to the prison block," I said conversationally. "What cell were you in, Dad?"

"Two thirty-one." His voice wasn't quite as cheery as mine, but I imagined he was thinking about getting out. That was something I had stopped worrying about once I stepped through the gate.

We shuffled over the threshold, a tightly knit trio in lockstep like mindreaders synchronized to a common heartbeat, then took the stairs immediately across the hall. Our footsteps echoed through the concrete stairwell, clanging on the metal steps. Doors at the bottom clicked open for us, and we stepped out into a short hallway. There was a wide-eyed guard in an enclosed security checkpoint next to an iron-barred door. He was shield protected, but he gaped at us like he couldn't believe what was happening.

"Tell them to let us in, Vellus," I said.

"We need access to the prisoner level," Vellus said into his comm-link. The guard pressed two fingers to his ear, obviously listening to his own commands. He shut his gaping mouth and must have mentally activated something, because the door buzzed and slid open.

We frog-marched Vellus down the hall and through the door, passing through a disruptor shield along the way. When we arrived at the central prisoner area, it was like the view from the pressroom: two stories of cages filled with jackers in pale-green prison garb. An audible murmur swept through the air as jackers caught sight of us. I mentally reached ahead. There weren't any disruptor shields on the cells: every jacker was in a physical cage but each could reach all the other jackers for a hundred feet in every direction. It was madness, a recipe for death and mayhem. It was a wonder there were still people left alive here. I sensed a few were juiced, but most were fully functioning mentally, enough to react to my lightest touch and shove me out.

There were no guards that I could see, but the door had also shut tight and locked behind us. Whoever was calling the shots probably figured there was nowhere for us to go.

The jackers watched us carefully as we strode down the center aisle between the cages. Some leered at Vellus, others stared in disbelief. A few rested their elbows on their cage bars, their arms hanging out casually, as if having Senator Vellus paraded in front of them at gunpoint was an everyday occurrence. Or perhaps they had simply given up and didn't care anymore.

No one surged us, but I was in the awful position of having to mindguard Vellus to make sure no one killed him before we got him to Sasha.

"Pick up the pace, Vellus." I urged him and my dad a little faster toward the cell where I saw Sasha peering through his bars at us. "And you better hope Julian is still alive, because if he's not, you'll have a hard time living out your normal lifespan in Jackertown."

"So, you're taking me to Jackertown?" Vellus said, with an *I'm-the-snake* tone slipping into his voice. His thoughts tripped through scenarios like a high-speed computer, trying to figure out what I would do next.

"If you're lucky. Or we could just leave you here." I tilted my head toward a particularly large jacker inmate who looked like he could eat Vellus for lunch.

The truth was I wouldn't leave Vellus anywhere. I wasn't entirely sure Sasha would be able to scribe Vellus, but if he couldn't, I would be true to my word and not hesitate in killing him. It was still my primary mission here, and I would take the consequences from there. Especially with the plans Vellus had set in motion, there was no way I could allow him to walk out of here alive, unchanged.

Walk out of here... *oh no. Kestrel!*

I clenched Vellus's arm tighter. He wanted power and glory, but Kestrel... he was a true jacker-hater, even though he was a jacker himself. If Kestrel wasn't dead, then there was one place I was sure he was going: the water pumping station. Vellus seemed to think Kestrel was only following orders, but I knew Kestrel the way you know someone who's been the focus of your hate fantasies for such an intense period that you've forgotten there was a time before hating them. And *that*Kestrel, the one that I had killed a hundred times in my head, would never let something as small as the capture of his boss by jacker revolutionaries stop his years of work. Kestrel loathed jackers with the kind of hatred which could only come from somewhere deep, dark, and pathological.

He wouldn't stop until I put a bullet in him.

As we approached Sasha's cage, I called out to him, "We come bearing gifts."

Sasha smiled bright white. "You didn't bring much of a rescue party, that's for sure." The J on his cheek didn't stand out against his dark skin as much as my dad's did, but it stabbed my heart nonetheless.

"The rescue party is in need of a little rescuing themselves," I said. There wouldn't be anyone else coming for us today.

Sasha's face visibly grayed. "Is Ava all right?"

I cringed and lied as convincingly as I could. "She's fine." It was possible. She might be fine. Or she might be dead. There was no time to explain, and even if I had hours, there was no way I was telling him Ava had been on a mission trying to save him when the water station was taken. He needed something to live for.

Sasha took a shaky breath and nodded.

However, I did need to bring him up to speed on everything else, so I reached out to link in to his head and ran smack into a disruptor barrier around his cage. Then I noticed Sasha stood back from the bars, not sticking his hands through like the jackers in the cages behind us. In fact, the stretch of cages ahead were all the same as I skimmed along. All blocked by disruptor shields.

This must be the maximum-security section. I saw why Sasha would be here, but it would complicate things considerably. Sasha needed to touch Vellus, and physically reaching through the bars while the disruptor shield was up would scramble his mind. I couldn't reach through the shield either, so boosting his ability was out as well.

"Tell them to open the door," I hissed in Vellus's ear. He scrambled to relay the command to the comm-link. There was a long stretch of silence that had me second-guessing this plan.

I resorted to speaking out loud, but quietly. "I have a job for you, Sasha, but if you can't do it, then I'll have to do it for you." I hoped he could decipher what I was saying. *If they don't let you out to scribe Vellus, I'm going to have to shoot him.*

Sasha's face settled into a mask. "Well, that was always part of the mission, wasn't it?" It had taken a circuitous route, but he was right: we were still on the mission. He knew from the start that we might not come back from it, just as I did. As long as we eliminated Vellus, it would be worth it. However, my dad didn't sign up for this. I flicked a look to him and linked in to his head, but he was way ahead of me.

Make sure you shoot him in the head, Kira. I don't want him making a miraculous recovery.

I pressed my lips together and gave him a short nod. My dad

and Sasha both had to know that if I shot Vellus, there would be nothing holding back the prison guards anymore. We would likely all end up dead on the floor. The entire prisoner wing had fallen silent, the whisperings quieted as if everyone knew it. With a hundred jacker minds jostling one another, they probably did. It was an odd feeling, like back in my days in school when rumors surged in waves through the adolescent minds in the cafeteria.

I moved my gun from Vellus's ribs to his temple. "You had better hope they open that door very soon," I said quietly.

Vellus shrank away from me, and my dad pushed him back upright again, none too gently. Vellus tapped his comm-link several times like he didn't think it was working properly. "Command! Command, you need to open the cell!"

Nothing happened. I waited, finding myself slowly counting in my head. I moved my finger to the trigger. If I got to ten, something was wrong. They were probably finding a way to shoot me first, or gas the prisoner cells, or something... Suddenly, the door to Sasha's cell clicked and slid open. I tried not to let the relief show too much on my face.

Sasha hurried out of the cell as soon as it had opened wide enough.

I brushed his mind and he quickly let me in. *Can you scribe him? He's still under the gas, but he's a handler, Sasha.*

Sasha narrowed his eyes, measuring Vellus like he had transformed into a cobra ready to strike. *I should be able to. I've never scribed a handler before.* Given that Julian was the only other handler any of us had met, I wasn't surprised.

233

Well, no time like the present to find out. I cast a look up and down the jacker prison, checking for signs of snipers or SWAT teams waiting to rush in and rescue the senator.

Sasha reached his hand toward Vellus, who threw up his cuffed wrists to fend him off.

"Wait!" Vellus cried out. I couldn't tell if he had guessed what Sasha planned, but Vellus's mind was a terrorized scramble. If necessary, I'd jack him into lying prone on the ground, so he better not make much of a fuss about it.

He turned to me. "Kira, there's... there's something you don't know. It's about the water station."

"I know, Vellus."

"What?" he asked, more confused than afraid. "How could you... what do you think you know?"

"I know that whatever the problem is, you're going to help us solve it."

I nodded to Sasha. He dashed two fingers to Vellus's forehead, the lightning strike of a mongoose on the kill bite. Vellus jerked in surprise. Then his eyes glassed, just like Molloy's had when Sasha scribed him from being a vicious clan leader to a lumpy teddy bear of a jacker who we had to keep under careful watch in Jackertown, just to make sure someone didn't use him for their own evil purposes.

All the things that made Vellus who he was—all the plans, all the evil acts, all the threats of retribution, all the political scheming and years of turning good men like my dad into tools for his quest for power—all of it faded under Sasha's mental washing.

I couldn't help but wonder what was happening at that moment. Sasha must have access to the hidden depths of Vellus's brain. I could imagine the tangled connections that controlled every process in the mind: the simple, the automatic, the instinctual, the learned. All of it was one big mess in our heads. How did Sasha find his way through it? How did the people he scribed come out anything other than a vegetable?

For the first time, it occurred to me that Sasha wasn't a merchant of death for the soul. He was a *healer*. Someone who found the evil and excised it from your mind with the precision of a laser and the good intentions of a saint. Anyone else would be tempted to do far less and far worse. It made something inside me squeeze in recognition. It was an understanding, but an elusive one, like it was at the tips of my fingers but slipping away.

Sasha released him and Vellus blinked several times.

Then his soft brown eyes met mine. "Kira, there's an antidote."

I frowned. "What?" I wasn't sure if I had heard him properly, or maybe Sasha's mental scalpel had slipped while he was in there.

"There's an antidote to the serum," Vellus said with complete urgency, seizing hold of my shoulders with his fervor. "But only Kestrel knows where it is."

My stomach clenched tight.

It was time to break out of Vellus's prison.

Chapter TWENTY-TWO

I shrugged out of Vellus's grip, adjusting my shirt afterward. Even though I knew Sasha's scribe had taken hold of him and turned him into one of us—which he should have been all along, considering he was a handler like Julian—I still didn't like him touching me.

The jackers in the cages around us murmured again, and I felt the energy building. I wished I could free all of them, but that wasn't going to happen today. I didn't want anyone else over-hearing, so I linked in to Sasha, my dad, and Vellus all at once. It was a combination that I had never expected to experience.

Kestrel has some kind of plan to poison the water at a pumping station that feeds into Jackertown. I'm sure he's on the way there now. We need to get out of here and stop him.

I know! Anguish rippled through Vellus's thoughts, turning his fall-leaf mindscent sour. *There are so many people who will be affected... how could I have been so wrong... why did I let Kestrel...*

Focus, Vellus. I didn't have time for his remorse. *Is it already done? Is the poison already in the water?*

No, he thought. *Or at least... I don't think so. The plan was to wait until the plant was secure and cleared out. We didn't want too many eyes on the operation. If Kestrel has already dumped it in the water, the antidote should be able to reverse the effects.*

Okay, good. My heart was pounding through Vellus's explanation. Maybe we weren't too late after all. *We need a way out of here. We can negotiate your release with the warden, or whoever's in charge now...*

Yes, yes! He practically gushed happy thoughts in his desire to help. Sasha may have tuned him up a little too much. *You can release me and then I'll tell them to let everyone go!*

I sighed and threw a look to Sasha. He shrugged. *It's not an exact science.*

Now he tells me.

But I want to help! Vellus protested. *I... I can help you stop Kestrel.* Then confusion spun his thoughts as if this sudden desire to help was a completely foreign animal inside him.

Sasha indicated Vellus's head. *And there were some serious issues in there to deal with.*

Vellus looked at Sasha's finger as if it were a fly he wanted to swat.

They won't believe anything Vellus says, I linked to Sasha and my dad, ignoring Vellus and his flailing at Sasha's hand while staying in his head to keep tabs on him. He was still under the effects of the tranq dart, so he wasn't terribly dangerous, but he seemed... unstable. *The prison officials know he's been jacked, although once they have him back, they may not suspect that it's permanent. If he keeps acting this way, they might put him in a padded psych cell. They're probably debating whether to shoot us all right now.*

Sasha nodded and my dad frowned. I didn't see a way out either.

We should bring him with us, my dad offered. His thoughts wandered to unpleasant things he'd like to do to Vellus once we were free. The coldness of his thoughts bothered me, but I didn't have time to think about my dad's desire for vengeance.

We might have to, I linked to all three of them. *Vellus is the only thing keeping us alive right now. We can try walking out with him, but I'm sure they'll have snipers in the courtyard. At some point, if they can get a good line of sight, someone's going to take a shot.* In spite of our dismal chances, a warm flush of satisfaction ran through me—we had stopped Vellus, one way or another. Even if we didn't make it out, he would never work against jackers again. If they didn't send him to the demens ward, he might even do some good. I could just picture Vellus in the Senate, working for jacker rights.

Julian would love the irony of that.

Julian... My heart wrenched.

He was captured, maybe dead. Kestrel was on his way to poison all of Jackertown. And we were trapped inside the Detention Center with dozens of twitchy guards ready to kill us.

It was looking pretty grim.

The hydrocopter! Vellus's thoughts burst out into a single clear pulse, and he clapped his hands like a small child discovering there was cake for dessert.

My dad, Sasha, and I all turned to him. *Excuse me?* I asked.

My hydrocopter, Vellus thought, with an emphasis on the possessive part. He seemed delighted to have our attention again, as if it were a spotlight shining on him. I had a sense of what Sasha meant by issues. *The copter is quite impressive. Big and black and very powerful-looking. It used to transport the president before they upgraded to the new fusion-powered ones that can perpetually circle the earth. You know, in the event of a domestic attack or nuclear crisis—*

Vellus! I cut him off. *You have a hydrocopter? Here at the Detention Center?*

My mouth hung open, a look that was mirrored on my dad's and Sasha's faces as well.

Oh yes! His million-watt smile beamed at me, full of pride over his toy. *It's on the roof! We can use it to fly directly to the water pumping station and stop Kestrel before he dumps all those nasty genetic inhibitors of his into the water.*

I rubbed the shock off my face and peered up into Vellus's. *How good of an actor are you?* I shook my head. Stupid question. *Scratch that. Call it in, tell them that's our demand. A hydrocopter ride off the roof. Then we'll let you go.*

I'm not going with you? He seemed disappointed.

I gritted my teeth and did my best Julian impression. *We*

need you to fight for the cause here, Vellus. You need to undo all the things you've done before, okay? You can start with getting these jackers, your fellow jackers in the Detention Center, released. That's the best way you can serve the JFA. His face lit up. *But you need to be mesh about it!*

His face fell, then took on a crafty look. *Mesh. Yes, I can do that. But you need to take me with you, Kira. You know they'll track you, right? And probably try to intercept you.*

Then it's a good thing we don't have far to go.

You'll only be safe, you'll only reach the water station at all, if you have me on board.

I took a breath and let it out slowly. I didn't want to admit it, but Vellus was right. *Okay. You can come with us. Lie to them, tell them we'll let you go if they have the hydrocopter ready. But they'll suspect you're, uh, changed, know what I mean? You need to be convincing.*

Don't worry, Kira. He grinned. *I can be persuasive if I need to be.* He was back to that sunshiny smile that was just a little too happy. And, heaven help us, he was a handler. Who knew what he would do with that once he was off the tranquilizer.

I was starting to think I should have shot him anyway.

Vellus spoke into his comm-link. "The terrorists are demanding that the hydrocopter be ready to go once they reach the roof." He spoke in a calm, even tone. "Along with a pilot to take them where they need to go." A pause. "Yes, I understand your reluctance, Warden, but I assure you they have no intention of letting me walk out of here alive, otherwise." Another pause. "And if I *were* jacked? Would that make their demands any less pertinent to solving this crisis? Surely allowing a few jackers to release early from the Detention Center is worth my life. Or would you rather see a senator die on your watch?" Another pause. "Thank you for your concerns, Warden. When this is finished, we can discuss the soundness of my mind."

My mouth was hanging open, so I shut it. Ok, maybe Vellus would do all right after all. My dad and I took up positions on either side of him, our guns pressed not quite so hard into his side, but hopefully still convincing. Sasha followed close behind. Vellus put on a good show of fear and trepidation.

As we approached the door at the end of the prisoner level, it buzzed and slid open. Vellus guided us out and to the right, heading down a corridor and past another guard station. Behind the glass, the guard watched us go, his lips moving as he spoke into his comm-link. Another door buzzed open for us, and we marched up a stairwell.

I didn't like it. The feeling of being confined in too small a space was starting to crawl down my back. We managed to climb three flights of stairs, though, with no problems. When we reached the top, I tried the guard's badge and it swiped us into another hallway. At the end was a door with a window out into the bright afternoon sun. I saw the hazy blue of the Chicago winter sky outside. We had made it to the roof.

We crept down the hall, but something was wrong. It was dead silent. We should be hearing the hydrocopter by now if they were truly letting us go. When I had coptered off the roof of the Tribune Tower a zillion years ago, the vibrations could be felt all through the top floor. I reached ahead, but the outside of the building was blocked by a shield. I beat on my brain, trying to remember if the entire building had been shielded when I came in or only the outer perimeter.

I linked in to all three of their minds—Sasha, Vellus, and my dad. *Something's wrong.*

Agreed, thought Sasha. He darted a look down the hall behind us, then up ahead. *I'm going first.*

My dad handed Sasha the dart gun as he edged past us. He stole up to the outside door, trying to peer around the edges of the window. As he got close, the door buzzed and clicked unlocked. Sasha reached for the door handle, paused, then flung the door open and led with his dart gun.

A hand shot from the side of the door and grabbed his arm with the gun. Another person—a SWAT guy in full riot gear—grabbed Sasha by his jumpsuit, lifted him off his feet, and slammed him against the door, stunning him.

I yanked Vellus to the side of the hallway, pushing him in front of me to block any bullets that might come my way. My dad quickly tucked behind us. Up ahead, Sasha was wrestling with the two SWAT guys, but losing fast. They forced him to the ground right outside the doorway, and a couple of more SWAT guys swarmed around him, pointing rifles at his head.

He stopped resisting.

Then Vellus's comm-link squawked. "They want to make an exchange," Vellus said in a breathless voice over his shoulder.

"They want to trade Sasha for me. Then they promise to let you all go."

The hydrocopter wasn't even started, so I knew that was a complete lie. As soon as they had Vellus, they would shoot us all. The only question was whether it would be with dart guns or bullets.

Sasha was twenty feet away, pinned to the ground, but I wasn't sure if he'd overheard Vellus. He seemed to figure it out quickly enough, though, given that he wasn't already dead. He turned his head to stare right at me.

"Kira!" he shouted. "Don't let them take me! Please!"

What? I reached out with my mind, but he was outside the shield. I linked to my dad and Vellus instead. *We can't just give them Vellus. If we do, they're going to kill us all, including Sasha. Or at least take us into custody.*

Yes, they will, Vellus thought. I threw a look to him. He shrugged. *It's what I would have done before.*

I agree. My dad peered over my shoulder at the door. *There has to be another way out of this.*

The SWAT guys hauled Sasha to his feet. There was one on each side of him, holding him fast, and two more behind. They were still outside the shield.

"I mean it, Kira!" Sasha called again. "Vellus isn't worth it! Just give him up!"

Were they jacking him? No, the SWAT guys were all wearing anti-jacker helmets.

Sasha has to know they'll kill us, I linked to Vellus and my dad. *He's got a plan. I think we should trust him.*

My dad nodded.

"Okay," Vellus said into his comm-link. "Don't shoot! They've agreed to exchange me for the prisoner!"

My dad and I edged forward, still gripping Vellus. My attention was glued to Sasha. He very slightly moved his head side to side. I stopped, pulling Vellus to a halt with me. We were only a dozen feet from the door.

"You, at the door," I called to the SWAT guys holding Sasha hostage. "Meet us halfway, or no deal."

They looked at each other, and I heard the comm-link chatter again in Vellus's ear. "They want you to send me ahead."

"Halfway or no deal!" I shouted at the SWAT team. We started to move, but slowly. They hesitated, then edged forward. They had to squeeze together to get all three of them through the doorway, but they kept a firm grip on Sasha.

As soon as Sasha was past the shield, I mentally flung myself into his head. *What are you thinking?*

Dose me, Kira, he thought, his mind racing.

What?

Adrenaline dose me! Now!

I plunged deeper into his mind, going down the levels, searching for his adrenaline center. His mind was so complicated... but I remembered the thread I had found before, raced along it, and dosed him with a massive shot of adrenaline. I yanked back out of his mind because I had finally figured out what he was planning.

As soon as I was free, Sasha grabbed the hands of the two guards holding him, managing to get his fingers on the bare skin of each. Then he jerked backward, shoving them through the doorway and outside the shield so he could access the minds of the other two SWAT members behind him. I had no idea if Sasha could scribe four guards, two without touching, all at the same time, even with the adrenaline, but I wasn't waiting around to find out.

Run! I linked to my dad and Vellus, hauling them with me as I lurched after Sasha.

We reached the doorway and crossed the shield, stumbling out onto the roof to find all four guards sprawled in the gravel and Sasha lying facedown on top of them.

"Sasha!" I gasped and bent down to him. I heaved him over, but he was staring unseeing up at the bright winter sun.*No, no, no...* My gaze flitted across his mint-green jumper, but there weren't any gaping holes, no bright red spots of blood seeping out...

My dad snagged one of the SWAT team's rifles, and he and Vellus sprinted for the hydrocopter. I linked quickly to my dad. *Get the hydrocopter started! Vellus, come help me with Sasha!*

Vellus pivoted on his heel to run back to my side while my dad went ahead. I prayed there would be a pilot there since I was pretty sure flying hydrocopters was not one of my dad's skills in spite of his time in the Navy. I linked in to Sasha's mind, but it was a tornado of thoughts and images.

Sasha! It was like calling into a hundred-mile wind.

Kira? His thoughts were faint. They bounced around his head like he was lost in a faraway place that held an infinite number of rooms.

Sasha! What's wrong? How do I fix this? I asked.

Kira...? He was searching for me in the maelstrom, but I couldn't tell where he was.

The hydrocopter started beating the air into gusty waves that tore at my clothes. *Sasha, we need to go!*

Vellus was hovering over us. "Help me get him to the hydrocopter!" I shouted over the increasingly noisy blades. Vellus bent down and hoisted Sasha up, bracing his shoulder under Sasha's arm. I grabbed his other arm and looped it across my shoulders. His prison shoes dragged along the gravelly roof.

Sasha's head hung, and his body was dead weight. *A-va...?* Sasha's thoughts were choppy, like they were being beaten to bits by the wind whipping our faces from the hydrocopter. Or the hurricane in his mind. Either way, it was bad.

Ava's not here. You need to pull it together, Sasha.

But there was no answer. I searched and searched inside his mind, but it was just floating bits of memories and thoughts. He was splintered into a thousand pieces, and I had no idea how to put him back together again. My heart beat painful thuds against my chest in time with the copter blades. I didn't know how to fix him, but maybe Ava would. She knew him better than anyone.

The only problem was she might be in no shape to help, either.

Vellus carried Sasha up the five-step ladder into the hydrocopter, and I climbed up after him. My dad helped Vellus lay Sasha out on the plush carpet inside. A pilot peered out of the cockpit, nervously watching us. His anti-jacker helmet lay on the roof at the bottom of the steps where my dad had clearly tossed it out. Vellus was right—the hydrocopter was big and black and looked presidential on the inside, with a dozen white faux-leather seats stretching down the length of it and a gleaming steel-and-glass kitchenette at the entrance. I braced my hand against the cockpit doorway and linked in to the pilot's head. I would jack him if I had to, but he was afraid, not suicidal. He would take us wherever we wanted to go.

Take us up. I would let him know where we were headed once we were in the air and free of the airspace around the Detention Center.

My dad knelt by Sasha. Vellus took one of the luxurious seats and gazed out the window as we lifted into the air. His grin was unsettling, like he was a small boy on a grand adventure, eager and full of expectation and the thrill of possibility.

It was creepy, but having him on board was probably the only thing that gave us any hope of getting to the water plant in one piece.

The hydrocopter blades beat the air and pummeled our eardrums as they wound up for takeoff. My dad punched the button that closed the hatch door and muffled the sound to a low throbbing. I watched through the cockpit windshield as the roof slid away. We tilted and zoomed across the courtyard. I held my breath until we were out of rifle range, beating a path through the air over the city. The fact that we were putting space between us and the Detention Center seemed nothing short of a miracle.

We would need a couple of more before this was done.

Chapter TWENTY-THREE

We were flying low, only a few hundred feet above the rooftops of the city. I linked in to the pilot's mind, giving him just enough instruction to head him in the right direction: the water pumping station where I was sure Kestrel had gone when he slipped away.

And where I might find Julian lying dead.

My heart twisted, and I tried to focus my thoughts on our goal: stopping Kestrel. If there was anything Julian wouldn't forgive me for, even in the afterlife, it was failing on this particular mission. The diamond of hate inside me, forged when Vellus had ordered the assault on the water station, had lost some of its bite. Vellus hung on the edge of the faux leather seat next to me, looking down at the rooftops of Jackertown. Chicago's winter sun had frosted them white, and they were almost too bright to look at. His grin was carefree and boyish, like this was his first hydrocopter ride. The Vellus I loathed had disappeared under Sasha's touch. I thought it would be difficult to see, but the change was plain on

248

his face and even more obvious in his thoughts. It was impossible to hate him like this, grinning like a fool, off to save the day with us. But if Julian had been hurt in the raid that Vellus ordered, I might end up putting a bullet in the senator anyway.

I would cross that moral dilemma when I came to it.

So, what exactly is Kestrel putting in the water? I asked Vellus. My dad stood near the pilot, watching the airspace in front of us, but he was linked in to Vellus's head too. It wasn't like the senator could keep us out, being just a linker, and my dad clearly didn't trust him.

Genetic inhibitors, Vellus answered, a scowl settling on his face. *He's been working on the serum for years. They will weaken anyone with the jacker gene, reversing the gene expression that was triggered by the hormone change that occurred at adolescence.*

So he's flooding Jackertown with these genetic inhibitors to make jackers easier to control.

Easier to control, yes, he thought. *More importantly, they'll be less likely to rebel against our plans to incarcerate them. We didn't want them fighting back and us ending up with piles of bodies. If jackers believe their cause is hopeless, it will be easier to gain their compliance.*

So these inhibitors mess with their heads too? I asked, confirming my suspicions about my time in Kestrel's cell. *What is it, like some kind of depressant?*

No, although I did make a suggestion to mix in an antipsychotic medication. Vellus's face held no guilt or remorse, as if his prior self were some other person who he had no connection to. *Kestrel wouldn't agree to that; said he didn't want that getting out into the general population. Then we found that depression was a side effect of the inhibitor anyway. Once the natural gene expressions were reversed, some patients had suicidal tendencies.*

Something nagged at me about Kestrel not agreeing, as if he was in charge, not Vellus. More pressing was what Vellus said about the inhibitors breaking loose. *The general population?* I asked. *I thought you were targeting Jackertown.*

We are, Vellus thought, then shook his head as if that was an unpleasant thought he could swipe from his mind. *Kestrel is. I'm trying to stop him.* I wasn't sure if he was trying to convince himself or just reminding us. Sasha was right—Vellus's head was a mess, even after Sasha cleaned it up. *Kestrel is targeting Jackertown, but once the inhibitors are in the water, they won't stop there.*

I leaned away from him. *What do you mean?*

Well, where does the water go after you drink it, Kira? The patronizing drift of his thoughts rubbed me the wrong way, except I only vaguely knew the answer.

In the sewer?

And then?

I don't know—the lake? All of Chicago New Metro got its water from Lake Michigan, which seemed like a horrible idea, now that I thought about it.

It goes to the treatment plants, my dad offered, *and then gets dumped in the Chicago River. What are you getting at, Vellus?*

The treatment plants may remove the inhibitors, Vellus thought. *Or they may not. If not, they will eventually end up in the Mississippi River. Pharmaceuticals in the water are notoriously difficult to control.* He gave a wry grin as if that was terribly ironic.

The idea was giving me chills. *So these inhibitors could spread beyond Chicago New Metro?* Which had to be Kestrel's intention all along. He wasn't the kind to think small.

Yes, Vellus thought. *Which is why Kestrel made sure they were tailored to only affect jackers. And he developed an antidote as well.*

An antidote you were planning on keeping for yourself, my dad thought. Which was my thought, too, tasting bitter in my mind. Maybe it wouldn't be so hard to shoot Vellus when we were done.

And for Kestrel, Vellus thought simply. *And the other jackers left in control, like you, Kira, and your dad, if you had joined us. That really was the plan all along. I always believed you would understand everything in the end. That you would see we were doing the right thing for humanity.* He frowned, looking like a young child baffled by a massive conundrum. *At least, I thought it was the right thing for mankind before.*

I shook my head, suddenly sickened by the whole conversation. I ignored Vellus's vortex of confusion as he tried to parse out why he was evil before, but not now. That was his problem.

Susan Kaye Quinn

Then an image of a Senate chamber flashed through his mind, and his face lit up. He leaned closer. *There's something else you should know. This plan with the inhibitors in Jackertown—it's just a trial run. Kestrel had to cut off his experiments earlier than he wanted to, and this was our final test to see if the inhibitors would work on a larger population. If the test worked, then we would expand it to other cities. And eventually the entire country.*

You mean all the water, everywhere? It was one thing to try to poison jackers or accidentally have the inhibitors leak out into the regular waterways, but to intentionally poison the water of the entire country? I couldn't wrap my head around it.

That was the only way to make sure we reached all the hidden jackers as well. Vellus's face was somber. *We had to guarantee that every jacker would be contained.*

Guarantee? I asked. *To who?*

To some very powerful people. For several months now, there have been high-security meetings behind closed doors in the Senate about a "permanent solution" to the threat that jackers pose.

Permanent? I asked, horrified. *You mean they're going to kill us.* I had suspected it all along, but to hear Vellus say it sent chills skittering across my body.

Yes. Vellus's face paled as he realized for the first time that he truly was part of "us." *I meant what I said about the bloodshed and trying to keep it to a minimum. The defense secretary has been pressuring the president for a while to consider military options. So far, the president has resisted, but as the JFA has grown stronger, the military option has gained support in the president's cabinet and the Senate. I've been trying to convince them of other options. Kestrel's experiment is our last-ditch effort. If the inhibitors work, if the threat of jackers is contained, it would reassure the president and his supporters in the Senate that jackers can be dealt with using incarceration alone. If the experiment fails… the president will likely move forward with a preventative military strike against Jackertown before the JFA becomes too powerful. That's why the National Guard was on standby—not just to fence in Jackertown, but to coordinate the assault in the event the command is given.*

They're simply going to attack us? I asked. *How can they possibly justify that? People will be outraged.*

No, Kira. Vellus's shoulders dragged down. *They won't. The public isn't on the side of jackers, and you played right into the government's hands by taking the water station.*

The truth of his words pulled me back into my seat, the faux-leather sucking me in like a malevolent flower trapping me in its hold. We were already water-terrorists. The feds could justify any action they liked—it wouldn't be hard to make up a pretext for how Jackertown was a threat to the surrounding suburbs. Any public outrage would come after the fact, after the government had wiped out the JFA.

I swallowed. All along, Julian's talk of rebellion had been stoking fear in the highest levels of the government. *So, if we stop Kestrel, if we keep the inhibitors out of the water, the government is just going to attack Jackertown anyway?*

Vellus frowned. *I'm afraid so.*

My dad's face was taut with the agony I was feeling. *If the feds attack Jackertown,* I linked to him, *we'll be slaughtered. We won't stand a chance.*

They'll have a lot less chance with damaged brains, my dad thought.

I gave my dad a small smile. *Then we better make sure we're fully armed.* Maybe we couldn't save the people in Jackertown from imprisonment or death, but we could at least give them a fighting chance by not letting Kestrel weaken them with drugs.

There's another possibility, Vellus thought. *For now, we need to stop Kestrel, or at least get the antidote. Then, once I'm back in the Senate, I can try again to stall the military action. Find another solution besides the inhibitors. It will be difficult...* His thoughts wandered to my announcement on the tru-cast about him being a jacker. *That might complicate things.*

At the very least, they'll know you've been jacked, Vellus.

True, Vellus thought. *But they won't expect the jack to hold once I'm free. I truly have been working all along against the military option, Kira. That won't be a radical change from my position before.*

I leaned forward, propping my elbows on my knees and scrubbing my face with my hands. Were we really doing the right thing, stopping Kestrel? Wouldn't it be better to have everyone still alive, even if they were damaged by Kestrel's drugs? Even if they couldn't jack anymore? It was horrible, but it seemed better than ending up with a bullet to the head like Jameson. Then again, I couldn't imagine standing by and letting Kestrel poison everyone I loved.

Okay, I linked to my dad and Vellus. *No matter what else happens, Vellus, you go back to the Senate and try to come up with another option besides a military strike on Jackertown. If that doesn't work, the JFA's going to need every jacker in his right mind to have any hope of surviving.* Even as I thought it, our chances appeared bleak at best.

Vellus nodded. *Which is why we need to stop Kestrel first.*

I agreed, and my dad glanced at the cockpit. The pilot's thoughts showed we were approaching the water station, so I reached forward, trying to get a heads-up about what was happening on the ground. We could land on the roof, avoiding the legions of National Guard that were milling around outside the pumping station, but getting to Kestrel would be tricky. Assuming he was actually inside.

We were within my range, so I carefully skimmed the minds outside the station. They were all helmeted, so I couldn't sense if they knew who we were or what had just gone down at the Detention Center. The key would be getting inside the water station quickly, before anyone realized we weren't supposed to be there. Unfortunately, the shield was back up around the perimeter of the building. I had no idea what was waiting for us inside.

We'll need to move fast once we land, I linked the thought to Vellus and my dad.

What are we going to do about Sasha? my dad asked.

I bit my lip. I didn't like leaving Sasha unprotected on the rooftop. He was defenseless until we could find Ava and hopefully fix whatever had gone wrong when he scribed the four SWAT members. But getting Ava up to the rooftop had to be second to stopping Kestrel.

Once we disembark, jack the pilot to lock the hydrocopter, then knock him out. That way, only a jacker will be able to revive him and get to Sasha. Unless they break into the hydrocopter. That will at least slow them down, and we might need a way off the roof when we're done.

My dad nodded.

We'll use Vellus as a hostage again, I continued, *to get us inside, then work our way to Kestrel.*

Maybe I can reason with him, Vellus thought. *Convince him that we were wrong all along.*

Yeah, I linked, *I wouldn't count on that, but you can try. All you need to do is get us close to him.* I didn't plan on talking to Kestrel. I would prefer shooting him as long as he hadn't already put the inhibitors in the water. If he had, we would need the antidote, and that might buy Kestrel a little more time to live. Of course, I couldn't tell Vellus that—his mind was too wide open.

As we hovered over the water station, a voice crackled over the hydrocopter comm. "This is restricted airspace, order of the governor." They sounded very official. "State your intentions."

I linked to the pilot. *Tell them we're landing on the roof, and we have Senator Vellus on board.*

The pilot relayed my message in a shaky voice, to a noted silence on the other end. We were only fifty feet or so above the roof. It wouldn't take much for them to bring us down in a fiery wreck, which might or might not damage the water station but would definitely be the end of our plans.

Finally, a flat voice came over the comm. "You are cleared to land."

The roof seemed to rush up at us, stopping right before we touched down. My dad activated the hydrocopter hatch, and the beating sound of the blades swept in. We walked Vellus down the short steps to the roof, the artificial wind of the blades flapping our hair and clothes and the sun making us squint. I held a gun to Vellus, and my dad was armed with the rifle he had lifted from the SWAT team back at the DC. Vellus put on a good show of being our hostage again, but there was no one on the roof to see it.

My dad reached back to jack the pilot, who closed the hydro-copter hatch behind us.

If I remembered the layout correctly from earlier in the day, the door standing in the middle of the roof led to the third floor of the water station. The roof was shielded, and the electrical buzz from it worked its way through my boots, a slithering itch that was crawling up my legs. Ava had once said that long-term contact with the shield made her throw up, and now wasn't the time for that. A quick scan of the surrounding buildings showed spots of anti-jacker helmets positioned in all the sniper points where I had placed our own people not long ago, an irony that left me wanting off the rooftop in a hurry.

I held tight to Vellus, my gun clearly to his head, as we inched toward the door. The hydrocopter blades came to a rest with a decaying whine of the engine. A huff of wind curled up over the edges of the roof and buffeted us. No bullets or darts came whizzing from the sniper positions. In fact, the air settled into a dead silence.

My dad yanked the rooftop door open and swept the inside with his rifle. There was no response. Again, complete quiet, which was now ramping up my nerves even more than the vibrations from the roof shielding. We crept across the threshold, barely squeezing through, Vellus in the lead. The disruptor shield buzz drained from my boots, then lifted the small hairs on my arms as we passed through the shielding across the doorway.

It took a moment for my eyes to adjust from the blinding white of the roof to the too-dim third floor where shadowed railings overlooked the giant green pipes below. Now that we were inside the shield, I flung my mind out. Just as I felt, rather than saw, the anti-jacker helmets on the floor with us, a familiar rippling nausea surged through me. Vellus tipped sideways into me, all six-foot-plus weighing me down like an avalanche. He crushed me to the floor, and my dad thumped down heavily next to us.

The nausea still gripped me as boots scuffed the floor. The helmeted Guardsmen skittered out of their hiding places. They had used a thought grenade—my hard head had protected me, but Vellus and my dad had just had their brains electronically scrambled. Of course, the Guardsmen were readers, so they were unaffected even though the thought grenade could reach through their helmets. Vellus's arm muffled my face, but my gun hand was free of his body. I fired blindly, guided only by my mental reach. A cry, a scrambling noise, and a thud that shook the floor told me I'd hit something. The anti-jacker helmets gave away their positions, so I fired again, the crack of my shot mixing with another cry as my shot went true. I shifted under Vellus's weight, keeping him between me and the Guardsmen. I counted three helmets. Vellus's body was probably the only reason they hadn't fired back.

Peering over Vellus, I saw two of the Guardsmen on the floor, unmoving. I shouted to the third, "Unless you want a dead senator on your hands, you'll let us pass!"

The third Guardsman crouched behind a big metal tube that stuck out from the wall. He didn't respond. Was he waiting for backup? They had lured us into this confined space, waiting for us with armed guards and a thought grenade. This must have been their rescue plan for the senator because they thought he was a reader and wouldn't be affected by the thought grenade. Only it didn't work the way they expected. That, plus my dead-on aim, was giving the third gunman some pause.

We needed to move *now*, before he figured out what to try next or reinforcements showed up to help. With Vellus's mind a scrambled electrical mess it would be near impossible to jack him up to consciousness. What I really needed was an adrenaline med patch. Unless... maybe I could jack deep enough into Vellus's mind, plunge past those top levels where all the conscious thoughts were an electronic haze, and find a trigger for his own adrenaline to rouse him out of this induced coma.

A scraping of boots sounded from the far side of the room near the door. Reinforcements had arrived. My reach told me there were two of them, one on either side of the door, but my eyes had adjusted enough that I saw their rifles held ready and pointed at me.

I hauled Vellus on top of me for protection and inched back toward the wall, dragging him with me, my gun still held to his head. "Don't, or I'll shoot the senator." Hysteria was climbing up my throat, and sweat was trickling down my back with the effort of dragging Vellus's two-hundred-pound body. The Guardsmen didn't move, holding motionless, waiting. I took a breath, braced my back against the wall, and plunged fast and hard into Vellus's mind.

The swirling electric vortex sucked me deep and spun me around. My stomach lurched. If I hadn't been jacking so strongly, I would have been stuck in that maelstrom in his mind, but I pushed through to the relatively calmer deep levels. I quickly hunted down the trigger for his adrenaline, dosed him, then hauled myself up out of his mind again. I barely made it out before the electrical storm could sweep me away.

I was panting, but so was Vellus, moaning and slowly coming out of his unconscious state. I cast my mind out, searching the floors below. Maybe the jackers from the assault team were there. I could let them know what I was trying to do; maybe they could help. There was nothing but helmets, some huddled on the bottom floor, some in the control room below us on the second floor. That meant either Kestrel had decided to wear a helmet, or he wasn't here at all. And the JFA were either gone from the facility or they were dead.

I fought an empty weariness that threatened to pin me to the floor.

Vellus mumbled, then jerked in my arms. "Don't!" I gripped him around the neck and he froze. I dropped my voice. "You've been knocked out. They're watching us. We're still following the plan." He nodded, and I slowly released my hold on his neck. Together we eased up from the floor, my back flat against the wall and Vellus's body providing plenty of cover. He tried to say something, but his mouth wasn't working yet, still garbled by the effects of the grenade.

"You!" I called to the third Guardsman. "Hiding behind the tube! Come out! You and your friends by the door are going to go back downstairs where you came from. The senator and I are taking a trip to the second floor." I nudged Vellus forward, inching toward the open doorway of the room. "If you get too close, I'll start shooting different parts of the senator's body."

We nearly stumbled over my dad's inert form, and I desperately wanted to check if he was okay, but we had to keep moving. Who knew what would happen to my dad—or Sasha in the hydrocopter—for that matter. I had just one mission, one goal, before a Guardsman managed to put a dart or a bullet in me: stop Kestrel.

The third Guardsman shuffled out of his hiding spot, hands

held out, his weapon pointed at the ceiling. He backed toward the door and retreated into the hallway.

The stairs were only a short walk down the hall, and the control room was just one flight down. It felt like an impossible million exposed miles. There was nothing left to do but bluff my way there and hope I could keep the Guardsmen in front of me.

Boots shuffled around the doorway and the rifle tips disappeared. I heard them retreating down the hall. Once Vellus and I were over the threshold, we moved more quickly with me tucked tightly behind him. The scraping of our shoes along the linoleum floor and my own labored breathing magnified a hundredfold in my ears, but my mental reach told me the Guardsmen were adjusting their position, shifting backward as we worked our way down the hall.

We made it to the stairs, but then Vellus's legs tangled and he nearly went down. I sensed the Guardsmen shift forward again, encroaching up the stairwell toward us.

I quickly jacked into Vellus's mind. *Tell them to back off!* His mindfield was still a dizzy vortex from the thought grenade, but less so. The adrenaline must be fighting off the effects, and it was more like linking in to the mind of a demens: nauseating, but tolerable.

"I promise you, she'll kill me if you shoot!" Vellus clenched the railing with both hands to keep upright. We clambered down the steps, awkward in Vellus's uncoordinated movements. By the time we reached the bottom, he was a little steadier. The Guardsmen had retreated to the hallway, the bare whisper of them talking into their comm-links carrying over the stillness of the building as if it were collectively holding its breath.

The control room was across the hall, halfway between our stairwell and the one where the Guardsmen were holding their position—the same stairwell I had marched up earlier, that led to the ground-level floor.

We edged out into the hallway, angling so I could see through the open door of the control room. My mental reach showed three figures inside—one pacing a narrow pattern, the other two holding stock-still. They were around the corner of the door, out of sight. Four more helmets in the back office closest to the door were all unmoving. The windows into the office showed nobody inside, but as we crept closer, I saw several pairs of legs lying on the floor.

Bodies. I prayed they were no one I knew, but was certain that they were.

One had a delicate, pale hand, palm up and unmoving on a fan of long blond hair. My view of her head was blocked by the angle of the doorway, but I recognized the cargo pants and the boots the size of a child's.

Ava.

I had no time for the tears that her name welled up, so I swallowed them down. She was helmeted—it didn't make any sense. Why would you helmet a dead body? Unless... unless they were alive, just unconscious. *Helmeted to keep them from jacking.*

I tried to beat back the hope that surged up in my chest. I didn't have time for that, either.

The pacing figure stopped. It was time to make our play. No sense waiting around for a trigger-happy Guardsman to finally decide he had a good shot on me. Vellus and I shuffled to the threshold of the control room. The Guardsmen hovered at the top of the stairwell.

I clenched the back of Vellus's shirt and linked in to his mind. *I'm going to swing you into the control room with my back to the door frame,* I thought. *It's got to be quick, or they might try to take a shot at me. Are you ready?*

Ready.

I pulled out of his head before the dizziness got to be too much and quickly pivoted him into the control room. My back was now up against the propped-open door, giving several me inches of door and control-room wall to protect my back from the Guardsmen while Vellus's tall frame covered my front.

I still held the gun to his head where everyone could see it.

Our sudden entrance into the control room pulled the attention of the helmeted figures. I peered over Vellus's shoulder, but I could only see two. One was a Guardsman, decked out in a flak jacket and with a rifle now pointed at my head.

The other was Kestrel.

He was ashen but alive. His face was lit with fury and a hyped-up tension that felt like a mirror of what was rippling through my own body. His G-man jacket was gone, and his starched shirt was rumpled, but I could see a corner of the bulletproof vest underneath.

Now I knew to aim for his head.

His attention was drawn back to the manual-interface board on the table in front of him where he was tapping. That's when I noticed that his other hand held a gun, and it wasn't pointed at me.

It was pointed at Julian's head.

My breath caught in my throat. *He's alive.* I reached out without thinking, but ran into the helmet on his head. He sat cross-legged on the floor, leaning against the corner of the table, his hands tied behind his back to the metal leg. His head hung down, tilted slightly away from the gun pressed to the back of his neck, and he appeared to be examining the tile floor in front of him. His flak jacket moved in and out with the breaths he drew in through his teeth.

I sucked in a shaky breath, which drew Julian's gaze to mine. I saw the muscles in his arms flex as he tested the ties binding him. Color quickly darkened in his face. Kestrel pressed the gun harder, forcing Julian's neck to bend down again.

"Patience, lover boy," he said. "I don't want to shoot you just yet."

Kestrel's icy voice sent shivers through me. If I was quick and my aim was good, I might be able to shoot him. The Guardsman would probably shoot me in return, or maybe not, with the senator for hostage. But I didn't know if I could do it, not with Kestrel's gun to the back of Julian's head. Besides, if Kestrel had already poisoned the water, it would be for nothing.

I scanned the screens behind him, filled with security images of the water plant, plus control panels and a large schematic of twisting blue lines. Two control panels were lit up green, and I remembered what Julian had said about those: Kestrel was flowing water to both Jackertown *and* the suburbs. For Kestrel, this had never been just about Jackertown. He wanted the inhibitors to reach jackers in the suburbs from the start. Kestrel's steely blue gaze bore into me as if his anti-jacker helmet and my hard head were no obstacle to the venom of his hate.

"I told the senator that you weren't worth the trouble," Kestrel said. "That you were far too dangerous."

"Agent Kestrel—" Vellus said.

Kestrel cut him off. "She clearly has you under her control, Senator." His gaze didn't waver from me. "Something that will soon come to an end. Just remain calm and everything will be fine."

Kestrel's hand flitted across the manual interface pad on the table in front of him. Then I saw it: an unfamiliar tension in Kestrel's normally cool eyes. The twitch of his cheek. Those told me as much as the screens behind him: he was buying time.

I jacked into the mindware interface of the controls, the metallic taste of the electronics stinging the back of my tongue as I searched for a way to stop whatever Kestrel was doing. Only I wasn't sure what I was looking for. I randomly flipped switches and pulled up controls, desperate to figure it out. I found a holding tank that Kestrel had set to drain. It was labeled *chlorine*, but it was disconnected from the main line that dispersed to the suburbs and Jackertown alike. I tried to shut it down, whatever it was, but my interference caused a display to pop up behind

Kestrel. He was helmeted, so he couldn't reach into the mindware to stop me.

Kestrel cursed and motioned to the Guardsmen holding a rifle pointed at my head. "Hit the manual override!" he barked out. The man hesitated, then with his gun still pointed at me, shuffled over to a gray metal panel next to the screens. My link to the mindware interface cut off abruptly. Kestrel stayed at his controls, jabbing in commands so hard the manual board jumped under his fingers.

Vellus was talking again. "Kestrel." He sounded more like a senator now, more authority in his voice. "You need to stop. We can't do this, not like we thought. We have to find another way to keep the peace."

Kestrel's face was turning purple from his frustration with the controls, but Vellus's words whipped his gaze back to us. His eyes narrowed at Vellus, then he seemed distracted by something moving on the screens. His mouth fell open. Before I could figure out what he was looking at, he turned back.

Kestrel raised his gun from Julian's head and fired at us.

Vellus was yanked sideways into the free space of the doorway. My grip on his shirt pulled me into the hall with him, and we fell together to the floor. A second shot rang out and I ducked. I grabbed the front of Vellus's shirt and wrestled him up to sitting, pulling him close to me for protection. I dragged us both away from the control room and braced my back against the wall just outside the door, hugging Vellus's body for a shield. The Guardsmen at the end of the hall crept out from their spot at the top of the stairwell.

Susan Kaye Quinn

My gun wavered in their direction. "Stay back!" They drew back into the stairwell, shielded from my shot.

Vellus's head lolled to the side, and I struggled to keep his six-foot-plus frame upright, propped against me as I sat with my back against the wall.

Kestrel had shot *Vellus*.

I blinked as my mind wrapped around that idea. I blindly felt the front of Vellus's shirt. It was slick with wetness, and my hand came away stamped red with blood. Then I saw it trickling down Vellus's side to the floor in a slow, hiccupping stream. I pressed my hand against his chest, searching for the hole where the bullet had gone in. I had no idea what I was doing, I just wanted to stop the pulsing of blood out of him. I pressed harder. Vellus's breath came in small gasps.

He tried to turn his head to see me behind him. "It wasn't supposed—" He stopped to gasp. "—to be like this."

Vellus's body shuddered and a sick feeling washed through me. Vellus was shot. Kestrel was poisoning the water and holding a gun to Julian's head.

We weren't going to make it after all.

Chapter TWENTY-FOUR

I stared down the sight of my gun at the Guardsmen lurking by the stairwell.

"I was going to fix it, Kira," Vellus whispered next to me. "I was going to fix everything." Gasps pulled the air from his throat faster than the words could come out, making them fade at the end. Then his breath wheezed too softly to form sound. I linked in to his mind.

There were never supposed to be any readers. His thoughts were weak, and one thought-whisper echoed through his rapidly emptying mind. *Accident.* Then his body shook so badly I could feel it in my bones. His mind became a black hole, sucking me in. I yanked out before I was pulled into that empty space with him.

His body went still next to mine.

The echo of the emptiness of his mind reverberated through me, and my mind clung to his last thoughts. *There were never supposed to be any readers.* What did that mean? The first mindreaders were triggered by leftover pharmaceuticals in the water, but it wasn't an accident. More like an environmental disaster that caught us by surprise.

I didn't understand, but it didn't matter. In the end, I hadn't been the one to kill Vellus after all. Even more stunning, I didn't actually want him to die. He took with him any chance of stopping his friends in the Senate from using their military option to solve the "jacker problem" once and for all. The feds would find some excuse—maybe even Vellus's death—to attack Jackertown. They could wipe it out with one fast bombing run. It wouldn't take much to kill us. No matter how strong our minds, they were nothing against bombs and bullets.

Maybe Kestrel, with his plan to poison jackers with his inhibitors, would be able to stop the feds from outright killing everyone. Maybe jackers would all end up in Vellus's Detention Center, but at least they would be alive.

My gun hand wavered, still pointing at the Guardsmen on the stairs. Despair was a weight dragging on my arm, wanting me to put the gun down. Give up before the Guardsmen decided it was safe to shoot me. Maybe giving up would save Julian, too. My head seemed to float above my body, and a fuzzy fatigue pulled on my eyelids.

Popping sounds, like fireworks on the Fourth of July, went off in the distance.

I blinked my eyes open. The blood leaking out of Vellus was spreading across the floor by my knee. It had slowed to a small, ebbing ooze, presumably because his heart had stopped forcing it to flee from his body. The fireworks cracked again, a rapid string of them, and a thought flitted through my mind that they were somehow connected. Vellus was dead, and the fireworks were celebrating it. Only it was a macabre dance of sounds that were wrong, shifted in time and purpose from where they really belonged.

Shouts, closer now, snapped me out of my fugue.

Someone was downstairs. And they were making a real ruckus. The Guardsmen had disappeared from the top of the stairs, drawn to whatever was happening on the first floor. A scuffle of steps, grunts, and the pop-whoosh sound of dart guns came from downstairs.

Dart guns!

I flung my mental reach to the ground floor, only to find a tight squad of jackers working their way up the stairwell. I swept them quickly—Anna and three of Hinckley's military converts— then pushed a sweep to the rest of the floor and the grounds outside. Anna had brought dozens of jackers with her, and they were everywhere, swarming the street and running between the stationary helmets of the Guardsmen. She arrived at the top of the stairs and did a quick peek-check around the corner.

Her eyes went wide when she saw me. I finally let my gun arm drop and relaxed my grip on Vellus's body. The three bulky jackers behind her fanned out to cover the hallway. I waved to Anna with my free hand, not remembering it was covered in blood until her gaze fixated on it. She slowly shuffled down the hall, making sweeps with her rifle. Then someone else peeked around the corner of the stairwell—possibly the last person I expected to see.

"Mom?" Dressed in a flak jacket and JFA gear with her gray hair tied back under her combat helmet, she looked like a strange mixture of PTA mom and revolutionary. The flood of relief I had at seeing her alive was overpowered by a pulse of anger that Anna had brought my mom on an op.

"What in the world, Anna?" I asked, my voice low, when she crouched next to me.

"Your mother insisted on coming," Anna whispered, pointing with her rifle over my shoulder to the open door. "Is the control room secure? I sense helmets, but they're not moving."

I shook my head. "Kestrel's in there with a Guardsman," I whispered back. "He's poisoning the water. I tried to stop him, but he's got Julian. The other helmets are captured JFA, but they're all out. My dad's on the third floor, and Sasha's on the roof. They need help, but we need to stop Kestrel, or at least not let him escape, but don't kill him—he's the only one who has the antidote."

She nodded and signaled two of her jackers. They stole on silent boots toward the door of the control room. The third stayed back by my mom, who started shuffling toward me, so I motioned her back and quickly linked in to her head. She pushed me back out.

She... *pushed me back out.*

My mouth hung open. A sly smile crept up on my mom's face as I brushed her mindbarrier—it was soft like a changeling's but firmer than a mindreader's. This time she let me in.

Mom, you... you're... what the...?

I changed, Kira. When the Fronters attacked you, I don't know, it was like something was triggered inside me. Of course, I couldn't help you because they had those helmets on. Xander convinced them that I had been tested and was a mindreader—

"I would be happy to put a bullet in your brother, Ms. Navarro," Kestrel's voice cut through my mom's thoughts. "So I wouldn't come any closer if I were you." Anna and her two jackers stood in front of the control room, their rifles pointed inside, holding perfectly still. I struggled out from under Vellus's body and up from the floor, leaving a bloody smear on the wall as I tried to keep the room from tilting under me. I stumbled toward the door and edged up to the corner.

Kestrel had tipped the table up on end and was crouched behind it, using both the table and Julian as cover. When I appeared in the doorway, Kestrel locked gazes with me. There was a demens sparkle in his eyes. "So, tell me, Kira—did Vellus explain to you about the antidote?"

I didn't answer him. What was he playing at? I couldn't imagine Kestrel would tell me where the antidote was if I asked nicely, or even at gunpoint. Julian's insistent stare captured my attention, then he looked with only his eyes toward the screens. There was a bar graph slowly rising. Julian was telling me to stop Kestrel. But shooting Kestrel would just end up with Julian dead and no antidote.

When I didn't answer Kestrel's question, he smirked. "There is no antidote, Kira. There never was. It was a small lie, but one that Vellus needed to hear."

No antidote. Was Kestrel lying to me or had he lied to Vellus? There was no way for me to know. And why was Kestrel telling me this now? My gaze flicked to the bar graph on the screen again. There was a schematic of a tank next to it, like the chlorine tank Kestrel had been draining before, filling now instead of draining. Filling with the inhibitors was the only logical thing. If the inhibitors were already on their way, he wouldn't be stalling; Kestrel still needed time for his plan to work.

My mind linked back to my mom, counting on Anna to hear my thoughts in her head. *He's stalling until the poison is all done transferring or whatever. We have to stop him, but with Julian in the way...*

If only we could get your mom close to him, Anna's thoughts rang in my mom's head.

My mom? I asked. *What in the world, Anna?*

I'm a scribe, sweetie, my mom thought.

My brain stalled out. *What? How can that be possible—*

"I can understand why you wouldn't believe me," Kestrel went on, conversationally, as if my lack of response and look of disbelief were directed at him. "Vellus easily believed the lie. It worked well for both of us. He needed to think he would still have a place of power when it was all done, and I needed him on board with the rest of the plan. But Vellus never understood the truth: that there was never going to be a way out of this. For any of us."

My mom's thoughts broke through. *Kira, I really am a scribe! When the Fronters let us go, I went to Mr. Trullite for help. I accidentally figured out I could scribe when Mr. Trullite wasn't as helpful as he could have been. Xander helped me sort through it.* She paused. *And I'm pretty sure I could do it again, if I can just get close enough—*

That's crazy! I linked. Sasha's mind had been completely scrambled by his scribing, and he knew what he was doing. My mom was a brand-new changeling. I had no idea how that was possible, but I was sure she knew nothing about how to control her power—

Julian's voice interrupted my thoughts. "Kestrel's right, Kira. There's no way out of this for any of us."

Kestrel hit Julian on the helmet with the grip of his gun. The dull thud sound of it made me flinch. "No one's asking you, Mr. Navarro."

Julian's brilliant blue eyes were still focused on me, peering up from under his bowed head. He wanted us to shoot Kestrel, to not worry about whether he got shot as well, but I couldn't do it. All this talk, all of it, and the tank on the screen kept filling. When it was done, Kestrel wouldn't have any reason to stall anymore. Which meant Julian would have no value left as a hostage. When that happened, I had a feeling Kestrel would start shooting people and would keep going until someone stopped him with a bullet.

I have another idea, Anna thought. *The thought grenades we used back in Kestrel's cells, to break out...*

They can reach through shields! I thought, relieved and excited at the same time. *Which means they'll reach through*

Kestrel's helmet. And they'll work on him, because he's a jacker. Do you have some?

Hinckley used to carry one, Anna thought, *in case a jacker went rogue, but I can't find him.*

Wait... the Guardsmen... they used one coming in!

I'm on it. I heard Anna's footsteps flying down the stairs.

I turned my attention back to Kestrel, gripping my gun tighter. "So you're poisoning the water to stop a war?" I asked, to keep him talking until Anna returned. If she didn't get back in time, I should shoot Kestrel and hope I could get him before he shot Julian. Only I didn't know if I could force myself to do it.

"Poison is such a harsh term," Kestrel said.

"I didn't know jackers could go demens, Kestrel, but you've proven me wrong."

He laughed, and it actually sounded lighthearted, like the burden of a hundred years had been finally lifted. "Demens? I'm the only right-thinking one here, Kira. Jackers won't be destroyed, just weakened. The evil part, the jacking part, carved out of us. Excised. I would have thought you would realize what a good thing that is by now," he said and waved his hand in the air, "what with all the horrors you've seen jackers perpetrate. The only solution is to strip all jackers completely of their abilities, so the balance of power can tilt back to what it was before. That will eliminate the need for war, Kira, something you and your revolutionary friends..." He nudged Julian's head with his gun, making me twitch. "...don't seem to understand. But there are so many jackers, more every day. And I had to be sure to get everyone, you see, which was why I had to test it on so many mindreaders as well. Lucky for me, Vellus was all too willing to help. His testing stations have been very useful in expanding the reach of my experiments, not to mention the extra help the Fronters were eager to provide, bringing in new subjects."

I sucked in a breath. Vellus had said Kestrel had to cut his experiments short, but he had just shifted them to the testing stations. How many people had Kestrel already infected with the genetic inhibitors? My mom had crept up behind me, and I involuntarily glanced at her.

Let me try to get to him, Kira, she thought.

Don't be demens, Mom, he'll shoot you. Kestrel peered at her, now that she was visible in the door, like he was trying to figure out who she was. Which I didn't like at all. *The thought grenade will work,* I linked to my mom.

What if Anna can't find one? she asked. *Maybe we can bargain with him. If he surrenders, we'll scribe him but let him live.*

I wasn't entirely sure Kestrel wanted to live, but it was worth a shot.

"Look, Kestrel," I said, putting on my best game face and glancing at the two jackers still holding rifles pointed at his head. "This isn't going to end well for you. You have to know that. No one's letting you walk out of here alive. If you're lucky," I said, hooking my thumb over my shoulder at my mom, "we'll only scribe you and let you live, like Vellus." Which wasn't the best point to make, given that Vellus was dead at my feet. Then again, it was Kestrel who shot him, not me.

"You'll *only* scribe me? That's not much of an offer, Kira." Kestrel flicked a look to my mom and frowned. "Besides, I know your mother is a mindreader."

"Yeah, well, not anymore."

"Mindreaders don't change late in life." His voice was patronizing. "And your mother is suddenly a scribe? That's not much of a bluff, Kira."

"Like I said, getting scribed is only going to happen if you're lucky," I said. "If you put the gun down now. Because I guarantee that if you kill Julian every jacker in this building will want you dead. So, what'll it be, Kestrel? It's the only offer you're going to get today."

He flicked looks between my mother and me, as if trying to figure out a puzzle, but it was pretty simple the way I'd laid it out. My mom had a freaky earnest look, like she was itching to use her new scribing skills on him. Then a strange realization dawned on Kestrel's face and his mouth fell open. He hastily glanced at the screen, then stabbed at the manual interface on the floor with sudden, jerky movements.

I frowned. "Change of heart, Kestrel?" I checked the screen. What was he doing?

Anna's footsteps came pattering down the hall and her thoughts filled my mom's head. *I've got it!* She slipped the tiny, bullet-sized thought grenade into my hand, then hurried back to the top of the stairs. *I'll be out of range, just in case you get taken out too.* She leaped down the stairwell steps.

Suddenly, Julian whipped his head back, knocking into

Kestrel's arm and sending the manual-interface board skittering along the floor out of Kestrel's reach. Kestrel growled and bashed Julian's helmet with his gun hand. The blow tipped Julian sideways, but he was held upright by the wrist ties. Kestrel brought the gun around to Julian's neck again. I panicked and slammed the thought grenade against the doorjamb. Nausea ripped through me as everyone crumpled to the floor, including and, most importantly, Kestrel. The shot from his gun, intended for Julian, must have missed, because I heard it ricochet, and a black divot marred the tile floor next to Julian's feet.

I lurched into the room, leaving the bodies of Anna's two jackers in the doorway, along with my mom, who had fallen on top of them. My mom, the jacker—if I needed any more proof, there was the fact that she had been taken out by the thought grenade. I stumbled past Julian, who was tipped over sideways, and stepped over Kestrel, the nausea from the thought grenade still pulsing through me. There was a dead Guardsman hidden behind the table. Kestrel must have shot him, too, probably after he shot Vellus.

He really hadn't planned on leaving the water station alive.

The bar graph on the screen had frozen. I nearly tripped over Kestrel's body on my way to the manual control panel on the side. I flipped the mindware interface back on, jacked in, and verified it: Kestrel had stopped the poison from filling the secondary tank, and it hadn't been connected to the main line yet.

Trying to weaken jackers everywhere was Kestrel's life's work. He never had an antidote, not even for himself. He was crazy, willing to take whatever outcome came of it. He relished it, in some kind of demens atonement, hoping to excise the jacker within him along with everyone else.

So, why, at the last moment, had he stopped it?

I glanced back at my mom. He couldn't believe that she had changed into a jacker. I couldn't believe it, either, but it was incontrovertible, what with her lying on the floor with the rest of them. *When the Fronters attacked you, I don't know, it was like something was triggered inside me,* my mom's voice echoed in my mind. She had just left the testing station... where Kestrel had been experimenting with the inhibitors.

I flashed back to the jacker at the Mediation Room: he claimed he was a reader, fresh out of the testing station, too. Then he had run into a JFA patrol and wiped them out. That attack had somehow triggered the change, turning him into an extreme jacker. It was just like my mom, when we were attacked by the Fronters, changing into a scribe. The inhibitors were changing people, under certain conditions, into powerful jackers, even though they were way past the age where it should be possible.

Kestrel was creating jackers, entirely without meaning to.

I looked at him, crumpled on the floor. He must have figured out that something had gone wrong, and that he was about to flood the world with genetic inhibitors that would weaken jackers everywhere... but create newer, more powerful ones out of mindreaders as well. It was the extreme opposite of everything he had worked for. Kestrel knew that the only thing stopping the feds from rolling out their military option was his inhibitors. He was ready to die for his cause; I was sure he would rather have all jackers die with him than run the chance of creating new super jackers.

No wonder he had stopped the inhibitors.

This will eliminate the need for war, Kestrel had said of his grand plan.

I stared at the screen. The inhibitors would weaken jackers who I knew and loved, maybe create the dead spots in their brains that I'd seen too many times as the result of Kestrel's experiments. I'd already felt the effects myself when I was trapped in his cells, losing my mind to the effects of the drugs. But the inhibitors would also create new jackers, stronger ones. Jackers who might give us a fighting chance in the war that was coming no matter what.

How much of a chance? I glanced at Kestrel passed out on the floor. Enough of a chance that Kestrel was willing to destroy his life's work to stop it from happening.

This is about fighting to survive. Julian's words welled up in my mind. *But you've always known those were the stakes, haven't you?*

Maybe the new jackers would be enough to tip the scales in our favor long enough for us to survive. And we would need every weapon we could get to have any chance at all.

You're poisoning the water to stop a war. Somehow it didn't sound so crazy when I said it to myself. I quickly linked in to the mindware interface before I lost my nerve.

I searched for the switch, hesitated, then gave a mental nudge to the pump that stood frozen. It chugged in to operation and I watched the tank fill. When it reached completion, a valve switched and it dumped into the main line. A chill pulsed up and down my body. Fear? Uncertainty? It was too late for any of that now. The genetic inhibitors were on their way to change the balance of the war in a way that Kestrel hadn't foreseen.

I looked down at Julian, the jacker revolutionary I loved. He had tried to find a way for us to survive, to live, to not be annihilated before the tipping point could be reached. The day he was sure would come, when everyone would eventually turn into a jacker.

You were right after all, Julian, I thought. *It was inevitable. Just not the way you imagined.*

Anna scurried into the room, just missing the bodies in the doorway, then quickly knelt next to her brother. She checked his pulse, then looked up at me. "Did we stop Kestrel in time?" she asked, scanning the screens and trying to decipher their meaning.

"No," I lied. We stared at the screens together as the poison raced to fill the waterways of Chicago. I would tell her the truth later.

I just hoped that she and Julian could forgive me.

Chapter TWENTY-FIVE

I lurked like some kind of demens stalker behind the bushes near Raf's house. If anyone saw me hunkered down in my camouflage-and-black ultralite jacket, they would call the police to come pick up the peeping praver in their neatly manicured suburban yard, and rightfully so. My ability to reach long distances had quickly wasted away under Kestrel's inhibitors and now, almost a month later, I had to be practically at Raf's front door to check in on him.

Of course, it was my own fault, having put the inhibitors in the water in the first place. But no one knew that, except me, Julian, and Anna. They had sworn to take the secret to their graves and, eventually, had forgiven me, although Anna broke a few things first. Her reaction made sense—it was Julian's forgiveness that I still didn't understand. After all, what I'd done wasn't something that could ever truly be forgiven.

I had understood that part when I pushed the button.

I shifted my crouch as my muscles protested my hunched

position next to the hedge. This would have to be the last time, I told myself. Or I would end up getting caught. And that would be far too embarrassing, even if I could jack my way out of going to jail for peeping.

I brushed Raf's mind lightly so he wouldn't detect me. Now that he had turned, his mindbarrier was getting harder—more the firm gel of a jacker changeling than the soft nothingness of a mindreader. His skills were getting stronger too, but they weren't anything extreme. Just a normal jacker: something that was extraordinary all by itself.

I stayed out of his head and dipped into his mom's instead. He was jacked in, so I heard his thoughts clearly there. I was lucky he hadn't mastered his skills enough to sense me.

There are more and more people changing now, Mama, Raf's thoughts rang in her head.

I know! Her mind was inching up to panic. *The world is going to hell in a handbasket.*

Whoa. If Mama Santos was swearing, they must have been at it for some time. But Raf was right. The inhibitors were flowing through the watery arteries of the country, and they had worked just as Kestrel had promised and exactly as he had feared at that last moment: normal readers all over Chicago New Metro had been turning into extreme jackers. But no one had expected what came after that. The demens were turning as well, and a large percentage of them had extraordinary abilities. Julian was coming up with new names for them every day.

It's not as bad as you think. Raf's lilting Portuguese accent came through in his thoughts, and it pulled at memories buried deep inside me. *These are our neighbors, Mama. They're normal people. They're just... different now.*

Different? You mean evil! his mom thought. *It's like the devil himself has come up and is spawning his children all over the neighborhood!*

Raf didn't answer. So he still hadn't told her that he had changed. But it was reassuring to hear Raf had found other jackers nearby. He would have someone he could turn to in order to navigate his new skills. Someone who could help him.

Someone who wasn't me.

The dull ache in my chest made itself known, but I tucked it away. I settled into the dirt next to the bush and swept the neighborhood as far as I could reach, which was actually only as far as Raf's cranky next-door neighbor. Thankfully, he hadn't noticed me peeping from the bushes.

A broken white stone poked out of the grass beside me, and I idly picked it up. It had once been round and smooth and whole, but a piece had been chipped off. The jagged part left an interesting shape to it, almost like a heart. I rubbed my thumb over the rough part, the broken part, tempted to keep it. Something to take back with me. Instead, I tossed it back into the grass where it buried itself.

I really needed to not come back here anymore.

Everything was about the future now, as Julian liked to say, and in that future, eventually everyone would be a jacker. The world had gone a little demens—although that term had a new meaning now, with so many of them changing. Healing. It made me wonder if they were meant to be jackers all along, only something had not quite gone right.

There were more questions than answers these days. The world had turned upside down, yet it was strangely calm as everyone felt their way through the change. The threat of war had evaporated like a black cloud that was cleared out by the morning sun. It was one thing to contemplate locking us up, or even killing us, when "us" was a strange group of dangerous people in a small corner of Chicago New Metro. But when "us" was Aunt Mildred, who could suddenly jack into her niece's mind two states away, or Grandma Jane, who had taken to winning her golf games by mindjack, it forced people to stop and think. And argue and debate and worry. But it had ceased all talk of a war on mindjackers mid-thought.

The tipping point had well and truly been reached.

I wondered if it had felt this way to my great-grandfather, the one who had lived through the first mindreader camps and survived to experience the aftermath when everyone was a reader. Was this sudden absence of strife and fear in the wake of the change what peace felt like?

Yet peace had a cost.

I was luckier than most jackers: my impenetrable mindbarrier was still intact, along with most of my jacking strength, minus the extended reach. I hadn't shied away from drinking the water, in spite of Julian's attempts to stop me. It wasn't like any of us could really escape it; the chemicals weren't just in the water we drank, but the showers we took, the food we ate, the dishes we washed. *Pharmaceuticals in the water are notoriously difficult to control.* I understood Vellus's thoughts better now.

The way I saw it, I was responsible for everything, and that responsibility came with an obligation to be one of the first affected. It made logical sense, even though Julian had fought against it. I was less sure that Julian would still forgive me once the effects of the inhibitors were fully understood, regardless of his reassurances. But I was one of the few who could reach inside my own head and inspect the contents there, to know exactly what I had done in that split second of time when I had tipped the fate of our world.

I smiled. I should have my head examined for coming here, spying on Raf and selfishly taking time for this one last connection with the past, when there was much more important work for the future that I should be doing in Jackertown. I linked back in to Mama Santos's mind. It was blank, numbed out of thoughts, just repeating the words that Raf had put into her head, over and over.

I'm a jacker too, Mama.

My breath caught, a surge of emotion I hadn't expected. He'd told her. Finally. She wasn't freaking out, at least not yet, still caught in the shock of it.

Good for him.

I pulled out of her head, starting to feel like the praver I appeared to be. I hadn't realized I was waiting for this moment, but now that it had arrived, I knew I wouldn't need to come back. I could finally leave behind all that had happened in that before-time: back when Raf was only a mindreader with stolen memories, back when he thought I had jacked him into loving me, back when he had threatened to brand me a jacker.

It was a new world for him now, and he would be fine in it. He didn't need me anymore.

I was sure Sasha had never imagined the privacy rooms he'd built at the JFA headquarters would be used this way. The jacker sitting next to me on the worn couch bounced her leg and pulled over and over at a thread sticking out of the fabric. Her name was Crystal, she wasn't much older than a changeling, and she was very nervous. But that was how they all looked in the beginning. It wasn't easy to trust someone you didn't know, especially enough to let them into your mind. And it was almost impossible when you had lived through Kestrel's mental torture experiments.

Something of which I had a firsthand understanding.

"It's okay," I said. "Everyone's nervous the first time. It's natural." I kept my voice gentle and soothing, like my mom, when I talked to patients.

No one feared my mom when she was a mindreader, but now that she was a scribe, people heard a quiet menace carried on the soft velvet tones of her voice. It was really just their fears speaking. My mom was an excellent scribe, precisely because of her gentleness. Only someone with great compassion should be allowed to have that power. Most people didn't know my mom was a sweet, self-sacrificing person. They thought the power owned the person, turned them. That was probably what people thought of me too. Like Crystal, in front of me, who probably thought I would do irreparable damage once inside her head.

"Primum non nocere," I said with a small smile, hoping she might understand the Latin. Back when I was still in school, all the mindreaders bound for college had to learn it, but I didn't know if she was old enough to have taken the classes. I guessed not, by the way she froze as if I had thrown an ancient curse over her in addition to threatening to invade her mind.

"First, do no harm," I translated, trying to keep that soothing tone. It was something I already believed in from that long-ago time when I'd wished I could read minds, so that I might someday become a doctor. It was strange to be herenow, doing the one thing I never thought I would be able to: healing. I clearly had already caused enough harm, but that just made my commitment even more ironclad to do no more.

"I promise, I will only work on things that are already broken." I laid a hand on her tapping leg to still it, careful to just touch the part that was covered by her thick wool pants. Touching bare skin had no effect but it made them even more skittish.

"Think of me as someone who can fix what's in here," I said, tapping my temple with my other hand, "without having to get out a scalpel or anything scary like that."

She nodded and flicked a look to my assistant, Anna. She

had traded her camouflage for hospital scrubs, but it didn't help much with the scary, intense look on her face. I was training her to help me, and a small, selfish part of me hoped to win back her respect along the way. It would help with the enormous task ahead if Anna could learn to heal, but we wouldn't get anywhere if she made the patients more nervous.

"I can send Anna out if it would make you more comfortable," I said. "She's only here to observe me, but she can sit in with the next patient."

Anna wrestled a smile onto her face, but Crystal's shoulders had already relaxed. That word—patient—seemed to have that effect. I didn't like to call myself a doctor, but it helped if they pictured me that way: confident, calm, assured that I knew what I was doing. I needed her to trust me. When I dove into my own head, generally speaking, I didn't get in my own way. But when I was tunneling into the depths of someone else's mind, all kinds of barriers were thrown up, even when the patient consciously allowed me in. The subconscious was almost like a beast that roiled underneath the conscious mind, and I needed it not to fight me.

The mind was a tricky thing that way.

"Okay," I said. "I'm going to close my eyes because it helps me concentrate. You can do the same if you would like, but you don't have to." I closed my eyes as I spoke and I reached out to Anna. She knew the drill and met me halfway, our mind fields synching up. *Look, but don't touch,* I reminded her.

Look, but don't touch, she echoed back, indicating she was ready.

I pulled her mindfield along, and we slipped into that synchronization where our thoughts became melded like one person. I was dominant, because I had to be, but it was still hard to communicate without using the plural.

"We're going to reach toward your mind now," I said to Crystal. "Are you ready?"

"Yes." Her voice was just a whisper but when we touched her mindbarrier, she let us in.

Very good, Crystal, we thought. *You're doing fine. We're going to slip below your conscious thoughts now, down deeper in your mind where the damage is so we can fix it. You won't feel a thing. In fact, you may get bored waiting for us to finish, so try thinking about something that will occupy you. Maybe sing one of those new synchrony songs that are so awful.*

We could feel her relax. Humor always helped to lower their defenses, especially the subconscious ones.

All right, we thought. *We'll let you know when we're finished. Don't get too bored while we're gone.*

We dove slowly into the deeper levels of her mind. When we were two, it was important not to break the connection while we were so deep in our patient's mind. Plus, going slow helped us to slip under the patient's natural defenses. We found the spaghetti mess of threads that tied together all the connections of Crystal's mind. There were a myriad of them, bewildering to the weaker one of us, but the stronger one knew exactly how to tell them apart.

We can sense the flavor of each, we thought. *Like strawberries, this one is pleasure centers, none of our concern. This one...* A nudge sent a vibration down the length of one string, a tiny signal just pinging to show that it was active. *It tastes of mint, a memory string. Also not what we are looking for. But these ones that flavor of nothing, these ones are broken. Their function, their flavor, is lost. We will search the string till we find it, the breaking spot.*

The stronger of us let the weaker one lead as we traveled the string. We knew that at deeper levels the strings were made of neurons, connecting each one to the next, but at this level, they formed a circuit. Only this live wire had lost its spark of life. We found the break, a sudden end that tasted of death. It wasn't chalky or burnt or some kind of sulfurous decay. Death tasted like the acrid residue from an electrical fire. It was the flavor of something that used to be living and vibrant, but was now gone. It was a ghost.

This, in the break where death sat, was where we set to work.

I left Anna behind and tunneled deeper for the most detailed work. I microscoped in, but it took a full minute to find a new neuron that would properly connect to the dead end of the broken link. The beautiful part was that, as soon as I did, the brain itself did the rest of the work. Once I reconnected the dead ends to living cells, the brain quickly sought out a connection, like a lightning strike searching for ground. I had to watch for it, backing off as soon as the connection was made.

It hummed with electric life. I smiled.

I drew back until I synced with Anna. *We are done with this one now,* we thought. *Let's find another.* Anna's focus was intense, and her thoughts approved of the quick progress we were making. I tried to hide how much that approval made me glow, but it was tough with our minds twined together. We pressed on, and after two more repair jobs, we decided Crystal had been waiting long enough, and we should pull out of the depths of her mind before she became too concerned.

When Anna and I pulled completely out of Crystal's mind, I opened my eyes. "All done for today," I said in a bare whisper, knowing better than to startle the patient.

She still winced and popped open her eyes.

"It went really well in there." I gestured to her head, and she raised a hand to touch her temple as if she could feel what we had done. "It may take a few more sessions before you notice the difference, but your mind seems eager to heal itself." I glanced at Anna, who was wearing a true smile now, and it didn't even look too scary. I couldn't help returning it, but I ducked my head and turned to Crystal, using my smile to reassure her. "We hardly had to work at all. I think you'll be jacking again in no time."

A small grin crept up on Crystal's face. I patted her knee and reassured her once or twice more before I left her with Anna, closing the door behind me to let her take her time in deciding when she was ready to leave.

I leaned against the wall between two of the privacy rooms, resting my head back and closing my eyes. It left me tired deep inside, doing the healing work that I alone could do, and I alone was responsible for. It wasn't so much the focus and the energy, but the tension of making sure I got it right. *Primum non nocere.*

It didn't help that the patients came in with wild expectations of what I could do based on rumors that had swirled since I had started healing. As much as I pretended to be an expert in front of the patients, I was just a novice. With no one to teach me but myself. The idea that I was training others, like Anna, would be faintly amusing if it wasn't the only way to reach everyone who needed to be healed.

I had done some minor repair work on my own mind, but my long-distance reach was less important for the work that I most urgently needed to do. I worked mostly with changelings who had suffered damage under Kestrel's experiments. They had more mental destruction as well as the most potential for healing because their brains were still growing, trying to build new neural pathways to compensate for what Kestrel had done. Like Crystal, whose mind was so responsive to my efforts. But there would be others, many others. An impossibly large number, so I tried not to think about it most days.

I still wished we had scribed Kestrel first and asked questions later. We hadn't learned nearly enough about his experiments in that short time after the crisis at the water pumping station. The information we had managed to retrieve verified a few things: the inhibitors were truly designed to weaken jackers but not destroy them, Kestrel had been pressured by the formation of the JFA to speed up his experiments, the side effect that turned some readers and almost all the demens into jackers was unexpected, and there truly was no antidote.

There was more information locked in his brain, gleaned

from all that experimentation, and we could have learned more, but things were pretty chaotic in the beginning. A contentious debate had raged about whether scribing was the right choice for Kestrel or whether we should put a bullet in him for all his crimes. Unfortunately, he managed to kill himself, ending our debate rather finally. We never quite figured out how he managed it, locked in a room, under heavy guard. Maybe he just hated himself to death, if the thoughts in his head during interrogation were any indication.

In the end, it didn't matter. Any answers died with him.

I would probably spend the rest of my life trying to fix the damage that he and I had accomplished together. Every time I worked on a changeling, I couldn't be sure if the damage in their brains was his or mine. On a bad day, I still questioned whether it was the right choice to put the inhibitors in the water. But when I could make those neurons come back to life, I finally felt like I was doing what I was put here on the planet to do.

"I leave you alone for a few minutes," a voice said, soft and close, "and here you are, slacking on the job."

I grinned with my eyes still closed, turning toward the sound of Julian's voice. "Can't a girl get a moment's rest without being bossed around by uppity jackers who think they own the place?"

I opened my eyes when I felt him move closer. He slipped an arm around my waist and kissed me quickly on the lips. It was a mere ghost of a kiss, gone before it had even announced its presence. He gave a quick look down the hall to make sure we weren't putting on a show. As if anyone cared. But Julian was more and more cognizant of how "things looked" these days.

"Afraid someone's going to see the newly elected senator of the Free Jacker State of Illinois making out in the hall?" I grinned when he flushed, not sure if it was his new title or the public making-out part that made him the most embarrassed. Knowing Julian, probably a little of both. The thirty-year-old age requirement for the US Senate had to be relaxed to allow the nineteen-year-old leader of the JFA in, but then there wasn't much precedent for many of the things we were doing.

His embarrassment quickly faded, and that intense look commanded his face, the one he had when discussing politics or jacker freedoms. Or sometimes when he looked at me like I was a feast after a hundred-day fast.

He pressed me into the wall with his kiss, holding my cheek with one hand while the other snuck behind and pulled me into him. It welled up the same lightness of being that flooded me every time he kissed me like this. Like I was at exactly the right spot at the right time, and all the universe's troubles had melted away, leaving only the two of us, fused together. When he released me, it felt like being pried apart. Not just our bodies, but our hearts and minds, even though we rarely mindlinked.

He held me loosely but with restrained power, like a tiger at the limits of its cage. "What does a guy have to do," he whispered, his words caressing my cheek and floating into my ear, "to get an appointment with you in one of these privacy rooms?"

I smiled, heat running up my neck at his suggestion. I

bunched up the starched fabric of his shirt and pushed him away, but without enough strength to actually move him.

"Get in line," I said. "There are a lot of people ahead of you, mister." In the strictest sense, Julian would never need to visit my jacker clinic; he was one of the few unaffected by the inhibitor, something I gave thanks for every day. He said it was because his jacking came out of a different part of his brain; all I knew was I wouldn't have been able to stand it if he was hurt with no way to get into his head to fix it. Julian had forgiven me from the start, but it wasn't until the effects were known and we had reached the tipping point, that I dared to hope his forgiveness would hold. And even then, if he had been damaged, I would have never forgiven myself.

Julian let me put a tiny distance between us, but no farther. "I know..." He kissed me lightly on the lips. "...the work you do is so important, Kira. It's holding everything together." Which wasn't true. My healing didn't come close to righting all the wrongs that had been done. It was Julian who held everything together, but that thought was lost when he kissed me again. Then he pulled back and whispered against my lips, "Your ability to heal is making a difference to jackers everywhere." Another kiss, longer this time. "And I wouldn't dream of pulling you away from your work, not even for a few minutes, during a short break, in between patients—" Then he couldn't talk anymore because my hands were tangled in his hair, and our kiss was growing.

If he kept talking like that, I *would* pull him into a privacy room with me.

A light clearing of a throat behind Julian made us both stumble mid-kiss. Ava stood behind him, trying to hide her smile and look businesslike.

"Julian, you're on in five minutes." Her smirk was finally defeated by her pleasant-but-determined executive-assistant demeanor.

When I found out that Ava had suffered the same loss of long-distance viewing that I had, it felt like someone had ripped a chunk out of me with an ax. I wanted to fix her, offered to do it even before I knew that I could. She refused, insisting I help the changelings first. But *I* needed to fix *her* more than anyone else—beyond Julian, who thankfully didn't need my help, and my dad and Xander, who were only weakened and already finding their place in the JFA. Ava finally agreed to let me heal her once I had worked through all the changelings whom Kestrel had experimented on.

Even that would take me years.

Meanwhile, she seemed happy to serve as Julian's personal assistant, and Julian certainly needed someone to keep all his appointments straight.

"Doing another chat-cast?" I asked Julian and Ava both, wagering that Julian wouldn't know.

It was Julian who answered. "No," he said, putting on his serious face. "I'm holo-casting into the Senate floor today. They want an update on the treaty negotiations between Illinois as a Free Jacker State and the federal government. We're the model for the other states that are considering treaties, so we need to get it right. They also want another report on the effects of the inhibitors." I finally noticed that Julian was wearing his most-starched high-collared shirt, the one with the boardroom-ready tailoring, along with the trim pants he wore whenever he was doing official business.

I smoothed down the wrinkles that our fevered kiss had pressed into his shirt, feeling a little guilty. "Didn't you just send a report to them with all our knowledge about Kestrel's research?" I asked. "What more do they want?"

"They want me to tell them that the inhibitors will only affect Illinois."

"But that's not true." Julian wouldn't lie to them, especially not about this. "The demens are changing all up and down the Mississippi. What do they think? It's just happening by accident?"

"No." He sighed. "Eventually they'll have to recognize what's happened. But the less..." He searched for the word, tapping his fingers on his chin. "...threatened they feel in the meantime, the longer we have to build peace while we wait for the effects to be fully felt."

I nodded. "Sounds like you've got it under control."

Sasha had crept up behind Ava and wrapped his arms around her. "Yes, the senator has everything under control," Sasha said with more than a little sarcasm. "Unless he's late, in which case he has to deal with Ava's wrath. And I wouldn't recommend that, my friend."

Ava gave him a dirty look and shrugged him off. The rest of us were trying hard not to smirk.

"Well," said Julian, "I'd better get going then. If I leave Ava to handhold a bunch of mindreading senators and their assistants, they'll have her voted into office by lunch and I'll have to find a new job."

Ava rolled her eyes and tapped her foot expectantly.

Julian threw me a look full of promise that made me tingle down to my toes. I nudged his shoulder to interrupt that look before it set my face on fire with embarrassment. "Go make your speech, Senator."

He grinned and turned away with Ava, heading to the main chat-cast room in the back where Hinckley had set up a permanent studio.

Sasha watched them go, then tilted his head toward the door of the privacy room. "How are the rooms working out?"

"Perfect." I looked him over. I couldn't see any change in his dark eyes, but then I didn't really expect to. "How are you?" I asked.

"Never better."

"I'm serious, Sasha."

"So am I."

I stared at him. He crossed his arms and leaned against the doorframe.

"The offer is still open," I said. "And I'm getting better at the finer-detailed repair work. I'm pretty sure I can do it." With my mom's help, Ava had gathered up and brought the scattered bits of Sasha's mind back into coalescence. Then the inhibitors hit, and in his weakened state, they had a bigger impact than they would have normally. He could still jack, but his scribing ability had been destroyed. At least he could still hover protectively over Ava, and I welcomed that now that she had lost her abilities. But it didn't seem right for him to lose so much.

"No offense, Kira," he said with a small smile, "but I don't want you in my head."

"No offense taken." I paused. "It's just that—"

"Kira." He pushed up from the wall, suddenly serious. "It's better to let the monster sleep."

In the hands of someone lesser, Sasha's mind could be—and had been in the past—a weapon of mass mental destruction. But Sasha was like my mom: he deserved the power.

"You're not a monster, Sasha," I said softly.

"Not anymore." The smile was back, and he patted the door to the privacy room. "You should go help someone who needs it."

He brushed past me, and I turned to watch him go. Someday I hoped to convince him to let me fix him, but for now, he seemed to be telling the truth about being happier this way. In the meantime, he was right. There were other people who needed—and wanted—the kind of fixing that I could do.

I took a breath and smoothed down my clothes, trying to drape on the reassuring doctor-persona for my next patient. Another changeling with dead spots in her brain, some of which were put there by Kestrel, some by me. Dead, broken pieces that I was going to stitch back together one by one, making right all the wrongs that had been done before. The inhibitors hadn't killed any jackers, but they had pushed us into the next era of human evolution.

Only it wasn't evolution. It never had been.

Accident.

That's what Vellus called it. A hundred years ago, someone else—like me—had put something in the water that triggered the first wave of mindreaders. Was it an industrial accident? Had the government tried to create mindreaders, then accidentally flushed their experiments down the drain? The cover story—the one that everyone in the world believed—was that it had happened spontaneously, an unforeseen result of our carelessness with the cocktail of all our antidepressants, antipsychotics, and just plain aspirin that we allowed to pollute the water.

What was the truth?

We would never know, just like the people who came after us would never know what really happened that day at the water pumping station. Maybe they would remember that a madman, Kestrel, had poisoned the water and then taken his own life. It was as good a story as any. Or maybe they would come to believe, as Julian had all along, that it was fate, or evolution, or the cosmos telling us that it was time for us to change into something new. After all, jackers had started popping up in the population long before Kestrel brewed up his genetic inhibitors to stop them and accidentally sent us to the tipping point.

I understood the drive Kestrel and Vellus had to put the genie back in the bottle. Who knew what would happen now, what the long-term consequences would be? I certainly didn't know what the future held, any more than I had before. But one thing I knew for sure: you couldn't bottle up something once it was set free, whether it was chemicals in the water or people changing into something new.

I put a smile on my face, pushed the door open, and went to see my next patient.

If you enjoyed *Free Souls*,
please leave a review.

For more Mindjack fun, check out the
Mindjack Origins Collection

Want more Julian? Wondering how Sasha's ability really
works? Looking for EXCLUSIVE DELETED SCENES from
Free Souls? This collection is for those craving a bit more
of the characters and drama of the Mindjack series.

Includes
Mindjack Novellas
Mind Games (Raf's story)
The Handler (Julian's story)
The Scribe (Sasha's story)

TWO EXCLUSIVE DELETED SCENES
from *Free Souls*
(published nowhere else!)

PLUS
mindjack flash fiction
a conversation between Raf and Julian
jackertown slang

Want to see the Mindjack concept on screen?

The Mindjack Trailer

Prod. MIND JACK
Roll 01 Scene 1.M Take 1
Director BETH SPITALNY
Camera L. KAPLAN
Date 11/6/12 48 / Night Sync /

a live-action trailer
directed by award-winning director
Beth Spitalny
with a 20+ member cast and crew

Check out the Mindjack Trilogy website
www.MindjackTrilogy.com
or
find all of Susan's stories on
Amazon, Barnes&Noble, Kobo, Smashwords, and iTunes

Acknowledgements

Finishing a trilogy is like completing a book, only more so: more tears, more startling the cat by laughing out loud at your own words, more warm rush of satisfaction when the story reaches its end. With this book, it was particularly important to me to write the ending that the series deserved; I hope my readers will agree that I achieved that goal. And while it is tough to part with characters I love, Kira's story has been told, and other characters beckon with theirs.

My first thanks go to my readers. Your reviews and facebook posts and chapter-by-chapter tweets as you read the books inspired me and reminded me why I write in the first place. Thank you for your amazing support in spreading the word about the trilogy, something that's vital for any author, but especially critical for an indie one like me.

Once again, my fantastically talented cover designer, D. Robert Pease, has made a gorgeous package for the book. Thank you, Dale, for lending your artistic talents to my work and for being a great friend as well. Thanks to Anne of Victory Editing for compensating for my severe lack of understanding when it comes to hyphens, as well as my comma abuse. Any errors that remain are mine alone.

My critique partners aren't just trusted story advisors—they're fast friends and fellow journeymen and women in this business of creativity. A special thanks to Dianne Salerni for answering my frantic midnight emails with sage, rock-solid advice. Many thanks to Rebecca Carlson, Adam Heine, and Sherrie Petersen for reading that early draft. Someday I'll send you a manuscript that isn't wearing a ragged bathrobe with no makeup and bed hair... but then I'd miss out on all your amazing advice. Thanks to Leigh T. Moore, Elle Strauss, Megg Jensen, and Rhiannon Frater for helping fix the stuff that still needed fixing, and much gratitude to Sheryl Hart for fitting me in, copyediting in pieces, and generally being a lifesaver. A tip of the hat to Lenny Lee for letting me borrow his name for a certain police negotiator.

Special thanks to my son Adam Quinn, who takes time from writing his own novels to critique mine—I think your notes are more entertaining than my story! To my sons Sam and Ryan: thanks for wanting to read Mom's book, even if it has that icky romance stuff in it. And a final thank you to my husband, who still won't let me dedicate a book to him, even though he deserves it. Maybe if I write a novel about robots, you'll let me. Oh, wait...

future works by
SUSAN KAYE QUINN

Third Daughter

(steampunk fantasy romance)

Expected Publication: Summer 2013

For National Novel Writing Month 2012, I had ridiculous amounts of fun drafting this fantasy romance novel (you can check out my Pinterest Board — Susan Kaye Quinn — to get a peek at this east-indian-flavored steampunky world). I hadn't planned on writing this book until 2013, but my mom was interested in NaNo, so I told her I would do it if she did. We completed NaNo together—I'm super proud of her for taking the leap! I'll be revising Third Daughter in the first half of 2013.

for fans of the mindjack stories

Singularity Series
(young adult science fiction)
Expected Publication: Late 2013

The unnamed first novel of this multi-part series will revolve around a future world that is post-Singularity (the Singularity is the event horizon when computers become more intelligent than humans). I've plotted out the series, but won't start writing until 2013. I think these stories will appeal to fans of the Mindjack novels, with plenty of cool technology and future world dreaming, all told through the viewpoint of a legacy human boy.

Check out my Singularity page
or
subscribe to my mailing list for future releases:

www.susankayequinn.com

About the **Author**

Susan Kaye Quinn grew up in California, where she wrote snippets of stories and passed them to her friends during class. Her teachers pretended not to notice and only confiscated her notes a couple times. She pursued a bunch of engineering degrees (Aerospace, Mechanical, and Environmental) and worked a lot of geeky jobs, including turns at GE Aircraft Engines, NASA, and NCAR. Now that she writes novels, her business card says "Author and Rocket Scientist" and she doesn't have to sneak her notes anymore.

Which is too bad.

All that engineering comes in handy when dreaming up paranormal powers in future worlds or mixing science with fantasy to conjure slightly plausible inventions. For her stories, of course. Just ignore that stuff in her basement.

Susan writes from the Chicago suburbs with her three boys, two cats, and one husband. Which, it turns out, is exactly as much as she can handle.

I love to hear from readers!

Like my Facebook page, follow me on Twitter,
or subscribe to my newsletter to be the first
to hear about new releases. Links for these
can all be found at my author blog:

www.susankayequinn.com

16750360R00183

Made in the USA
Charleston, SC
09 January 2013